DEBBIE MACOMBER

The Perfect Christmas

Includes the story
Can This Be Christmas?

MIRA®

Recycling programs
for this product may
not exist in your area.

ISBN-13: 978-0-7783-1924-5

The Perfect Christmas

Copyright © 2016 by Harlequin Books S.A.

The publisher acknowledges the copyright holder of the individual works as follows:

The Perfect Christmas
Copyright © 2009 by Debbie Macomber

Can This Be Christmas?
Copyright © 1998 by Debbie Macomber

For questions and comments about the quality of this book, please contact us at
CustomerService@Harlequin.com.

www.MIRABooks.com

Printed in U.S.A.

First printing: November 2016
10 9 8 7 6 5 4 3 2 1

Midnight Sons
VOLUME 1
  (*Brides for Brothers* and
  The Marriage Risk)
VOLUME 2
  (*Daddy's Little Helper* and
  Because of the Baby)
VOLUME 3
  (*Falling for Him,*
  Ending in Marriage and
  Midnight Sons and Daughters)

This Matter of Marriage
Montana
Thursdays at Eight
Between Friends
Changing Habits
Married in Seattle
  (*First Comes Marriage* and
  Wanted: Perfect Partner)
Right Next Door
  (*Father's Day* and
  The Courtship of Carol Sommars)
Wyoming Brides
  (*Denim and Diamonds* and
  The Wyoming Kid)
Fairy Tale Weddings
  (*Cindy and the Prince* and
  Some Kind of Wonderful)
The Man You'll Marry
  (*The First Man You Meet* and
  The Man You'll Marry)
Orchard Valley Grooms
  (*Valerie* and *Stephanie*)
Orchard Valley Brides
  (*Norah* and *Lone Star Lovin'*)
The Sooner the Better
An Engagement in Seattle
  (*Groom Wanted* and
  Bride Wanted)
Out of the Rain
  (*Marriage Wanted* and
  Laughter in the Rain)
Learning to Love
  (*Sugar and Spice* and *Love by Degree*)

You…Again
  (*Baby Blessed* and
  Yesterday Once More)
The Unexpected Husband
  (*Jury of His Peers* and
  Any Sunday)
Three Brides, No Groom
Love in Plain Sight
  (*Love 'n' Marriage* and
  Almost an Angel)
I Left My Heart
  (*A Friend or Two* and
  No Competition)
Marriage Between Friends
  (*White Lace and Promises* and
  Friends—And Then Some)
A Man's Heart
  (*The Way to a Man's Heart*
  and *Hasty Wedding*)
North to Alaska
  (*That Wintry Feeling* and
  Borrowed Dreams)
On a Clear Day
  (*Starlight* and
  Promise Me Forever)
To Love and Protect
  (*Shadow Chasing* and
  For All My Tomorrows)
Home in Seattle
  (*The Playboy and the Widow*
  and *Fallen Angel*)
Together Again
  (*The Trouble with Caasi* and
  Reflections of Yesterday)
The Reluctant Groom
  (*All Things Considered*
  and *Almost Paradise*)
A Real Prince
  (*The Bachelor Prince*
  and *Yesterday's Hero*)
Private Paradise
  (in *That Summer Place*)

Debbie Macomber's
  Cedar Cove Cookbook
Debbie Macomber's
  Christmas Cookbook

CONTENTS

The
Perfect
Christmas

To
Gary and Marsha Roche
and
Bob Mullen
who have shared their love of
Civil War history
with Wayne and me.

CHAPTER ONE

"Who mails out Christmas cards before Thanksgiving?" Cassie Beaumont lamented to her best friend.

Angie Barber looked up from her microscope and seemed to take an extra moment to consider what Cassie had just said. "You got a Christmas card? Already?"

Cassie wheeled her chair back to her station. "Can you believe it?"

"Who from?"

"An old college friend. You wouldn't know her." Cassie shrugged. "Jill married Tom two weeks after we graduated."

"They have children?"

Cassie caught the wisp of longing in Angie's voice and answered with a nod. "Two, a boy and a girl, and of course they're adorable."

"Of course," Angie echoed.

The Christmas card photo showed the four of them in matching outfits of green and red. The mother and daughter wore full-length green dresses with red-and-green plaid skirts. Father and son had on three-piece suits with vests in the same fabric as the dress skirts. It was too adorable for words.

"There was a letter, as well."

"Everything in their lives is perfect, right?" Angie asked.

"Perfect in every way," Cassie grumbled. The unfairness of it all was too much. Jill, who worked as a financial planner, held down a forty-hour-a-week job, kept a meticulous house and *still* managed to be a terrific wife and mother. Despite all the demands on her time, she'd mailed out her Christmas cards a full month in advance.

"Is there a reason the perfect Jill sent her Christmas cards so soon?" Angie asked.

"Jill and Tom just moved into a new home and wanted to update family and friends with their address change. Oh, and there was a photo of the house and it was—"

"Perfect," Angie finished for her.

"Perfect doesn't begin to describe it."

Angie watched her closely. "Do I detect a slight note of envy?" she asked.

"Slight envy? Me?" Cassie asked, exaggerating the words. "Heavens, no. What you're hearing is a full-blown case of jealousy. The green-eyed monster is alive and well." Cassie rolled her chair to the end of a counter filled with an assortment of microscopes, test tubes, slides and other equipment, then stood, hands propped on her hips. "Do you realize how long it's been since I've been on a real date?"

"You went out with Greg last week," Angie reminded her.

"Greg isn't a man," Cassie blurted out. "I mean, he is, but not in the sense of someone I'm interested in," she said. "Greg's…completely unsuitable as marriage material." She didn't need to explain that, at thirty-four, the ticking of her biological clock got louder by the year.

Angie sighed. "I agree."

He was eligible in practically every way but he happened to be divorced and in love with his ex-wife. Unfortunately, he hadn't figured that out yet. The entire date, if
it could even be called a date, was spent rehashing the trag-
edy of his divorce. He went on and on about how much
he missed his three kids—and his ex-wife, if the number
of times he mentioned her name was any indication. The
night had been sheer drudgery for Cassie. It was her first
and last date with Greg.

"The problem is, we don't meet many guys here at work,"
Angie said. Cassie was well aware of that. Since they were
holed up in a lab eight to ten hours a day, working as bio-
chemists for a plastics company, the opportunities to social-
ize outside the job were limited.

"What really hit home," Cassie said, "after receiving that
Christmas card, is how badly I want a family of my own."

"I know." The longing was back in Angie's voice, too.

"I don't understand why it's so hard to meet men. I'm
reasonably attractive, right?"

Angie nodded enthusiastically. "Yes."

"Thirty-four isn't so old, is it?"

"Not really."

Cassie shook her head and wondered why she was still
single. She *wanted* to be married, and she liked to think
she had the full package—five-five, dark hair, dark eyes.
She was attractive, as Angie had confirmed, and she was
smart, with a successful career, an engaging personality (if
she did say so herself) and plenty of friends. "I blame my
mother for this."

"Your mother?"

"I blame my father, too, even if he didn't stick around all that long."

"Or maybe *because* he didn't stick around."

"Yeah, I guess. After the divorce, my mother was so down on marriage, the whole idea terrified me."

"But it doesn't anymore, does it?"

"No. I want a husband and I'd really like children." She grinned. "The ironic thing is, my mother's remarried."

"Marriage seems to terrify your brother, too. Shawn should be married by now, don't you think? He's older than you are."

"I'm not so sure about Shawn." Cassie sometimes wondered if Angie might be interested in her brother. There was actually nothing to indicate that, but every once in a while Cassie had this *feeling....* "He travels so much that maintaining a long-term relationship would be difficult for him."

"True," Angie said.

Shawn was a well-known artist who painted murals all over the country. Brother and sister were close and kept in touch, calling each other two or three times a week. Currently Shawn was in Boca Raton, Florida, painting the side of a building that stood next to the freeway. He'd sent her photos of the mural from his cell phone—an ocean scene, which Cassie knew was his favorite. Whales rising up out of the crashing waves. Dolphins and sea turtles and all kinds of fish frolicked in the sparkling blue water. His murals made headlines wherever he went and huge crowds showed up to watch him paint.

"Shawn's a different case," Cassie said. In her opinion, that summed up the situation pretty accurately.

"But if you were married, I bet he'd show some interest in finding a wife," Angie commented.

Cassie had never thought of their family dynamic in those terms. Perhaps, in some obscure way, Shawn *was* waiting for her to make the leap first. Angie might be right. It wasn't that Shawn followed her lead—far from it. They'd both been traumatized by the divorce and by their mother's reaction. Their father, who wanted his kids to call him Pete, had been in and out of their lives. Mostly out and yet...yet he'd had a powerful influence on his children, whom he rarely recognized as such.

"Shawn won't feel marriage is safe until he sees *you* happily married," Angie went on to say.

Cassie scowled at her friend. "What makes you so smart?"

"Just an observation," Angie said. "I may not be correct, but it seems to me that you and Shawn are afraid of love."

"Me afraid of love? Hardly." Not if the longing in her heart was anything to go by. Like her friend Jill, she wanted it all.

"Whenever you meet a man—no matter how perfect he is—you find fault with him," Angie said.

Now, *that* was categorically untrue. "Not so," Cassie argued.

"Oh, it's all wine and roses in the beginning, but then it's over before you even have a chance to really know the guy."

"How can you say that?"

"Well, mostly," Angie told her softly, "I can say it because I've seen you do it again and again."

"You're not talking about me and Jess, are you? The man had no class. He scratched his private parts in public!"

"Not Jess."

"Who do you mean, then?"

"Rod."

Cassie cocked her head. "Rod? Rod who?"

"I don't remember his last name. You went out with him a year ago."

"Not Rod Showers? Good grief, he was so cheap I had to pay for my half of the meal and tip the valet because he refused to do it."

"What about Charles…"

Cassie got the point quickly enough. "Okay, okay, so I have standards."

"High standards."

"Okay, fine. High standards." Cassie had made the effort, though. "I've *tried* to meet men."

"We both have."

"I had hopes for that online dating service." The advertisements had looked so promising. Cassie and Angie had signed up together and then waited expectantly to meet their perfect matches.

It didn't happen.

"I had real hopes for that, too," Angie returned sadly. "I thought for sure we'd meet really wonderful husbands."

Cassie sighed. That had been an expensive venture. Her expectations had been great and her disappointment greater. Angie's, too. In fact, Angie was the one who'd suggested trying the internet.

"The church singles group was a good idea," she said now.

"A great idea," Cassie concurred, "if there'd been any men involved." They'd gone there to discover the group consisted of thirty women and two men—both close to retirement age.

Angie nodded. "The pickings were few and far between."

"We've read all the right books," Cassie said. *"Dating for Dummies. How to Find a Man in Five Easy Lessons.* My personal favorite was *Lasso Yourself a Husband and Other Ways to Make a Man Notice You."*

"The only thing we managed to lasso was a hundred-dollar credit-card bill for all those books."

"Divided two ways," Cassie reminded her.

"They did make for interesting reading."

"They would've been a lot more interesting if we'd been able to make any of them work," Cassie said in acerbic tones.

"Yeah…"

"We've tried everything."

"I'm not giving up," Angie insisted. "And I won't let you give up, either."

Cassie sighed.

She was close to it. The Christmas card from Jill and Tom was the final straw. For too long she'd been convinced that one day soon, she'd be mailing glossy Christmas cards to all *her* friends and relatives. She, too, would have a photograph that showed the perfect husband, the perfect children, a boy and a girl, all looking forward to the perfect Christmas. But year after year it was the same. No husband. No children. And each Christmas with her embittered mother more depressing than the one before.

The time had come to step forward and find a man, she decided with new resolve. Maybe she did need to lower her standards. She couldn't allow another Christmas to pass without—

"There's something, or rather someone, you *haven't* tried," Angie said, cutting into Cassie's thoughts.

Cassie perked up. "Oh?"

Angie grew strangely quiet.

Cassie frowned. "Don't hold out on me now, Angie."

"He's expensive."

"How expensive? No, wait, don't tell me." She paused. "Who is this *he?*"

"A matchmaker."

"A matchmaker," Cassie repeated slowly. "I didn't know there was such a thing in this day and age."

"There is." Angie avoided eye contact. "In fact, more and more people are turning to professional matchmakers. It works, too—most of the time."

"Now tell me how expensive he is."

"Thirty thousand dollars."

"What?"

"You heard me—and apparently he's worth it."

"And you know about him because…" Cassie let the question hang between them.

"Because I went to him."

Cassie slapped her hands against her sides. "Clearly you wasted your money."

"It didn't cost me a dime."

"And why is that?"

Angie's gaze darted in every direction except Cassie's. "He wouldn't accept me as a client."

"He rejected you?" The man was nuts! Angie was lovely and smart and a thousand other adjectives that flew through her mind. "What's wrong with this guy, anyway?"

"He was right.... I'm not a good candidate and I would've been wasting my money."

"Why didn't you tell me about him before?"

"I... I didn't want anyone to know I'd been turned down."

"If he rejected you, then he'll probably reject me, too."

"No...he said he couldn't accept me because I have feelings for someone else."

"Do you?"

"I did—a long time ago," she said without elaborating further. "But don't let my experience dissuade you. Check him out. Like you said earlier, you've tried everything else. At least make an appointment and see what he has to say."

Cassie was tempted to ask more about this man Angie had feelings for, but her friend had clearly signalled an unwillingness to talk about it. As far as the matchmaker went, she wasn't convinced. "He actually does this for a living?"

"Yes. He has an office and an assistant. I asked him for his credentials and he has an advanced degree in psychology and—" Angie stared directly at her "—he guarantees his work."

"Guarantees?"

"Yes. If he doesn't find you a husband, you get a full refund. So make an appointment and see for yourself. Remember—nothing ventured, nothing gained."

"I'll consider it," Cassie said. She hated to admit that the idea intrigued her. Then again, it *was* rather archaic. Besides, if this man had rejected Angie, he couldn't be any good. Still it was an opportunity, and nothing else had presented itself.

When she got to her condo building that evening, Cassie

stopped at her mailbox in the lobby and immediately noticed that her newspaper was missing. No surprise there.
It vanished every Tuesday when the shopping ads came
out. Her neighbor Mrs. Mullinex took it, although Cassie
hadn't been able to prove that yet. On Wednesday morn-
ings, her paper mysteriously reappeared with the coupons
clipped out. Twice now, Cassie had met her neighbor in the
lobby. The grandmotherly woman didn't resemble a thief
and would've been above suspicion if not for the handful
of coupons she clutched in her gloved fingers.

Grumbling under her breath, Cassie headed for her apartment. She tossed the mail on the kitchen counter without
looking. The picture of Jill, Tom and their two children
smiled at her from the refrigerator door.

The perfect family having the perfect Christmas.

Jill's smile seemed to be telling Cassie "All this could be
yours, too."

"A matchmaker?" Cassie said aloud. "Am I really resort-
ing to this?"

Angie had given Cassie his business card and then for
good measure a hug and parting words of advice. "Just do
it. I don't think you'll be sorry."

Cassie hesitated and glanced over at the perfect family
posed in front of the world's most beautiful Christmas tree.
Oh, for heaven's sake, what would it hurt?

After rummaging around the bottom of her purse, she
found the engraved card that read: Dr. Simon Dodson, Professional Matchmaker.

Heart pounding, Cassie reached for the phone.

CHAPTER TWO

Simon says: A good matchmaker always knows his clients—especially after a background check!

Cassie had to wait a week before she could get an appointment with Simon Dodson. He made sure she understood that he was doing her a favor by squeezing her in at the end of the day. All right, to be fair, his personal assistant, Ms. Snelling, a rather unpleasant woman, made it sound as if an appointment was a terrible inconvenience. Frankly Cassie didn't hold out much hope for this, and who could blame her? The matchmaking psychologist had declined to accept Angie, who was probably the most decent, kindest person Cassie had ever known.

The day of the appointment, Cassie went home to change clothes. She dressed carefully, choosing a suit that made her look confident but not formal, and she refreshed her makeup. When she walked into his office, it was with her head held high. She'd done her homework and was keeping an open mind. She'd checked two references the Snelling woman had passed on and felt she knew what to expect.

Both couples had raved about Simon. The wives had warned her that Dr. Dodson wasn't the "warm and fuzzy" type. One of them had suggested that Cassie should be patient and not take offense. Hmm…that was unusual advice.

"Dr. Dodson will see you shortly," his assistant informed her primly after Cassie announced herself. The office had modern art decorating the walls, large green plants in the corners and soft leather furniture in a deep shade of brown.

"You filled out the paperwork I emailed you and brought it in?"

"Yes, I have it here." Cassie thought applying for a job at the CIA would've been easier. Simon was interested in every aspect of her background, from the name of her first-grade teacher to her current shoe size. Okay, maybe that was an exaggeration—a slight one—but she didn't see how most of the questions were relevant. Really, why did Simon need a list of any allergies she might have?

She handed the lengthy application form to the assistant, who scanned it, then took it into the inner office. Ms. Snelling reappeared a couple of minutes later and gave her a thorough once-over. Then, to Cassie's surprise, the woman offered her a reassuring smile.

Cassie studied the assistant. She guessed Ms. Snelling was in her late fifties; she seemed efficient and no-nonsense. Cassie sat with her hands politely folded in her lap. This might be the most important appointment of her entire life. The best Christmas present she'd ever get—even if it was from herself. A husband for Christmas. Hmm…

The great Dr. Simon Dodson kept her waiting a full thirty minutes. Cassie knew because she glanced at her watch every five minutes, crossed and uncrossed her legs and flipped through three magazines. By then, she'd grown impatient and irritable and had started to wonder if she'd made a mistake—or, worse, fallen for a scam. She wasn't accustomed to being ignored. She had better things to do than sit in a waiting room on what might turn out to be a fool's errand, a complete waste of time. She trusted that wasn't the case; still, the longer she waited, the less hope she had.

A buzzer made her jump. Ms. Snelling got smoothly to her feet, obviously used to such a peremptory summons. "Dr. Dodson will see you now," she said. She motioned toward the massive double doors that led into his office.

Cassie walked inside and her gaze went instantly to the man standing behind the large desk. The internet research she'd done hadn't included any photos, so she hadn't been sure what to expect—but not someone relatively young with shockingly good looks. He was easily six-two and loomed above her.

"Ms. Beaumont?"

"That would be me," she said, straining to sound cool and collected.

"Please don't sit down."

"Uh…" The door closed behind her.

"Walk to the far side of my office and then walk back."

Cassie paused, which apparently he didn't like because he gestured for her to comply.

"Do I need to say, 'Mother, may I?'" she asked.

He didn't so much as crack a smile. "That won't be necessary."

"Okay." She did as he requested and felt his eyes burning into her with every step she took.

"You could stand to lose five pounds."

"I beg your pardon?" What a jerk!

"You heard me and you agree with me, only I doubt you'd admit it."

Okay, maybe she *could* shed a few pounds, but her figure looked fine the way it was.

He continued to study her and his frown deepened. "That color doesn't flatter you."

How dare he! "I happen to like navy blue." This was her favorite suit and she'd purchased it at a closeout sale for seventy percent off.

He frowned. "Pale blue would be better." He came out from behind his desk and walked around her. "You should let your hair grow, as well. That style is becoming but you need more length."

"I'm glad you think there's *something* attractive about me."

"I didn't say that."

This man was too much! Cassie was tempted to turn around and leave. She might have, only she decided to see how many other ways he could find to insult her. It was becoming a game to her.

"Sit," he said.

"Please?" Someone needed to teach this man some manners.

"Sit," he repeated, more loudly this time.

"Sit, *please*," she returned pointedly.

A flicker of a smile showed in his dark brown eyes. "All right, sit, *please*."

"Don't mind if I do," she said pleasantly, taking the chair across from his desk.

After a moment he said, "I've read your application." He

sat down across from her, reached for the papers and leafed through them. "Tell me about your father."

"Why are you asking about him?"

He lifted his shoulder in a nonchalant shrug. "It's my experience that most women want to marry a man just like their father."

"Not me. Pete's a poor excuse for a father. I want as little to do with him as possible."

Simon immediately made a lengthy notation on a pad in front of him.

Cassie moved to the edge of the cushion. "What did you write?"

Simon looked up, a frown darkening his face. Clearly she'd offended him. She could only suppose he wasn't accustomed to anyone questioning his actions. "What did you say?" he said frostily.

"I asked if you'd tell me what you wrote down." She pointed at his notepad. "It was about me and my nonrelationship with my father, wasn't it?"

He flattened his hands on the desk. "These are my notes. I don't share them with clients."

The urge to stand and simply walk out the door was nearly overwhelming. Gritting her teeth, she said, "Has anyone ever told you you're rude?"

He grinned as if the comment pleased him. "As a matter of fact, yes. Several people have taken delight in revealing their opinions." He shook his head. "It has more to do with them and their hurt feelings than with me."

"What others think doesn't bother you?"

He gave a bored sigh. "Not particularly. Why should it?

Now listen, Ms...." He glanced down at the application in an apparent effort to locate her name.

"Beaumont," she supplied.

"Ms. Beaumont," he said impatiently. "This is my office and *I* ask the questions here. Kindly refrain from interrupting me."

She leaned back in the chair. "By all means, ask away." She waved in his direction as though granting him permission to continue.

He narrowed his eyes. "In as few words as possible, explain to me why you aren't married."

That was easy enough to answer. She thought of what Angie had said a few days earlier. "I've been told my standards are too high."

He raised his eyes from the page, his expression startled.

"I guess you could say I'm choosy," she amended. "I'm looking for a perfect match. Someone who's just right— for me. The perfect man, the perfect marriage...and," she added, almost in a whisper, "the perfect Christmas."

He didn't respond. "You're how old?" he asked, instead. He ran his finger down the application.

"Thirty-four. How old are you?"

He exhaled. "As I requested earlier, kindly refrain from asking questions. My age is not your concern."

"Answer me one question, and then I promise not to ask anything else."

He glared at her.

"Just one," she cajoled. "You can't imagine how uncomfortable it is to sit here and have you scrutinize me. It's only fair that I should know something about you."

Sighing, he set the application aside, but before he could speak, she blurted out, "Are you married?"

His eyebrows arched. "*That's* your one question?"

"Yes, and it's important."

"Why is that?"

"Well, first, if you haven't been able to find yourself a wife, what qualifies you to find me a husband?"

"All I will say is that a doctor doesn't need to have a disease in order to cure it. I'm good at what I do. If I wasn't, I wouldn't be willing to offer a refund if I'm unsuccessful in locating a husband for you."

"Are you always so stiff and formal—as if your underwear's been starched?"

He stood abruptly. "I believe that will be all for this afternoon."

"You're sending me away?" She blinked, disappointed. Cassie was just starting to enjoy this. His typical clients were probably more respectful, if not downright obsequious.

"This interview is over."

"Did I pass?" She'd rather know now than be left hanging. She guessed not. She wouldn't be surprised if he didn't take her on. And yet, disagreeable though he was, Simon Dodson intrigued her.

He hesitated. "I'll be in touch later this week."

This was a line Cassie had heard before. "In other words, don't call me, I'll call you."

"Precisely."

Cassie recognized her marching orders. She bent down for her purse and reluctantly stood.

As she drove back to her condo, she tried to make sense of her short interview. On her way up, she collected her mail and noticed once again that the Tuesday paper was missing. Mrs. Mullinex, no doubt.

She ran for the elevator and saw Mr. Oliver, who lived on the same floor, standing inside. Looking her right in the eye, he let the doors close instead of holding them for her. This wasn't the first time, either. He was an unsociable man; the most she'd been able to coax out of him was a muffled greeting, as if he begrudged every word he was forced to speak.

When she got to her condo, she saw that she had company.

"Shawn!" Her brother had made himself at home and was wolfing down a sandwich while standing over her kitchen sink.

"Hey, it's about time you got home. Where were you?"

Rather than explain, Cassie walked over and hugged her big brother. "I had an appointment. How long are you here?" she asked.

"Two days, maybe three."

Shawn often had only a few days' rest before he flew to some other town where another commission awaited him. She knew he was headed to Phoenix, Arizona, next. He had his own home in Portland, but every now and then he dropped in on her. In an effort to encourage his visits, she'd given him a key to her condo.

"I take it you're hungry."

"Starved."

"Let me fix you something decent." Cassie checked the contents of her refrigerator, then reached for a frying pan. She loved to cook and had a small repertoire of favorite dishes. This was one. "How does taco salad sound?"

"Like ambrosia from the gods." He sat on the stool and watched her move about the compact kitchen. "You're going to make some man a wonderful wife."

She whirled around to face him. "Funny you should say that."

Shawn went still. "You've met someone?"

"I would've told you!" They weren't in the habit of keeping secrets from each other. "My appointment this afternoon was with a professional matchmaker."

Her brother's head went back as if the announcement had shocked him. "Get out of here! A matchmaker?"

"I had my first appointment with the great and mighty Dr. Simon Dodson."

"How'd it go?"

Cassie set the onion on the chopping board and paused. "I'm not sure. Simon's pretty rude, but apparently he knows his stuff."

"Simon, is it?"

In her mind it was. "Yeah. He's not a medical doctor, even though he has a bunch of letters behind his name."

Her brother looked unconvinced. "You checked his references?"

"I did. I spoke with two couples who met through him. I was warned in advance that he isn't the most likeable fellow on the face of the earth, but they say he has this gift."

"How'd you hear about him?"

"Through Angie."

"Angie?" Her brother appeared as astonished by this as Cassie had been. "I wouldn't think she'd need a matchmaker. Did she go to him?"

Cassie nodded.

"When?"

"A little while ago. She didn't really say. What I don't get is why Simon rejected her."

"That's crazy! Angie's great."

"And I'm not?" she asked, her hand on her hip.

Shawn chuckled. "I'm staying as far away from that question as I can. What did the matchmaker say? If he rejected Angie, then what about you?"

That was the thirty-thousand-dollar question. "I don't know if Simon will accept me as a client or not. He said he'd phone, but…" The rest of her sentence was drowned out by loud rap music coming from the condo to the right of hers.

"Good grief, what's that?" Shawn covered his ears.

"My new neighbor," Cassie shouted back. She walked over to the kitchen wall and banged hard three times. Within half a minute, the music had been turned down to a more respectable volume.

"Jalapeño?" she asked next, hardly missing a beat.

"Might as well. My life could do with a bit of spicing up."

"Mine, too."

"So tell me more about this matchmaker. Do you like him?"

Cassie began tearing lettuce industriously. "The truth is, I don't. He's arrogant, snooty and definitely not my type. I'm not his, either. Not that it matters… But he doesn't like to be questioned or challenged. I could tell I irritated him."

"You heard he's successful, though, right?"

"Yeah." Until that moment, Cassie hadn't realized how much she hoped Simon would agree to work with her. "I don't know if he's ready for someone like me."

"What do you mean?"

She waved a lettuce leaf in his direction. "Like I said, I questioned his actions and his decisions. He didn't like it."

"I wonder why he rejected Angie," Shawn mused. "I mean, she's not annoying or—"

"Hey, stop right there."

Shawn laughed and leaned his elbows on the counter where he sat. "Who's that picture of on the fridge?" he asked.

Although she didn't need to turn and look, Cassie did. She tensed slightly as she stared at the photograph of Jill and Tom and their perfect Christmas. "That, brother dearest, is my inspiration."

CHAPTER THREE

A few minutes later, Cassie reached for her phone on impulse and dialed Angie's number.

"Hello? Oh, Cassie, I was hoping you'd call. How'd the appointment go?"

"Do you like taco salad?" Cassie asked rather than answering.

"Is there any food group I don't like?" Her friend had a smile in her voice.

"Silly question. Come join us."

"Us?"

"Yes, Shawn stopped by. I'm making a taco salad and if you have fresh tomatoes bring one. If not, we'll do without."

"Shawn's there? Your brother?"

"That's what I just said. Are you coming or not?"

"I'm on my way, and I've got a tomato," Angie said, "but when I get there, I want details about the meeting with Dr. Dodson."

Shawn grabbed an orange from her fruit bowl and tossed it in the air, juggling it with an apple and doing a poor job.

The orange hit the floor and rolled into the living room. "I'm glad you invited Angie. How's she doing?"

"You know Angie. She's always in a good mood."

Her brother retrieved the orange. "Well…it'll be nice to see her again."

Cassie nodded absently as she began to sauté the ground beef.

By the time Angie arrived, Cassie had the hamburger with taco sauce simmering together. The salad fixings were in a large bowl, awaiting Angie's tomato. Shawn was grating the cheese.

Angie brightened the moment she walked into the room. "Shawn, it's great to see you."

"You, too." He set the cheese down long enough to give her a brief hug. Cassie always forgot how tiny her friend was until Angie stood next to her brother, who was well over six feet.

While Cassie got out the bag of tortilla chips and assembled the rest of the salad, Angie set the table and Shawn filled their water glasses. "Sorry I don't have any sangria," Cassie said as she carried the large wooden bowl to the table. Smaller bowls of meat, cheese and chips followed.

"This looks wonderful," Angie told her.

"Allow me." Shawn pulled out Angie's chair. Then he hurried around to the other side of the table to do the same for Cassie.

"Since when have you acquired gentlemanly manners?" Cassie asked.

Jokingly Shawn checked his watch. "About five minutes ago."

"Perfect timing."

"I'm dying to hear how everything went this afternoon," Angie said, her fork poised over the salad. "How was the meeting with… Dr. Dodson?" She glanced toward Shawn as if she wasn't sure she should say any more.

"It's okay." Cassie nodded. "He knows all about it."

Shawn rolled his eyes. "Personally I think she's nuts. So, what's the story with you and this matchmaker?"

Angie ignored the question and returned her attention to Cassie. "Don't keep me in suspense. What was your impression when you met him?"

"He's abrupt and ill-mannered, don't you agree?"

"That's putting it mildly." She turned to Shawn. "He rejected me. I didn't make it past the initial interview. I'll admit it was a blow to my ego but I felt I had to tell Cassie about him."

"I can't believe he'd reject you." Shawn looked genuinely outraged on Angie's behalf. "I don't understand why either of you would have any interest in someone who seems to enjoy insulting you."

"Why?" Cassie answered. "We're getting desperate, that's why. It's not easy to meet decent men, you know!"

"Not at our age," Angie added.

"See that picture of Jill and Tom?" Cassie said, pointing to her refrigerator. "She has the perfect life, the perfect family and is about to have the perfect Christmas. I want all that."

"Me, too," Angie murmured fervently. "And so far I haven't even come close."

Shawn blinked. "You two are actually serious?"

"Serious enough to pay thirty thousand bucks to find the right man."

Shawn's eyebrows shot up. "*How* much?"

Cassie didn't feel like repeating it. "You heard me."

Shaking his head, Shawn muttered something about being in the wrong business.

Angie sighed. "It's a ridiculous amount of money, I know, but from what I understand, it's worth every penny—if you're accepted, that is. Now, Cassie, tell me about your meeting with Dr. Dodson."

Mentally reviewing the appointment, Cassie suffered more than a few doubts. "I don't think I went over well."

"But you have a second appointment, right?"

"Supposedly." Cassie shrugged. "He said he'd call...."

"Cassie, that's great! Dr. Dodson read my application, took one look at me and said he didn't have anyone who'd suit me."

That wasn't precisely what Angie had told her earlier. Simon had apparently said she already held feelings for someone. If that *was* the case, Cassie didn't have any idea who it might be. She wished she'd questioned her further, but at the time she'd been too interested in hearing about this matchmaker and now didn't seem appropriate. Especially since Angie was obviously reluctant to talk about her own situation. The man in question must've been someone she'd met years ago, which was what Angie had implied. It certainly wasn't anyone Cassie knew, and they'd worked together for six years.

"Tell us what he said," Angie urged.

"Simon was pretty rude," Cassie said between bites of her salad. She added another layer of crushed tortilla chips to the lettuce.

"How?" Shawn asked. "I want specifics."

"Well, he didn't seem to like a single thing about me. Not my body type, not my choice of clothes or the color of my suit."

"I love that suit!" Angie cried.

"I did, too," Cassie said, immediately noting that she'd used the past tense. Hard as it was to admit, he was right about that. She would've preferred it in a soft robin's-egg blue, but the only available color had been navy.

"Didn't he have *anything* nice to say?" Angie asked.

"Well…he did mention that my hairstyle suited me but it needed more length. That was as close to a compliment as he got."

"But you made it past the first interview," Angie said again, as though Cassie had managed a feat of unparalleled skill.

"What I don't understand," Shawn said, pushing back in his chair, "is why you'd allow this man to insult you. I mean, everything he said was just a matter of opinion. *His* opinion." He raised both hands as the women started to protest. "Okay, I understand you're feeling desperate—to quote you—but I don't get it."

Cassie and Angie shared a look.

"I think it's the promise," Cassie said.

"The promise," Shawn repeated. "What promise?"

Angie leaned forward, folding her arms on the table. "Dr. Dodson guarantees that he'll find you a match."

"Someone who'll be a perfect match…"

"Someone who's as eager to meet us as we are them," Angie explained.

"The thing is," Cassie said, "I can't help wondering if the man of my dreams is actually out there."

"Of course he is," Shawn insisted. "Frankly I think all of this is nonsense. How can anyone *guarantee* that he'll find you a *perfect match?*" Sarcasm dripped from his words. "I can't believe you're willing to pay the guy that much money when you're completely capable of finding yourself a husband."

"Where?" Cassie asked, opening her arms and gesturing widely. "Tell me where he is and I'll send a search party to bag him."

"I'll volunteer," Angie said. "Maybe there'll be an extra man hanging around for me."

"Where?" Shawn ignored their teasing. "There are men, decent men, everywhere. You can meet him at work—" they shook their heads simultaneously "—well, then, at...at the grocery store. Or on the street. Or in a bookstore. Or..."

Angie cocked one finely shaped eyebrow. "Did you hear what I just heard?"

"I did," Cassie confirmed.

"What?" Shawn looked from one woman to the other.

"You used the word *meet,*" Cassie told him.

"Not marry," Angie said.

"Now, just a minute—" Shawn started to speak but Cassie cut him off.

"You're a prime example of what we're talking about."

"Me?" Shawn placed a hand over his heart. "I'm too busy for a wife and family. I'm constantly on the road. That's no life for kids."

"You don't feel the need for companionship, then?" Angie asked.

"Not really."

"Men don't," Cassie complained. "They don't know they're miserable until we tell them."

"So I'm miserable now?" Shawn laughed as if she'd made a joke. "Too bad I've never noticed."

Cassie wasn't about to argue with him. "Men aren't on the same timetable women are, and when they finally wake up and realize they want the same things we do, *they* can still father children."

"A woman has biological limitations," Angie said, "if she wants kids."

Her brother's look sobered. "You two aren't kidding."

"No way," Cassie said. "In fact, we're willing to put up with the criticism and scrutiny of someone like Simon Dodson in the hope of finding a good man we can share our lives with."

Shawn grew thoughtful. "I don't understand why he'd reject *you,* Angie. It seems to me you'd be an ideal candidate."

"Well, he did, and it's his prerogative," she said briskly. Then she smiled at Cassie. "I can hardly wait until you have your next appointment."

"Now, just a minute," Shawn said again. "You should've asked me to set you up before you went to all this trouble."

Cassie's eyes widened. "You have someone you want me to meet?"

"Well, sure. I know a dozen eligible men. I could've introduced you."

Cassie glanced at Angie. "He only thinks to mention this now?"

Angie frowned. "Do you really trust your brother to find you a husband?"

Cassie shook her head. "My idea of what I want and what he has to offer might be worlds apart."

"Hey, you two," Shawn said, breaking into their conversation. "I'm sitting right here. If you have any doubts, you can address them to me directly and not to each other."

"Okay," Cassie said. "Tell me about one such man."

"All right." He appeared to be deep in thought.

"I don't think he can scrounge up even one," Cassie whispered, raising her eyebrows.

"Give me a minute, would you," he snapped.

"Notice how testy he gets when challenged."

Her brother silenced her with a look.

"There's Riley," he declared triumphantly. He beamed a smile at Angie and then Cassie.

"I've always liked the name Riley," Angie said.

"Riley." Cassie threw back her head. "You're joking!"

"What's wrong with Riley?" Angie wanted to know.

"He's an artist friend of Shawn's. He's got two ex-wives, a gambling problem and he drinks too much. You're scraping the bottom of the frying pan if you're suggesting either of us should marry *Riley*."

"He's reformed."

"Yeah, right. And when did this happen?"

Shawn seemed unsure. "Not too long ago. He said he's through messing up his life. What he needs now is a good woman."

Cassie exhaled slowly. "Tell him to talk to one of his ex-wives, then."

"Sorry," Angie said, "I'm not interested, either."

"You're going to have to try harder than that," Cassie informed her brother.

"What about Larry Upjohn? You couldn't meet a nicer guy if you tried."

"Do you know Larry?" Angie asked her.

Cassie nodded. "He's Shawn's CPA and in a word… *b-o-r-i-n-g*."

"You didn't say you were looking for a stand-up comic," Shawn said, obviously annoyed.

"Call me superficial, but I don't want to date a man who wears knee-high socks with his sandals and a pocket protector in his pajamas."

"A little personality would be helpful," Angie said in a defeated voice. "As you can tell, it's not as easy as it seems."

"Warren!" Shawn's face lit up. "What about Warren?"

Once more Angie turned to Cassie.

She nodded, but without enthusiasm. "Warren's a… possibility."

"What's wrong with Warren?" Shawn cried.

Cassie shrugged. "Nothing really. He just doesn't ring my bells. He might Angie's, though."

Shawn leaned back, throwing out his arms in an expansive gesture. "I can introduce you, if you like."

"Tell me about him first," Angie said.

"He's Shawn's agent," Cassie explained. "He's a nice guy."

"*Nice* isn't a word I'd use to describe Warren," Shawn commented. "He's a tough negotiator."

"But a real kitten on the inside," Cassie said. "He's also divorced. Recently, if I remember."

"He and Clare split last year. I don't know many guys your age who aren't divorced."

"That's reassuring," Cassie muttered. Warren was the best of the rather shallow pool of Shawn's male friends and acquaintances. Shallow pools, as everyone knew, were usually the slimiest, too. This was exactly why she'd decided on the matchmaker.

"Warren's got a couple of kids. His wife has custody."

"Thanks, big brother, but I'll stick with Dr. Dodson."

"I appreciate the suggestion," Angie said, "but I'll pass on Warren, too."

"If I think of anyone else, I'll give you a call."

"You do that," Cassie said, although she didn't expect he would. "On second thought, phone Angie."

CHAPTER FOUR

Simon says: I can find the right mate for everyone. Even you!

Simon kept Cassie waiting forty-five minutes on her next visit. His assistant, Ms. Snelling, had called the day after her first appointment. It was now Friday. Since she'd been on pins and needles for three whole days, an additional forty-five minutes didn't bother her. Today would be when he'd announce whether he'd found her a match.

She couldn't figure out how, based on their brief conversation, Simon would be able to match her up with the perfect man. Maybe, as Angie said, it really was all about his ability as a psychologist, his scientific study of her lengthy questionnaire.

For three nights now, she'd been like a kid at Christmas—only instead of sugar plums dancing around in her head she saw men's faces. Men who were enthralled with her. Men who'd go through the same insulting rigmarole she had for the chance to meet her. Men who were just as eager for the very things she wanted—a home and family, security, a sense of belonging and a lifetime filled with love. And one of those men would be her perfect match.

"Dr. Dodson will see you now," Ms. Snelling said in the same crisp tone she'd used on Cassie's first visit.

Cassie bounded up from the chair as though she'd been ejected. Despite her eagerness, she tried to move slowly and calmly. When she entered his office, she found Simon sitting at his desk.

Without looking up, he gestured for her to sit, too.

Cassie did, perching on the very edge. She didn't expect an apology for being kept waiting and wasn't disappointed. When Simon eventually looked up, she noticed streaks of gray in his hair that had escaped her notice previously.

"What are your plans for Christmas?" he asked.

Of all the things Cassie had expected him to say, this wasn't it. "Ah… I'm not sure yet."

"Family plans?"

"Not really." She hadn't talked to her brother yet. Her mother and stepfather lived in Hawaii and it was unlikely that they'd fly in for the holidays. Her father…well, she hadn't spent Christmas with him since she was five or six. "There's just Shawn and me."

"And Shawn is?"

"My brother. It's on the questionnaire. He's—"

"Ah, yes," Simon broke in. "What did you do last Christmas?"

"Well, let me see…" She tried to remember where she'd been and with whom. Was it last year that Angie—

"This shouldn't be so difficult," he said.

"It was eleven months ago," she snapped. His attitude irritated her. "As I recall, Shawn and I went out to eat.

Angie, a friend of mine, was supposed to join us but at the last minute she couldn't and we—"

"Yes, yes," he said, interrupting her again.

"And what exactly were *you* doing?" she demanded.

His eyes widened. "I beg your pardon?"

"Where were you last Christmas?"

"As I indicated during our previous session, I'm the one asking the questions."

Cassie made an effort to hold her temper. "I guess that slipped my mind. But I was allowed one question then, so I assume that's the case today, and I'm asking it now." She took a deep—and necessary—breath. "Where were *you* last Christmas?"

He exhaled slowly. "Right here in Seattle."

"With friends and loved ones?"

"That's more than one question." He looked pointedly in her direction. "Shall we continue or not? The choice is yours."

Knowing she was fighting a losing battle, Cassie tried to regain her equilibrium. "Yes, let's continue, although I don't understand what last Christmas has to do with anything."

"That's not your concern."

"Are you always this dictatorial?" She realized she was asking yet another question, but she couldn't stop herself.

"I am when I feel I can find the right match for a client. An exasperating one, I might add."

"Really?" That was worth all the insults he could issue, Cassie decided. She slid so far to the edge of the chair that she was in danger of falling onto the carpet. "You actually have someone in mind?"

"I do." This was said in a clipped, businesslike way.

She waited, but he wasn't any more forthcoming than that.

"Before I introduce you, there are a few matters we need to attend to."

"Fine." Her heart felt as if it had moved into her throat.

"My fee is thirty thousand dollars."

"Yes, I know... That's a lot of money."

Simon glanced up. "I thought you were aware of my fee. If you can't afford me, then I suggest you leave now and save us both a lot of time and trouble."

The money was safely tucked in Cassie's savings account. "I put it aside for a wedding, but obviously there won't be one without a groom. I'm willing to make the investment."

"Good. Then I'll introduce you to John."

"His name is John?" John was a solid name, implying that he was a solid man; she liked him already.

"Before I introduce you—"

"There's a money-back guarantee, right?"

"I'll explain that in a moment."

"Okay, sorry, I didn't mean to interrupt." She wanted to capture every single detail of this meeting so she could repeat it all to Angie.

"I have three tasks I want you to complete first."

"Excuse me?" She wondered if she'd misheard him. Cassie was waiting to hear about her perfect mate, and he was talking about *tasks?* What was this, homework?

"These are qualifying tasks," he was saying. "I need to be sure you're the woman for John."

"But...no one said anything about needing to qualify."

He ignored her outburst. "Once you've fulfilled these three *simple* tasks, I will introduce you to John. The choice is easy—do what I ask and meet the man of your dreams or keep your money and walk away now." He sat back in his chair and clasped his hands, clearly regarding this as a take-it-or-leave-it proposition.

Cassie's head reeled. "Do you ask this of all your clients?" she cried, almost positive he didn't. Her nerves were quickly fraying.

"How often do I need to tell you? I'm not in the habit of answering questions." He paused and looked her straight in the eye. "However, I'll admit that I don't ask this of every client. Only certain ones."

"What made me so lucky?"

"Your motives. You expect to find the perfect husband, the perfect marriage and the perfect Christmas, correct?"

She remembered having said as much. She nodded.

"You're asking for the impossible."

"But...isn't that what you promised?"

"No. If you'll examine my website, you'll see that I promise the *right* mate. The most suitable spouse. But that's just the beginning. A happy marriage is about much more than the appearance of perfection."

Others had found true love. Jill and Tom had, so why couldn't she? "I can dream, can't I?" she muttered.

"Yes, you can dream as long as your dreams are rooted in reality."

"And you consider it your duty to drag me out of my happy fantasy and into the real world," she said sarcastically.

"What I consider my duty is to match you up with someone who'll spend the rest of his life thinking he's the most fortunate man alive to be with you."

"Oh." She swallowed tightly.

"Do you accept the three tasks or not?"

She hesitated. She needed more information before she agreed to anything. "What are they?"

"I'm not asking you to swim in shark-infested waters, if that's what you're worried about. It's nothing life-threatening."

"I won't have to eat anything disgusting, will I?"

He cringed. "Good grief, no. As I said, these are simple, ordinary tasks. It sounds as if you've been watching too much reality television."

"Actually, I don't. My friend Angie watches that stuff and then tells me about it the next day."

He ignored her explanation and reached for a slip of paper on his desk. "Here's your first task. I need you to volunteer for a four-hour shift as a bell ringer in front of the Southcenter Mall near Kent. Do you know it?"

"I know every mall within a two-hundred-mile radius of Seattle."

"I have no doubt of that."

Really, how difficult could a four-hour shift be? "Sure, that won't be a problem."

"It's the weekend after Thanksgiving."

"Great. The mall will be hopping."

"There's a quota the charity expects you to make, but I don't think you'll have any trouble with that."

"Okay. What's the second task?" The first one didn't seem too hard; the next one was probably along similar lines.

"You said on the application form that you're interested in a man who wants children."

"I am."

"Good. I'm going to give you the opportunity to spend

an entire afternoon with the little darlings. You'll be one of Santa's elves for a picture-taking session at the Tacoma Mall."

"An elf?"

"There's a costume. I apologize, but it's one of the requirements."

"Okay, fine, I can be an elf." She didn't like the idea of wearing some silly outfit with tights and pointed shoes but she could cope. "And the final task?"

He reached for another slip of paper. "I also saw on your application that you enjoy cooking."

"I do." And she was pretty good at it if she did say so herself.

"Excellent. For your third task, I want you to cook Christmas dinner. Turkey, stuffing, mashed potatoes with gravy, salad, vegetables...that sort of thing. Oh, and two different kinds of homemade pie."

"And who's going to be eating this huge meal?"

"Your neighbors."

"Ah." She raised her index finger in protest. "I don't have the friendliest neighbors...."

"Invite them, anyway."

"And who's going to check up to see if I've completed these tasks?" she asked. She suspected Simon hadn't thought this completely through.

"I'll be checking in on you during the first two tasks."

"You might as well come to Christmas dinner, then. Can I invite my brother and best friend, too?"

"Of course," he said, but he didn't respond to her admittedly reluctant invitation.

"Can they bring a contribution?" She was thinking

Shawn could scrounge up a cooked turkey somewhere and even Angie could manage stuffing out of a box.

"No, you will be providing the entire meal."

Cassie was afraid of that.

"Now that you know the tasks, do you feel you can handle them?"

"I guess so—but what exactly is the point?"

He smiled—a glimmer of a smile. "Each task will tell me something about you. Something important. However, you don't seem very confident. Can you or can't you? A yes or no will suffice."

Lifting her hand to her brow she saluted him smartly. "Aye, aye, sir."

Her gesture failed to amuse him, but he did relax somewhat. "Now that we've squared away that portion of our discussion, it's time to finalize the paperwork."

"All right. Oh—do I get to ask three things of you—small, easy-to-perform tasks?"

He sent her a withering look.

"Obviously I don't," she said under her breath.

"Let's make this clear," he said with exaggerated patience. *"You're* the one who sought me out. You came to me because of your desire for a husband and a family. I don't advertise. I didn't ask you to step into this office. You came of your own free will."

"I did," she concurred.

"Then we play this by my rules."

She resisted rolling her eyes for fear he'd demand she leave. "Rules," she repeated softly. "Is this a game to you?"

"No, this is life, yours and John's. He's a good man who wants the same things you do."

"Okay, I accept your rules."

"Thank you."

"Can I at least see his photograph?"

"No. You will meet when it's time. There will be no information exchanged before that official meeting."

Cassie didn't like it, but she didn't have any alternative. She nodded.

Simon opened a side drawer and withdrew a contract. "I advise you to have your attorney look this over before you sign it. This is a standard contract, stating what you can expect for your thirty thousand dollars."

"What if John and I don't gel? If we aren't a good fit?"

"That occasionally happens and it's a fair question. Your money will be refunded to both of you in full."

"In that case, will you introduce me to another potential mate?"

"No."

"No. No?"

"This is a one-shot deal."

"One-shot?" That sounded risky.

"If I offered choices, my clients would be wondering who else might be available. When I pick a mate for you, it's the best match I can find, someone I believe will complement your strengths, share your values and fulfill your desires—within reasonable parameters."

"And your success rate is?"

"High. I don't accept a client unless I'm confident I have the right person for him or her. It's as simple as that."

Cassie stared down at the contract. She'd feel better if she liked Simon more. The man was rude, arrogant and short-tempered.

It was as if he'd read her thoughts. "You don't need to like me, Cassie," he said. "In fact, it's preferable that you don't."

"Really?"

"Yes, really," he returned. "The last thing I want or need is for a client to fall in love with me. It only complicates matters, and I don't like unnecessary complications. Understood?"

"Now who's dreaming?"

A smile came and went. A smile that charmed her despite everything he'd said and done.

CHAPTER FIVE

Simon says: Maybe money can't buy love—but it can get you practically everything else.

On the Saturday morning after Thanksgiving, which she'd spent with Angie and her family, Cassie headed for South-center Mall. This was the venue for her first task and she was eager to prove herself to Simon, obviously a curmudgeon. Spending four hours soliciting money for charity couldn't possibly be that difficult.

Since she'd be standing outside, Cassie dressed in wool pants and a hand-knit sweater over her long-sleeved blouse. Between the shirt and sweater, she could barely get her arms inside the sleeves of her coat. She added a hat, gloves and a scarf, dressing for the cold. When she met her one true love, she wanted to make sure she didn't have a runny nose and a sore throat.

Cassie showed up at the mall at the required time and met the other charity bell ringers. Standing with her col-leagues, she glanced around. Some were being paid and frankly she thought they looked kind of shifty. Others, like her, were volunteers.

"Smile and greet everyone," the leader instructed. "Be friendly even if someone walks past you."

Filled with enthusiasm, Cassie could hardly wait to be assigned her post.

"Make eye contact" was the second bit of advice. "And ring that bell. Remind shoppers of those less fortunate."

"Got it," Cassie said aloud.

"This is one of the busiest shopping weekends of the year, so you shouldn't have any problem making your quota."

In the back of her mind, she recalled Simon's casually mentioning something about collecting a certain dollar amount and the way he'd made light of it. The recommended donation amount turned out to be $60 an hour. That was a dollar a minute! How was she supposed to know how much money she'd collected when the red pot was securely locked? It wasn't as if she could pry the lid off and count the cash.

"Are we ready?" their helpful leader called out.

Cassie's shout blended in with the others'. "Ready!"

One by one, they received their assignments. Cassie was told to stand in front of the Target store, which had an outside entrance. With bell in hand, she headed toward her designated post. This wasn't so bad. Not only was she helping the underprivileged but she was moving toward the man of her dreams.

She waited eagerly as a couple walked up. Smiling sweetly, she jerked her hand several times in succession, making the bell jangle. "Merry Christmas," she greeted them.

The couple avoided eye contact and entered the store via the door farthest from Cassie.

Their lack of generosity—and appreciation for her efforts—didn't faze her.

Not much later, a grandmotherly type approached her. "Do you have change for a five?" the woman asked.

"Sorry, we can't make change."

"Oh, dear," she said regretfully, "then perhaps I can give you something on my way out."

"Don't worry," Cassie said cheerfully, "I'll be here."

In her first thirty minutes, Cassie estimated that she'd collected less than five dollars, which wasn't even close to her hourly goal. She stomped her feet to ward off the cold. In an effort to liven things up a bit, she attempted to ring the tunes of popular Christmas songs.

She gave that up during "Frosty the Snowman" when a teenage boy walked past and reached for his cell phone. He said, "Hello. Hello. Hello," before he realized it was her bell and not his cell. He stopped in front of her and glared.

"Sorry," she said, and gasped when the youth shot her the finger.

"Well, Merry Christmas to you, too." Of all the nerve!

After an hour Angie came by and mercifully handed her a cup of steaming hot coffee.

"God love you," she said, gratefully accepting it.

"How's it going?"

If it'd been Simon rather than Angie, she would have declared that this was the most wonderful, rewarding experience of her life. With Angie she felt compelled to tell the truth. "I can't feel my nose."

"Can I get you anything else?" her friend asked, her expression concerned.

"Put some money in the pot. I'm nowhere near my quota."

"Oh, sure." Angie put in a hefty donation.

"Thank you."

"Do you want me to stand in for you? You look like you could use a break."

"No way." Simon Dodson was sure to find out about it and consider her unworthy of John. Cassie wasn't willing to risk that.

"You have a donation quota?"

Cassie nodded. "I bet that guy at the other entrance isn't having this problem," she muttered. Her breath made small whiffs of fog. Her nose wasn't the only body part in danger of frostbite. Even the knit cap wasn't enough to completely protect her ears. She'd swear those weren't earrings dangling from her lobes, but tiny icicles.

"I'll come and see you again later," Angie promised.

"Great, and thanks for the coffee." Cassie wondered whether anyone would notice if she stuck her nose in the hot liquid.

Angie disappeared inside the mall and Cassie rang her bell with renewed enthusiasm. It helped to remember that in less than three hours she would have completed one of the tasks that would bring her closer to meeting John.

In retrospect she wished she'd pushed Simon to show her John's photograph. Then again, she didn't want any predetermined impressions of him. He was already bigger than life in her mind. She pictured him at the head of a boardroom table or the helm of a sailboat. Or...

Suddenly, she noticed the scruffily dressed middle-aged man standing in front of her. He looked like he belonged to a motorcycle gang. He had on a worn leather jacket that barely zipped up over his protruding belly and a bandanna around his head. His hair, long and greasy and tied in a ponytail, reached to the middle of his back. He made a beeline for Cassie as if destiny had called him to her side.

Her bell ringing became a whole lot less enthusiastic.

He looked her slowly up and down. Then he smiled as if to say her waiting days were over; *he* had arrived. "Hello, there, pretty lady."

Cassie managed a weak smile in return. "Happy holidays." This guy didn't strike her as the charitable type.

"I bet you're real cold standing out here all by yourself."

She didn't respond but his gaze lingered on her, which gave her a decidedly uncomfortable feeling.

"I could find ways to keep us both warm."

"Ah...actually I'm warm as toast," she said. An outright lie. She hoped he didn't notice that, by this time, her nose was probably blue.

A mother and daughter scurried past her. Cassie thrust out her arm and rang the bell as if sounding an alarm during the great San Francisco fire. When the pair resolutely ignored her, she rang the bell using both hands. Still they walked past. In fact, it seemed to Cassie that they went out of their way to avoid her. In other words, she was on her own with the biker.

"We'd be grateful for a donation," she told him.

"I was thinking you could give me one."

"Me? What could I possibly give you?" As soon as she

asked the question, Cassie realized her mistake. "Forget I asked that," she said.

"What are you doing after this stint?" he asked.

Cassie could hardly believe this was happening and let her bell-holding hand fall to her side. "Are you trying to pick me up?" she asked incredulously. "You're old enough to be my father." She did her best to hide her revulsion.

"Hey, you can't blame a guy for trying."

"Yes, I can. Now kindly move along. You're discouraging donations." She scowled at him, letting him know she didn't appreciate that he was cutting into her hourly quota.

He chuckled as though amused. "You have no idea what you're missing."

Frankly, Cassie was grateful for the escape. She heaved a sigh of relief when he sauntered off. Her one hope was that when he left the mall he'd use a different exit.

As soon as Mr. Easy Rider was gone, donations picked up. Still, as far as she could figure, Cassie wasn't even close to making the recommended quota, despite her cheerful greetings.

Distracted, she didn't notice another man approaching.

"You should be ashamed of yourself," he said angrily.

Taken aback, she blinked, then asked, "I beg your pardon?" Obviously *he* wasn't the one standing in the cold, ringing his heart out, seeking donations for the poor.

"It isn't even December."

"And your point is?" she challenged, which she recognized almost immediately was a mistake. She didn't want to invite an argument, which she'd inadvertently done.

"Christmas is far too commercial."

"Ah…"

"Everyone's got their hand out. I've had it up to here," he said, slicing the air over his head, "with greedy beggars asking for handouts."

"Greedy beggars?" she repeated, growing agitated. "Don't you have any compassion for others? Where's your Christmas spirit?"

"It doesn't come out until December. Look at these shops! Most of them had their Christmas displays up before Halloween. All they're after is the almighty dollar."

"Go complain to them, not me," she urged, hoping to send Scrooge on his way. "And when you do, say hello to Tiny Tim for me."

"Who?"

"Never mind."

"Those greedy shop owners spoil the true meaning of Christmas. And you're no better than corporate America, stopping people as they're going into the store. Irritating them with that stupid bell."

"I'm not asking you for anything. The bell is to remind shoppers of the less fortunate. I didn't *stop* you—you're the one who came up to me. Furthermore..." She halted midsentence as it occurred to her that this man might be a plant of Simon's, that he'd purposely headed right over to chat with her.

Cassie eyed him warily. "Simon sent you, didn't he?"

"Simon? Who's Simon?"

"This is a test, isn't it?"

"Lady, I don't know what you're talking about."

"You can't fool me! Simon sent you to see how I'd respond. Well, you can tell him I saw through your little charade and it didn't work." She felt downright smug that Simon hadn't outsmarted her.

Scrooge stared at her, wearing a puzzled look. Then his eyes narrowed. "Lady, I suggest you seek counseling."

"Thank you, but I suggest you make an appointment first. You can tell Simon I said that, okay?"

He backed away from her as if he suddenly suspected she carried an infectious disease.

Donations were few and far between, and Cassie glanced toward her counterpart at the other end of the mall with envy. He had more business than he knew what to do with. She, on the other hand, felt like the Little Match Girl. Using her foot, she eased the red kettle ever so slightly toward the department store entrance. She was about halfway between the two when the other charity collector noticed.

Cassie eased her foot away from the pot and gazed in the opposite direction.

"Hey, you!" he shouted, pointing an accusing finger at her. "You stay in your half of the mall and I'll stay in mine."

Playing innocent, Cassie pressed her gloved hand to her chest. "Are you speaking to me?" she called.

"You drag that kettle one step closer, sister, and you'll live to regret it."

Cassie opened her mouth, then closed it. She'd been caught. There was nothing to do but drag the kettle back, one step at a time.

Eventually Cassie returned to her original spot and figured she'd probably lost thirty minutes in this attempt to find more fertile ground. With no option other than to follow her original plan, she continued to greet the shoppers, doing her best to display a cheerful holiday spirit.

A young couple approached from the mall parking lot and Cassie made eye contact with the man. The woman, who carried a cup of takeout coffee, didn't appear to see her, but he looked friendly enough, so Cassie rang the bell with renewed energy. These people seemed like the kind who'd dig deep into their wallets in order to help the less fortunate.

As they neared the store, just as Cassie had hoped, the man reached in his back pocket for his wallet. This was a good sign. Cassie smiled encouragingly.

The woman walked toward the store entrance, while the man paused in front of Cassie and slipped a twenty-dollar bill into the pot.

The woman quickly rejoined her husband. "How much did you put in there?" she demanded.

"Come on, Alicia, it's for charity."

"Charity begins at home. We've been through this, re-member? We're on a Christmas budget. We don't have extra money to be giving away."

The man grimaced apologetically.

"It's for a good cause," Cassie reminded the woman.

"As for you," Alicia said menacingly. "I saw the way you were flirting with my husband. You didn't think I noticed, did you?"

Cassie was too stunned to react. "I wasn't—"

"Don't bother denying it. I have eyes. Maybe the two of you are old *friends*."

"Alicia," the man snapped.

"That's it, we're finished. It's over." In a fit of anger she tossed the cup of coffee at Cassie.

She gasped and leaped back but not in time to avoid having coffee splash the front of her caramel-colored wool coat.

The man looked horrified, whispered something Cassie couldn't hear, then hurried after his wife. "Alicia, Alicia..."

In shock and denial, Cassie stared down at her coat. Some very unladylike comments formed in her mind. However, she didn't express them since that would reflect poorly on the charitable organization. Within minutes she was glad she'd kept her mouth shut. Because, to Cassie's astonishment, donations started to increase dramatically following the incident. She glanced at the other bell ringer, who was scowling at her. He rang his bell louder and harder.

Cassie retaliated with an all-out rendition of "Deck the Halls" and soon had a short line, everyone waiting to drop in donations. She wasn't sure what had changed but clearly there'd been a reversal. Perhaps her bell ringing was superior. Or perhaps that section of the parking lot had filled up. Whatever the cause, she was taking full advantage of it.

Toward the end of her shift, a sweet old lady sidled up to Cassie with a benevolent smile. She stuffed something inside her coat pocket and leaned close to whisper, "Use this to buy yourself a decent coat, dear. You poor thing."

That was it? People thought she was a charity case and had taken pity on her. Too bad the coffee incident had happened at the end of her four hours. Who knew how much she would've collected if it had occurred earlier.

She nearly laughed aloud when she realized one glove

was missing. Cassie didn't have a clue when that had disappeared or how.

Precisely four hours into her assignment, when she was
about ready to hand in her kettle and bell, she saw Dr.
Simon Dodson. He was walking across the parking lot and
headed directly toward her. And he was frowning.

CHAPTER SIX

Simon says: The best match for you is the one I *arrange.*

Just as Simon approached, an elderly gentleman stepped up to the pot and inserted a folded bill.

"Thank you and Merry Christmas," Cassie told him cheerfully.

"No, thank *you*," the old man returned. "You see, I was on a troop train in World War II and your organization met us at the station as we disembarked and handed out doughnuts and coffee. That small kindness meant the world to those of us going off to war. I've never forgotten it."

Cassie hardly knew what to say.

"A lot of us didn't come home from the war, but I'll bet you those of us who did will always remember the friendly smiles and support you gave us. I'm an old man now and I don't have many more years left." He grew teary-eyed as he spoke. "Merry Christmas, young lady," he whispered, gently squeezing her hand, "and thank you again for the sacrifice you're making on behalf of others."

Now it was Cassie who had tears in her eyes. She brushed

them aside as Simon came closer. The old man had disappeared inside the mall by the time he arrived.

"How was it?" he asked.

Cassie tried to swallow the lump in her throat. "My grandfather was in the Second World War, too."

"I beg your pardon?"

"That elderly gentleman," she said, sniffling, "the one who was just here. He told me about something that happened when he went off to war and thanked me as if I was the one who'd been kind to him."

"I didn't see any old man."

"You didn't? He was here a minute ago and was...just wonderful." She didn't understand how Simon could have missed him. It was unlikely that he'd have eyes only for her.

"What happened to your coat?" Simon asked, apparently not interested in hearing about the man who had touched her so deeply.

"Oh, that," she said, glancing down. "That was a lucky break. Well, to be honest, it didn't seem like it at the time, but I collected a lot of pity donations as a result."

He didn't ask her to elaborate. "Your shift is over. You can leave now."

"What about my substitute?" Cassie wasn't about to be lured away from her duty station until the next person was firmly in place.

"That would be me," a cheerful middle-aged woman said from behind Simon, the supervisor at her side.

Cassie handed over the bell, and the supervisor took her full kettle and replaced it with an empty one. "Good luck," Cassie told the new bell ringer and meant every word. She nearly added that the woman was going to need it.

"You didn't tell me how your morning went," Simon said. He walked into the mall with her.

Cassie stood just inside the sliding glass doors for a moment, soaking in the blast of warm air. Until now she hadn't fully realized how utterly cold she'd been. Four hours had felt like forever.

"You don't want to know," she said. Her teeth had only now stopped chattering.

"I don't ask questions if I don't want an answer."

"Okay, fine. I misplaced a glove, and my nose lost feeling in the first half hour." She looked at him and muttered, "It's still there, isn't it? My nose, I mean."

"Yes." His mouth twitched, but he didn't admit he was amused.

"My feet feel like blocks of ice. A jealous wife threw coffee on me and some sweet old lady slipped a fifty-dollar bill into my coat pocket because she felt sorry for me. I threw it in the pot," she added righteously.

Simon arched his brows. That apparently was his only comment.

"Furthermore, I recognized your plant."

"My...plant?"

"The man you sent. Okay, so I made that remark about saying hello to Tiny Tim. Oh, and about seeing a shrink. I probably shouldn't have, but I couldn't help it. He was obnoxious. Did you pay him extra for being rude?" she asked. That sounded like something Simon would do.

He eyed her speculatively, but didn't respond one way or the other.

"He told you, didn't he?" Cassie could easily picture Scrooge running to Simon to tattle on her.

As they walked past a Starbucks, Cassie stopped abruptly. "I would kill for a latte," she said and veered back into the store.

Simon followed, and they stood in line together. When they reached the counter, Cassie ordered her vanilla latte, along with two shortbread cookies. It was after two, and she hadn't had lunch yet.

Simon ordered a large black coffee and paid their bill. Although the small area was crowded, a couple left just then and they were able to secure a table.

Cassie sank gratefully into the chair. She crossed her legs, and removed one boot so she could rub feeling back into her toes, pausing occasionally to sip her latte. It tasted like heaven.

"About this, uh, plant you mentioned."

"Oh, him. Not to worry, I caught on fast enough. Well, maybe not as fast as I should have, but it was obvious that you sent him. He didn't try very hard to hide it, either."

"Not *that* obvious," Simon said mildly. "Because I didn't send anyone."

"Oh, come on. There's no need to carry on this charade."

He regarded her sternly. "I am not in the habit of lying."

She studied him—and realized he just might be telling the truth.

"I will repeat myself this once. I did not send anyone to test you."

"Oh." The man with all the complaints had been so unpleasant that it was a natural assumption.

To hide her embarrassment, Cassie tore the cellophane off her cookies and gobbled them both down.

"What did you learn from the experience?" Simon asked.

She rolled her eyes. "You didn't tell me there'd be an exam."

"It's not an exam. I asked a straightforward question."

"Well..." Cassie took a sip of her latte, then removed her other boot. "For one thing, I will never pass someone standing in the cold ringing a bell and not leave a donation. You wouldn't believe how many people simply look the other way."

"But you've ignored a bell ringer now and then, haven't you?"

"Okay, I may have, but I won't again. I don't think I've ever worked harder at anything."

The merest hint of a smile showed in his eyes.

"You find that funny? Why don't *you* stand out in the cold for four hours and see how you like it?"

"I prefer to write a check."

"Of course you would. It's much easier."

"Agreed. That's the point. Anything else?"

"Well, there was the lovely old man." She turned an angry look on Simon. "You must've chased him away."

"Like I said, I didn't notice any old man and I certainly didn't chase one away."

"He was definitely there. He reminded me of my grandfather. Grampa died when I was young, but I remember him so well." She grew introspective. "He was in the war, too. That old man made everything that happened today worthwhile."

She gestured at her stained coat and her stocking feet, then tentatively at her nose. "I think I'm finally thawing out."

"I'm glad to hear it."

He didn't sound glad. In fact, he sounded bored.

"Tell me about John," she urged.

Simon's deep sigh informed her that she was becoming tiresome. "What do you want to know?"

"Something. Anything. Did you assign him three tasks like you did me? What are they?"

"I won't discuss my other clients with you." The way he said it suggested she'd committed a major faux pas.

She forged ahead despite that. "Has John asked about me?"

Another sigh. "I should never have mentioned his name."

"But you did and now I'm curious. Come on, Simon, have a heart. Give me one small detail, one tiny tidbit, about my hero."

He glanced at her coat and, seeing the huge coffee stain, must have taken pity on her. "All right, if you have to know, he's an engineer."

"An engineer?" she repeated slowly.

"Your children will be left-brain geniuses."

"Children." Overwhelmed with excitement she grasped Simon's hand.

"Restrain yourself, please."

"Oh, Simon, loosen up a little, would you?"

He looked at her coldly, as though her comment didn't merit a response.

"Has John asked about me?"

He nodded.

Rubbing her palms together, she blurted out, "And what did you say?" After asking, she quickly changed her mind. "No, don't tell me—I'd rather not know."

"It wasn't unflattering, if that's what you're implying."

This was promising. "Really?"

"Are you looking for compliments, Cassie?"

"No…well, maybe." Then, because she was curious and she couldn't resist, she asked, "Do you like me, Simon?"

He regarded her for a moment, as though carefully weighing his response. "Not particularly. Wait—let me rephrase that. I don't have any feelings for you whatsoever. Except for the appropriate reactions of a professional toward his client, of course."

What would it have cost him to smile and say something nice? "You really are a dolt."

He stiffened. "I beg your pardon?"

"You heard me. You know, if you smiled more often you might look human. You're supposed to be a psychologist—haven't you heard that a smile is a positive way of interacting?"

"I don't see any reason to—"

"Forget it. You are who you are, and I am who I am."

"That was profound." He seemed to be making fun of her.

Cassie didn't care. Simon was a means to an end, and if he found her a decent man she could love for the rest of her life, then it didn't matter if he liked her or not.

"When can I complete the second task?" she asked, eager to hurry the process along. From the sound of it, John was equally excited about meeting her.

"I'm making the final arrangements next week. I'll be in touch as soon as everything's set."

"Okay." Cassie finished her latte and dabbed at the crumbs left over from her shortbread cookies. "You're not very good at relationships, are you? Personally, I mean, not professionally."

Acting as if she hadn't spoken, Simon shoved back his chair and seemed about to leave. "As I said earlier, I'll be in touch."

"Before you go, I'd like to ask how you came to this line of work."

"You already know I don't answer personal questions. This isn't about me."

"But it is."

"*Au contraire.* You came to me for services rendered. Do you interrogate your dentist about his background—or private life?"

"No, but—"

"You let him do his job and you walk away satisfied when he's finished. It's the same with me, or it should be. I perform a service, nothing more. I'm good at what I do and I enjoy my work."

"Always?"

"Some matches are more difficult than others. Some clients more trying." He looked pointedly in her direction.

"At least you can take comfort from knowing that once I meet John, you won't ever need to see me again."

"Yes, there is that...."

Cassie couldn't help it; she burst out laughing.

Simon seemed genuinely puzzled. "Why is that funny?"

"It wouldn't have been if you hadn't been so honest about it. You'll be happy to get rid of me, won't you?"

He stood and tossed his empty coffee container in the proper receptacle. "You did very well today, Cassie."

For a moment, she thought her ears had deceived her.

"Was that a compliment, an actual *compliment,* from the great Dr. Simon Dodson?"

"Not really," he said soberly. "It was a statement of fact. The truth is, I didn't expect you to last all four hours. You surprised me."

"I want to meet John," she told him, disregarding the implied insult in his words.

"So I gathered, and soon you shall."

Ten minutes later, they left Starbucks together and exchanged civil goodbyes.

Cassie could hardly wait to get back to her condo so she could talk to Angie. The minute she'd showered and changed, she reached for the phone and hit speed dial.

After several rings, she was connected to voice mail. That was odd. Angie hadn't said anything about going out—but then it wasn't as if Cassie was her parole officer.

Much later that afternoon she heard from Angie.

"Where were you?" Cassie asked right away.

"Shopping. 'Tis the season, you know?" Her friend seemed to be in high spirits.

"Did you find any bargains?"

"Lots. How'd the morning go?"

"Simon said I surprised him."

"You saw Dr. Dodson?"

"Yeah, he showed up to check on me. We had coffee afterward."

"You and... Dr. Dodson? Simon?"

"What's so odd about that?"

"I don't know," Angie said. "I just can't picture it."

"It wasn't like a date or anything," Cassie insisted. "More of a...debriefing. He said he'd be in touch next week with the details about my next task. I get to be an elf. That *has* to be easier than what I did this morning."

"I wouldn't be so sure of that," Angie warned her.

CHAPTER SEVEN

Her arms loaded down with groceries, Cassie hurried over to the elevator. "Mr. Oliver, hold that door for me!" she cried frantically, trying not to drop the quart of milk dangling from her index finger.

Mr. Oliver pretended not to hear, and the doors glided shut in her face.

Cassie ground her teeth in frustration. This wasn't the first time Mr. Oliver had purposely let the elevator close as she ran toward it. She'd watched him do the same thing with other residents. Obviously it gave him some kind of thrill. She might have imagined it, but Cassie swore she saw a glimmer of sadistic humor in his eyes as the doors slid closed.

She lowered one bag to the floor and pushed the call button. While she waited, she went to collect her newspaper, only to discover the slot was empty—and it wasn't even Tuesday. Apparently Mrs. Mullinex was now clipping coupons from the Sunday edition, as well.

Perhaps it was time to confront the retired schoolteacher.

Cassie took the elevator up to the fifth floor, brought her groceries to the kitchen, and walked down the hallway to

Mrs. Mullinex's unit. Outside her neighbor's door, she rang
the bell until she heard footsteps on the other side.

"Hold your horses," Mrs. Mullinex called out.

She answered the door, wearing her housecoat and slippers. Her head was covered in pink curlers and wrapped
with a bandanna knotted directly above her forehead. It
wasn't a look Cassie saw very often these days—if ever.

"Why, Cassie, how nice of you to stop by," she said pleasantly. "Can I offer you a glass of eggnog?"

"Oh, no, thank you." Cassie made an attempt to be
neighborly or at least polite. "Uh, I believe you have my
newspaper."

Her neighbor seemed startled, as if the suggestion that
she might have taken something not hers was a devastating insult. Mrs. Mullinex raised one hand to her mouth in
a gesture of innocence. "Oh, dear, was that *your* paper?"

Cassie held out her hand.

The older woman slowly retrieved the thick weekend
edition and reluctantly placed it in Cassie's outstretched
hand. "I was wondering, dear, if you wouldn't mind letting me have the section with the *New York Times* crossword puzzle."

Cassie clutched the paper to her chest.

"Only when you're finished with it, of course."

"I happen to enjoy doing the crossword puzzle, Mrs.
Mullinex."

"Oh."

Wondering if she'd been a little too inflexible, Cassie returned to her own condo, put away her groceries and made
a cup of coffee. She sat down with the paper, prepared to
relax. She'd just turned to the middle section, grabbed a

pen—doing the crossword puzzle in pen was a matter of pride—when the rap music started next door. The whole room seemed to vibrate. Cassie groaned. There was no question: the fates were conspiring against her.

Getting up from her chair, Cassie pounded her fist against the kitchen wall hard enough to rattle her dishes. She had to repeat the pounding twice before the music was lowered to a tolerable level.

Settled once more, she rested her feet on the ottoman, crossed her ankles and savored the first sip of coffee when her doorbell rang.

"Oh, for the love of heaven," she muttered, tossing down the pen. If it turned out to be one of her annoying neighbors—whom she'd be having dinner with all too soon, according to Simon—she didn't know what she'd say.

To her astonishment, it was her brother, toting a five-foot Christmas tree.

"Shawn, what are you doing here?" Normally she'd be fortunate to see him twice in four months, and this was his second visit to Seattle in as many weeks.

"Are you complaining?"

"Of course not!"

"I come bearing gifts." He thrust the Christmas tree into the room.

"So I noticed."

Shawn grinned. "I thought you could use a bit of Christmas cheer." He stepped into the condo and leaned the tree against the living room wall. "This also seemed like a good excuse to stop by so you could tell me how everything went yesterday."

Had it only been the day before that she'd stood in the

cold, soliciting donations? That didn't seem possible, and yet Cassie hadn't stopped thinking about the experience. What remained uppermost in her mind was the time she'd spent with Simon at the coffee shop. He'd been frank, unemotional, honest. She amended that to *brutally* honest. When she'd met him, she'd considered him rude and arrogant, but since then she'd had a change of heart. Simon, she decided, was simply...direct. He said what he felt and didn't moderate his opinions in deference to other people's flimsy egos. She'd never met anyone quite like him.

"Well?" Shawn prodded her.

"Who do you want to hear about first—Mr. Scrooge, who *wasn't* sent by Simon as a test," she added, "or would you rather I told you about the woman who threw coffee at me because she thought I'd flirted with her husband?"

Shawn flopped down on the sofa. "Both, and while you're up, I'll take a cup of that coffee."

"Sure," she said, while she got a mug and filled it to the brim. "You won't believe what he said to me."

"Scrooge?"

"No, Simon. I asked if he liked me and he said 'not particularly.' What's so funny is the fact that—"

"Funny? You thought this was funny?"

"Not at first," she admitted. "The thing with Simon is that he wasn't being intentionally rude. He's the most plainspoken man I've ever encountered."

"Sounds like a bore to me."

"I called him a dolt." She smiled at the memory. "He didn't much like that."

"So he can dish it out, but he can't take it?"

"Well, he certainly isn't used to it."

They chatted for a while, until Shawn eventually said, "I hope you realize that all you've done is talk about Simon. I've yet to hear a word about anyone else."

"Really?" Caught up in her musing, Cassie hadn't noticed.

"I think you might be falling for him."

"For Simon?" The suggestion was ludicrous. "Oh, hardly! If I'm focusing on him, it's because he's the man who holds the key to my happiness. He's going to introduce me to John—and I have high hopes for John. He's my perfect—oops, *most suitable,* which is what Simon calls it—match."

"Just in time for the perfect—or should I say, *most suitable*—Christmas."

Cassie suspected Shawn was mocking her a little, but she was too hopeful and too happy to care.

All at once he grew serious. "Don't build your expectations too high, Cassie. What if you and this John character don't really connect?"

"But we will. That's the beauty of it. Simon studied our profiles and concluded that we're ideal for each other. I think his success lies in the fact that he can be emotionally detached and even clinical. It's all quite scientific, you know."

"Uh-huh." Shawn nodded wryly.

"Did I mention Simon refuses to talk about himself? That's probably why he's so brilliant at this. He doesn't want to cloud the relationship between him and his clients. His sole focus is on finding the right person for them."

"Seems to me you've got him all figured out."

"I think I just might. Now wipe that smirk off your face," she said. Now that she'd thought seriously about Simon, and she'd been doing that for the past twenty-four hours, it all made a crazy kind of sense.

Simon made sense.

Simply put, he wasn't encumbered with the need to please others. His skill at matchmaking was based on his knowledge of psychology, as he claimed, but he obviously had good instincts, too. His success rate was impressive, and if he honestly felt John-the-engineer would make her a good husband, then Cassie didn't doubt it for an instant.

"He's an engineer," she murmured.

"Simon?"

"No, my match. Simon offered me a crumb of information yesterday."

"An engineer," Shawn echoed. "I guess your kids will be left-brained."

"That's what Simon said," she returned excitedly.

Shawn looked surprised. "You told him about your IQ?"

"No, but it was on the questionnaire." In high school, her high IQ had been an embarrassment rather than an asset. She always used to insist that scoring well on a test didn't make her any different from everyone else. She still felt that way—although it did get her through two chemistry degrees in four years instead of six.

"Mom was always proud of your intelligence," Shawn reminded her.

"It didn't matter to our father, though, did it?" As a child, Cassie had thought it was her fault their father had left the family. Although it made no sense for a seven-year-old to assume that kind of blame, she had. Later, she'd learned this was fairly typical in situations like this. They'd all been devastated, but she'd unconsciously taken on the role of scapegoat.

"Speaking of Dad…"

Cassie already knew what was coming. "He called you?"

Shawn nodded.

"His yearly sojourn into fatherhood! Lucky you. This year it was your turn to receive the great gift of his phone call. What did he have to say?"

"He saw one of my murals and wanted to tell me he was impressed."

Cassie shrugged. "That was nice."

"A surprise, actually."

Cassie knew how long Shawn had waited for any praise from their father. They rarely discussed him; the subject was still too painful for them both.

"Where was he?" The last she'd heard, he was living aboard his sailboat somewhere in the Caribbean.

"Hawaii."

Cassie chuckled. "Really? Wouldn't it be amusing if he ran into Mom on the streets of Honolulu?"

Shawn shook his head. "She's over him. She forgave him a long time ago."

"Mom's a better woman than I am." Talking about their father depressed her. "Can't we discuss something else? Something more cheerful—like bank foreclosures?"

Shawn snorted. "Very funny."

"I don't know why he bothers," she said.

"I thought we weren't going to discuss Dad."

"Right. Sorry."

Shawn drank the last of his coffee and stood. "I've gotta go."

"You mean you aren't going to stay and help me trim the tree?"

"Can't. I've got an...appointment."

From the gleam in his eyes, this so-called appointment involved a woman. "You've got a date."

"I'm not telling."

It really wasn't fair. Cassie had to pay tens of thousands of dollars to meet men, and her brother had women falling all over him. It must be those piercing blue eyes of his—plus, of course, the fact that he was talented, rich and eligible.

Cassie walked him to the door.

"Are you coming back here tonight?" she asked.

"Nope. I'm taking the red-eye to Phoenix."

"Will I see you at Christmas?"

"Sure. Where else would I go?"

"Call me, okay?"

"Will do. Besides, I want to hear all about Simon."

"John," she corrected. "Simon's the matchmaker."

"Right." That gleam was back in his eyes and Cassie suspected the slip had been intentional.

An hour later, Cassie had the Christmas tree in its stand and set by the window that overlooked the city. The big star above Macy's glowed in the dim light of late afternoon. She dragged her ornaments out from the guest room closet and decided to give Angie a call. Trimming a tree all alone wasn't any fun.

Her friend answered immediately. "Come on over," Cassie invited her. "Shawn stopped by to drop off a Christmas tree and then abandoned me to decorate it by myself. I've got hot apple cider and popcorn popping in the microwave."

"Oh, Cassie, I'd love to but I can't."

"Are you off shopping again?"

"No, I'm meeting an old friend. Sort of a last-minute thing. You could join us if you want."

"Anyone I know?"

"Um, not really."

"Oh, well, I've got an appointment with a box of ornaments, a bowl of popcorn and the DVD of *The Bishop's Wife*."

Angie sounded regretful. "I hate the thought of you trimming the tree alone."

"Oh, I don't mind." And that was true. She was in a good mood; in fact, she planned to give Mrs. Mullinex the Sunday paper when she'd finished—and she'd leave the crossword untouched.

"Think of next year," Angie urged. "You'll most likely be married by then."

"John and me." She filled her head with happy thoughts of a Christmas photo in front of next year's tree, the two of them smiling blissfully into the camera. The perfect Christmas. The first card she mailed out would be to Jill and Tom.

"You might even be pregnant by then."

"Whoa, you're moving a little too fast."

"Why? You're getting the best husband money can buy, aren't you?"

Cassie laughed. She hadn't thought of it in those terms but Angie was right. She was paying top dollar to meet John-the-engineer; by the same token, he'd been willing to pay top dollar to meet her.

And the one walking away with fistfuls of cash was Simon Dodson.

As far as Cassie was concerned, he would have earned every penny.

CHAPTER EIGHT

At the end of their brief telephone conversation, Angie had said she'd call Cassie once she got home Sunday evening. Although it'd been an offhand comment, Cassie was surprised when she didn't hear from her. Apparently Angie's last-minute meeting with her friend had turned into more of an event.

Cassie didn't think much about it until Angie showed up at the lab Monday morning. Her friend's face radiated... joy. Unmistakable joy.

"Well, well, well," Cassie said, watching Angie closely. Something was up, and it didn't take Sherlock Holmes to figure out that a man was involved. Clearly Angie had met someone special. The "old friend" from yesterday evening?

"Stop looking at me like that," Angie said, blushing.

"You're in love, aren't you?"

Angie's eyes widened. "You can tell? Really?"

Cassie nodded. "You've got the happy look. You know, the one we all get when we first realize we're falling for someone." She knew it had to be the "friend" Angie had seen last night.

Angie shyly glanced away. "The most incredible feeling

came over me this morning." Her voice fell to a whisper. "It's like...a sixth sense, a knowledge, that this man could be the one."

"That's the feeling I'm talking about." Cassie had never experienced it herself, but she'd seen it again and again with her friends.

A wistful happiness shone from Angie's eyes, but she didn't say anything else.

After several minutes Cassie couldn't stand it anymore. "Well?" she asked.

The reflective look disappeared and was instantly replaced by one that was far more guarded. "Well, what?"

"Aren't you going to give me details?"

Angie hesitated. "Of course...but not yet."

This confused Cassie. First, there was very little they didn't tell each other—except for Angie's meeting with the matchmaker and it was easy to understand why her friend hadn't mentioned that, since Simon had rejected her as a client. If it'd happened to her, Cassie wouldn't have announced it, either. But this was an entirely different matter. For some reason, Angie preferred to remain tight-lipped about this man in her life. Well, so be it. When necessary, Cassie could be patient. If Angie wanted to keep this mystery man to herself for a while, Cassie would respect that.

"I'll tell you everything soon," Angie said. "It's just that I'd like to hold on to this feeling for a little longer."

Still, Cassie couldn't help being curious. "Would it hurt to let me know how you met?"

Angie's face relaxed into a warm smile. "You'll love that part. We sort of stumbled upon each other. We dated for a while ages ago and decided it wasn't going to work. Or rather, he did, not me. So I began the search again."

"So this is the guy you've been in love with all along?"

Angie nodded. "You'll meet him," she said a second time. "I promise."

"Will you be seeing him soon?"

"No. It's a bit…complicated at the moment."

"Complicated?" Cassie didn't like the sound of that. "He's not married or anything, is he?"

Angie shook her head. "Oh, no! Nothing like that."

"Good." Cassie smiled, then glanced down at her feet. "Actually," she said in a low voice, "I was hoping to chat with you last night. I had a couple of questions."

"What kind of questions?"

"I wanted to ask you about Simon."

"What about him?"

"Basically… I was curious. Other than the information on his website, what do you know?"

Angie shrugged. "Not much."

"How did you hear about him?"

"He was a birthday gift—at least, the first consultation was."

"Who from?"

"My mother. She wants grandchildren and knew how brokenhearted I was when…this other relationship ended. She heard about Simon when he did a radio interview."

"Simon did a radio interview?"

"I don't think he does them often. This was around Valentine's Day a few years back."

"Oh."

Angie cocked her head to one side. "Why this interest in Dr. Dodson all of a sudden?"

Cassie didn't want Angie or anyone to suspect how intrigued she was by the matchmaker. She found her thoughts drifting toward him far more often than was comfortable. She told herself that once her curiosity was satisfied, he'd drift into the background where he belonged.

While she'd gone on to his website—the address was noted on his business card—she hadn't searched further.

That evening, she did. She logged on to the internet and immediately typed his name into Google. There wasn't a *lot,* but enough to answer some of her questions. He'd been a Rhodes scholar, attending Cambridge—after Harvard. He'd taught at a prestigious East Coast college. He'd written political articles for the *Wall Street Journal* and the *New York Times.* Just as she'd realized earlier, he had opinions about everything and didn't mind sharing them…in unvarnished prose.

According to Wikipedia, Simon had never been married. She found that…interesting.

Intent as she was on reading her computer screen, the phone startled her. "Yes," Cassie said, snatching it up. Her gaze stayed on the screen for fear she'd miss a single detail.

"Ms. Beaumont?" The female voice was vaguely familiar. "This is Dr. Dodson's office."

A chill raced down her spine. Simon knew she was online, reading about him! He was about to inform her that she'd forfeited her thirty thousand dollars. "I won't do it again!" she blurted without thinking.

"Excuse me?"

"Were you phoning because—" Cassie stopped abruptly,

aware of how absurd she'd been. How paranoid. "Can I help you?" she asked sweetly.

By now Ms. Snelling sounded utterly confused. "Would it be convenient for you to stop by tomorrow afternoon at four-thirty?" she asked.

"Ah, sure." That meant leaving work a bit early, which wasn't really a problem.

"Thank you. Dr. Dodson will see you then."

Rattled as she was, Cassie had hung up before she thought to ask what the meeting was about. She assumed Simon would be giving her the information regarding her second task. But why not call? Maybe he had her elf costume, although that seemed unlikely.

She felt a sense of expectation. She had to admit that Simon fascinated her, although she didn't especially like him—any more than he liked her. Perhaps he represented a challenge and she couldn't resist trying to make him aware of her as a woman. *Everyone* needed to be liked and appreciated, even Simon. That was probably what had led him into the matchmaking business. Certainly the couples she'd spoken to had expressed their appreciation—if not liking—for him. So maybe he couldn't achieve romantic satisfaction for himself but he could for others. It all seemed rather lonely.

On Tuesday, she kept checking her watch. Angie, who might otherwise have commented, was preoccupied, as well. Cassie had decided not to question her about this new, or rather resumed, relationship. When Angie was ready to tell her, she would. Cassie could only hope this man turned out to be everything Angie believed he was. Perhaps they could have a double wedding!

Because Simon had kept her waiting at their previous

appointments, Cassie didn't bother to show up until four forty-five. His assistant's disapproval was obvious. When Cassie stepped up to the desk, the older woman regarded her with distaste. "You're late."

"Well, yes… Simon, Dr. Dodson, was late the past two times and—"

"And you felt turnabout was fair play," he said, standing in the doorway leading to his office. "If you'll forgive the cliché." His arms were crossed and he looked more amused than annoyed.

It'd been four days since she'd last seen him and it struck her again how attractive he was.

He arched his brows. "You have nothing to say? Generally I can't get you to shut up and now you act as if we've never met."

"No… I figured you'd be late and—and I didn't want to waste time sitting here…" she stammered, embarrassed that he'd caught her staring.

"Don't let it happen again."

"Then don't keep me waiting again," she returned.

His shoulders relaxed. "Ah, I see the Cassie I recognize is back. Follow me. We have business to discuss." He walked into his office, Cassie close behind him.

Without waiting for an invitation, she took the visitor's chair across from his desk. She leaned back, legs crossed, trying to appear confident.

Looking stiff and formal once more, Simon sat down. "I asked to see you because I have the information concerning your agreement to work as Santa's helper."

She nodded. "Okay, but you could've phoned—unless you have my outfit."

"Outfit?"

"For my elf job."

Simon shook his head, and for the first time since she'd arrived, he seemed edgy. "There's been a small change in plans."

"Change? What do you mean?"

"The mall has experienced a decline in the number of parents bringing their children to meet Santa."

"Does this mean Santa won't be requiring my help, after all?" She did her best to keep her enthusiasm to a minimum. She wouldn't mind getting out of this; she liked children—in fact, she loved them—but if her tasks were limited to two instead of three, she'd be done that much sooner. Then Simon could introduce her to John.

Despite herself, she felt a twinge of regret at the idea of never seeing Simon again. But once he'd made the official introduction, his role would be over, his job done. She realized she'd miss his acerbic responses....

Simon frowned at her. "What are you thinking?" he asked.

Cassie answered a bit more sharply than she'd intended. "I'm sure you're not interested in my thoughts."

Again his brows shot toward his hairline. "I wonder how long it will take you to learn that I do not ask questions unless I *am* interested in the answer."

Cassie threw back her head. "All right, fine. I was just thinking that you're a very odd man. I find I'm rather... intrigued by you. Not in any romantic way, of course."

"Of course," he said dryly. "I can't tell you what a relief that is."

"It's more like...driving past a car wreck. Horrible though it is, you can't stop yourself from looking."

His frown deepened. "I can assure you my life is no wreck—nor is my car."

"Yes, well, I'm sure there's nothing wrong with your car."

Ignoring her comment and its implication, Simon picked up a piece of paper. "As I was saying, I heard from the Tacoma Mall regarding your assignment. There's been a slight change."

"Is this because of what you said earlier—that there's a decline in the number of children visiting Santa?"

"Yes. But here's what—"

"Oh, wait, I have a question," Cassie broke in.

Simon looked up at the ceiling as though his patience, which was always in short supply, had been sorely tested yet again. "No."

"That's rather dictatorial," she said. "How could a question hurt?"

"If you'd let me get a word in edgewise... I'm trying to give you some important information."

"About helping Santa?" Simon acted as if she'd have to smuggle top secret papers to the north pole.

"This relates directly to your assignment," he said, avoiding eye contact. "I need to know if you're afraid of heights."

How could that possibly pertain to her working as an elf? "Not really. Why?"

Simon paused. "Maybe you should ask me your question, after all, before I explain."

"I'd rather hear what you have to say first."

He sighed loudly. "I talked to the mall and—"

"Yes, yes, we've been through this."

"I did mention that a uniform—a costume—is required."

"Yes." His reluctance to get to the point was beginning to concern her.

"I wasn't aware anything like this would be asked of you, but I'm encouraged that you don't have any fear of heights."

"I don't have to swing from the top of the Space Needle, do I?"

"No…" He exhaled slowly, staring down at his desk. "The mall wants the first elf—that would be you—to arrive by wire."

Cassie swallowed hard. "You're not referring to a telegram, are you?"

"No."

"A wire…from where?"

Again he avoided meeting her gaze. "The ceiling."

Cassie frowned, attempting to picture it. "You mean they want me to fly in like Peter Pan?"

"Exactly."

"You're joking!" This was the most preposterous idea she'd ever heard.

"The reindeer will follow you."

"*Live* reindeer?"

"They're plastic, but the mall wants to make a real production of Santa's arrival."

"And," she said, swallowing again since her mouth was so dry, "I'm part of the production."

"Yes. Are you willing to do this?" he asked.

Cassie's fingers tightened around her purse strap. "Would I still meet John if I decline?"

Simon hesitated. "This wasn't part of our original agreement, so I'd need to find a replacement task. That might take a few weeks."

"I don't want to wait any longer than I already have to."

"Then I'll inform the mall there won't be a problem and they can expect you on Saturday morning around nine."

Her complete lack of reaction must have alerted Simon to the fact that she was having second thoughts.

"No need to worry," Simon assured her. "I've been told it's quite safe. The wire will hold up to four hundred pounds."

"Oh." Cassie couldn't believe she'd agreed to this. When she glanced up, she thought, just for a moment, that she saw a smile on Simon's face. She leaned forward. "Were you smiling?"

"Pardon me?"

"You were smiling, weren't you? You're enjoying this." The man should be arrested for deriving pleasure from her humiliation.

His mouth quivered, but Simon had the good grace to look away. "Actually, I was thinking you're going to manage this quite well. You're a woman who's destined for high places."

Unfortunately, his vote of confidence didn't excite her. And his joke didn't amuse her.

CHAPTER NINE

Simon says: The best match for you is the one I arrange—
because I know you better than you know yourself.

"This must be a joke," Cassie said, staring at the limp green tights. No way was she going to stuff her hips and thighs into those.

"Dr. Dodson gave us your size, miss," said an elderly woman, whose name tag identified her as Daisy.

"He did?" Well, if he assumed she wore a size four, then who was she to enlighten him with the truth? Besides, the material did stretch.

Daisy handed her the elf costume, which consisted of a short green dress, like a skater's, with white faux fur edging the hem and a wide red belt. A green Santa-style hat with a white fur ball dangling from the end completed the outfit. But the pièce de résistance was a gold-painted pair of slippers with curled-up toes.

"The changing room is this way," Daisy said as she guided her down the dimly lit mall corridor.

Cassie followed, clutching the uniform, the hat and shoes.

"I can't tell you how pleased we are that you agreed to do this," Daisy was telling her. "You already have an audience of children waiting."

This wasn't news Cassie wanted to hear. "Where will Santa be while I'm floating through the air?"

"Oh, he'll be right behind you."

"Great." So she wouldn't be doing a solo flight. If she was going to descend from the clouds, Santa should do the same.

"Only… Santa will be on ground level," Daisy explained.

This was unfair.

The woman stopped and, frowning, bent down to pick up an empty beer can. "Oh, dear," she grumbled. "I'm afraid Floyd's been at it again."

"And who is Floyd?" Cassie asked a bit fearfully.

Daisy's voice was a low whisper. "He's Santa."

Was she saying Santa was a *drunk?* Outrageous!

"Santa?" Cassie cried.

"Don't misunderstand me," Daisy hurried to say. "Floyd's a wonderful Santa and the kids love him. The problem is, the children can be a bit wearing…as you'll discover for yourself in a few minutes." Daisy led her through a dark tunnel to some kind of alleyway deep inside the mall. "There's a ladies' room back here where you can change into your costume. I'll wait outside and once you're done, I'll have one of the technicians help you into the harness."

Cassie gaped at her.

"We want you to be as safe as possible," Daisy said in a confiding voice. "The wire will lower you from the top level of the mall to the ground floor."

"Oh." Cassie couldn't recall if the mall was two or three

levels. One thing was guaranteed—she'd have her eyes closed the entire flight.

As if reading her mind, Daisy added, "You have to play this up, you know."

"Play this up?" Cassie asked skeptically. "What do you mean?"

"To the crowd. We want you to yell out that Santa's on his way and all the boys and girls will be getting a gift from him."

"We're giving them gifts?"

"Candy canes. The children look forward to receiving those."

A cheap candy cane was a gift? That seemed to be an exaggeration—but who was Cassie to quibble over truth in advertising?

They finally got to the ladies' room and Cassie went inside. She removed her shoes and then her jeans and sweater. She hung what she could on the hook of the stall door, then sat on the toilet in order to slip on the tights. *Force* them on was more accurate.

The fit was so tight, they felt like an extra skin. Unfortunately they didn't reach all the way to her waist. One wrong move, and Cassie feared they'd roll down and reveal features—like her butt—that she'd rather keep private. It helped a little to jump up and down and then prance around, pulling on the waistband as she did. She also did a couple of squats. Still, the tights didn't stretch quite as far as she would've liked.

"Is everything all right in there, dear?" Daisy asked.

"Just fine," Cassie told her. Thankfully, the minidress fit. The shoes were good, too. She adjusted the hat in the bathroom mirror and realized she'd need to secure it for the flight. Digging around the bottom of her purse, she located two paper clips, which worked—sort of. How long those paper clips had been there and where they'd come from would forever remain a mystery. Cassie could only be grateful for their presence.

She opened the restroom door, feeling more than a little foolish.

Daisy stood back and brought both hands to her face. "Oh, this is just perfect."

"I look okay?"

"You look *wonderful*. The children are going to be so excited." Daisy glanced at her watch, then led Cassie to an elevator. Silently they rode to the second floor, where a crew of men seemed to be waiting for her. Eight—or was it nine?—life-size plastic reindeer were lined up against the wall beside an authentic-looking sleigh.

Before Cassie had a chance to ask any questions, two of the men stepped forward and strapped her into a harness. They moved her arms, each grasping one, lifting them up and down.

One of the men murmured something in Spanish. She couldn't understand what he'd said, but got the gist of it when he made the sign of the cross and raised his eyes heavenward.

"Don't look down," the other man advised her tersely.

"You don't have a thing to worry about," Daisy said with a grandmotherly smile.

Suddenly a voice came over the loudspeaker system. "Boys and girls, moms and dads—is that Santa's sleigh I hear?"

The man next to her jingled bells and everyone looked up to where Cassie stood.

"Okay, boys," Daisy whispered and stepped back.

Suddenly Cassie was hoisted from the ground. Her feet made running movements as she scrabbled to find her footing and instead found only air.

"Play to the crowd," Daisy instructed in a loud stage whisper.

"Santa's on his way!" Cassie called out, doing her best to sound enthusiastic although she was absolutely terrified. "I can see him now! Look, here comes Santa."

And then it happened. Cassie gasped as her tights rolled down, catching on her thighs. She didn't know what to do. The tights slid farther down and everyone in the entire mall seemed to be staring up at her.

"I can see the elf's underpants," a little boy called, pointing at her.

Suspended above the ground, Cassie watched as several mothers covered their children's eyes.

"Get her to the ground fast," Cassie heard Daisy hiss.

The men released the rope and Cassie plunged downward. "Yiiiiiii!" she screamed, all the while struggling to pull up her tights. She'd partially succeeded—then saw that she was about to make a crash landing.

Just when it seemed she was destined to slam into the ground, a tall man emerged from the crowd and deftly caught her in his arms. The impact would have been enough to send them both sprawling to the floor if not for the fact that he'd braced his feet. Together they staggered backward until her hero recovered his balance.

Cassie opened her eyes to see that the stranger who'd

rescued her wasn't a stranger at all. Her startled eyes met Simon's, and they both breathed a sigh of relief. For a long moment, they stared at each other. Cassie's arms were tightly wrapped around his neck. It took time for her to find her voice and, when she did, it came out in a high-pitched squeal.

"You're paying for this," she told him, her pulse hammering in her ears. Why she'd ever agreed to this ridiculous scenario she'd never know. One thing was for sure; there wouldn't be a repeat performance.

Simon lowered her to the ground. "A simple thank-you will suffice," he said calmly.

Fortunately the audience was distracted by the flying reindeer, and no one could hear her X-rated response. Santa made his appearance, slipping out from behind a curtain. Santa Floyd carried a large bag over his shoulder, presumably filled with candy canes.

Santa ascended to his special chair, a huge cushioned monstrosity set up on the curtained dais, and Cassie took her place beside him. She looked around for Simon but he was nowhere in sight. The boys and girls lined up with their parents, and the photographer was ready with his camera.

The first boy clung to his mother. "He's a little scared," the woman explained, prying her son loose from her leg.

The poor kid was panic-stricken. Cassie couldn't understand why the mother felt it was so important to make him sit on Santa's lap.

"There's no need to be frightened." Cassie crouched down and tried to reassure the boy, who couldn't have been more than four years old.

"Go away!" he shouted.

Cassie straightened and stepped back. Her timing was perfect. The boy, without even a hint of warning, vomited on one of her shoes.

"Oh, dear. I'm so sorry," the mother said a dozen times. "I had no idea Jason was going to do that."

Cassie hopped around on one foot until the photographer produced a small towel. If Jason was any indication of what she should expect, Cassie could only imagine the rest of her day.

"Why don't you sit on Santa's lap with your son," the photographer suggested. The mother appeared eager to do anything that would remove attention from Cassie and the results of her son's queasy stomach. She clambered onto Floyd's lap, her son dangling from her arms.

After cleaning off her shoe, Cassie returned to her duties. The next few children had obviously had prior experience. They all told Santa their Christmas wishes, rattling off everything on their lists.

The line moved relatively well for the next half hour or so. There was the occasional crying baby and one pair of twins who took up more time than allotted, but all in all, it was a smooth-running operation.

Cassie had worked about two hours of her three-hour shift and was just beginning to think this job was tolerable. A lot of the children, while frightened, were eager to meet Santa. "Who are *you?*" a little girl asked as she waited patiently for her turn some time later. Cassie's shift was almost over by then, and there were only a few more kids in line. Other than a harrowing entrance and one small boy with a queasy stomach, it hadn't worked out so badly.

"Who am I?" Cassie repeated the question. "I'm one of Santa's helpers," she said as she handed the child a candy cane.

"Are you really an elf?"

Cassie nodded.

"You don't look like an elf."

"I don't?" Cassie said, surprised.

"You look more like a—"

"You pushed in front of me," the child's mother protested, elbowing the woman ahead of her in line.

"I most certainly did not!" The second woman elbowed the other one back as her son watched, eyes wide.

"Mommy, I have to pee." This plaintive declaration came from the first combatant's daughter, aged four or five.

"We are not getting out of this line now. I'll find you a restroom as soon as we're done," she said and shoved her way to the front, dragging the little girl.

"Would you kindly tell this person that I was ahead of her?" The comment was directed at Cassie by the other woman. The shoving match continued.

"Sorry," Cassie said, coming to stand between the two mothers. "I really wasn't paying attention, but if this goes on, I'm afraid I'll have to ask you both to leave." She said this with great authority and was rather proud of herself.

"Mommy," the little girl cried, her voice urgent now. "I can't wait anymore."

That was when Cassie felt the warm liquid soak into the top of her foot. She glanced down and saw a small waterfall raining down, ruining her shoe—the one unstained by vomit.

Letting out a yell, she leaped back and automatically shook her foot.

"Orange!" the woman shouted.

"It's okay. I don't have to pee anymore."

"Oh, dear…"

"Your daughter's name is Orange?" the other woman asked.

The first woman nodded. "We're from Florida."

The second mother backed away from the puddle on the floor, clutching her son's hand—and leaving Orange at the head of the line.

"I have a tissue." Orange's mother—Grapefruit? Cassie thought hysterically—offered her a crumpled wad.

"I'm fine," Cassie muttered. She intended to burn these tights once her shift was over. The shoes were probably goners, too. She wondered if Simon could possibly have known what this stint would entail.

After the two squabbling mothers had finished with Santa, a young girl, the very last one in line, approached Cassie all by herself.

"She hasn't paid," the photographer said as he returned his camera to its case.

Pleading eyes were raised to Cassie's. "I need to talk to Santa for just a minute," the girl whispered. "You don't have to give me a candy cane."

"How old are you?" Cassie asked, bending down so they were eye-to-eye.

"Eight."

Just a bit too old to believe in Santa Claus. And yet the child was so intent, Cassie didn't feel she could turn her away.

"Forget about the picture," she said when the photographer cast her a dirty look.

"Ho. Ho. Ho. And who do we have here?" Santa asked, ignoring the other man. He held out his arms to the child.

"Catherine," the child said softly. She walked up to Santa but didn't sit on his lap.

"And what would you like for Christmas?" he asked, playing his role to the hilt.

Staring down at the carpet, the child said, "I want my daddy to come home." Huge tears welled in her eyes. "He left and now my mommy says they're getting a divorce. All I want for Christmas is my daddy back."

Cassie felt tears burning in her own eyes. She looked at Floyd and wondered how he'd handle this.

"That's a mighty big order, Catherine," he said.

"I don't want anything else. I don't need toys but I need my daddy."

"Catherine?" A woman's voice echoed through the mall.

"I'm here, Mommy!"

The child's mother rushed up the steps to Santa's throne and fell to her knees in front of her daughter. She seemed about to burst into tears. "I looked *everywhere* for you," she cried. She threw her arms around her daughter's waist.

"I told you I was going to talk to Santa," Catherine reminded her. "I had to wait in line."

"I'm sorry if Catherine caused a problem," her mother said and, standing, took the little girl by the hand—but not before Santa whispered a few words in the child's ear.

"We're finished," Santa said as Catherine's mother led her daughter away.

Cassie must have looked as upset as she felt because Floyd gently patted her back. "Those are the tough ones. You did a great job."

Cassie doubted that.

"What did you say to her?" she asked him.

"I said her daddy still loves her and that he'll always love her. That it's not her fault he left." He stretched his arms high above his head. "Now this Santa has an appointment with Mr. Budweiser. Want to join me?"

"Thanks…but no thanks."

"Then you're free to go. Another elf will take over for you this afternoon."

Cassie nodded, eager to make her escape. As she started for the changing room, Simon appeared beside her.

Cassie realized she wasn't going to be able to control her emotions. Tears streamed down her face.

"What is it?" he asked. He seemed genuinely concerned.

"I was that little girl once," she said with difficulty. "All I wanted for Christmas was for my daddy to come home." She covered her mouth with both hands, trying to stifle her sobs.

They reached the doorway that led to the mall interior. Simon held open the door and Cassie slipped into the darkened hallway. Once inside, she leaned against the wall and let the tears flow unrestrained.

Simon stood next to her for several minutes, then tentatively placed his arms around her.

Cassie didn't care who he was; she needed his comfort. She rested her face against him, sobbing into his expensive wool jacket.

His hold relaxed and, after an awkward moment, he spoke soothingly into her ear. She couldn't make out what he was saying. It didn't matter.

As if by instinct, she lifted her head and gazed up at him.

He whispered something else, something that sounded like "It wasn't your fault." Then his lips, warm and tender, descended on hers.

CHAPTER TEN

Simon says: If you're the woman he's looking for, I will find you.

Simon's gentleness consoled her as he held her close. Cassie didn't want him to ever stop, and he didn't seem inclined to let her go. Time lost meaning, and Cassie didn't know how long he held her against him.

Then, just when she was least prepared, he seemed to snap to attention, become aware of his surroundings. He dropped his arms and stepped away. His movements were so abrupt that she nearly stumbled. She might have if he hadn't clasped her shoulders to steady her.

Speechless, she stared up at him, unable to make sense of what had happened in the past few minutes. Under normal conditions, Cassie didn't give way to emotion, and certainly not in public. But Christmas, that little girl and the memory of losing her own father had struck her hard and there'd been no stopping the barrage of deeply buried feelings. She told herself she was *not* going to react to that kiss.

"I need a cup of coffee," she murmured. Despite her tears her throat was parched.

Simon nodded.

"I'll change clothes and be right back." She was sure her voice sounded strained and unnatural. She hurried inside the ladies' room; once the door was closed she leaned against it and covered her face. Her whole body was trembling. Eventually, when she felt composed again, she straightened and began to dress.

To the best of her knowledge, this was the first time she'd ever cried over her father. Peter Beaumont had simply walked out of their lives one day as if it meant nothing. As if *they* meant nothing. The event had forever marked her and Shawn, and their mother, as well. And yet he seemed oblivious to the anguish he'd inflicted on his wife and children. His excuse was that he needed to "find himself." Apparently he couldn't manage that and be a husband and father at the same time. His was a solitary path, and it didn't seem to matter how many hearts he crushed along the way. Cassie made every effort to cast all thoughts of him out of her mind. But he was there, as much as she wanted to deny his existence.

When Cassie had finished dressing, she left her outfit neatly on a ledge near the sink and wrote Daisy a note explaining why the shoes and tights were in the garbage. Then she brushed her hair and repaired her makeup. Simon was pacing in the hallway outside the door. He stopped when he saw her and even in the dimly lit hallway she could see that he wasn't quite himself, either.

With his hand at her elbow, he escorted her back into the mall and toward an exit. "There's a place close by where we can have coffee." He reached inside his pocket for his car keys. "I'll drive."

Cassie didn't know what was wrong with the restaurants that were within walking distance. However, she didn't have the energy to argue, so she just followed him.

She wasn't surprised to see that he drove a black sedan with a black interior, which was meticulously maintained; she wouldn't have expected anything less. Simon wasn't the type of man who'd have hamburger wrappings and stale French fries littering his vehicle.

They didn't speak; he glanced at her for approval, then flipped on a CD. She recognized the calming strains of a Bach piano concerto. Again, she wasn't surprised, although she couldn't have identified the piece. She leaned back, eyes shut, letting the music flow over her. The restaurant wasn't really all that close, she noted a little later. It was perhaps a fifteen-minute drive along the Tacoma waterfront before he pulled into an exclusive housing development. He turned down several streets, then entered a driveway.

"This isn't a restaurant," Cassie said.

"No, it's my home."

"Your home?"

"I felt we'd both appreciate privacy for this discussion." He was probably right.

Simon ushered her inside. The house was spotless. It looked like one of those model homes with everything carefully arranged and color-coordinated, not a thing out of place. No Christmas decorations. Nor did she see a single photograph, and that seemed almost unnatural. Surely there were people in his life, people he loved and cared about.

Family. Friends. Then again, maybe he preferred to keep his distance from others. Maybe he felt his job required it.

"Make yourself comfortable," he said and gestured toward the sofa. Then he disappeared into the kitchen through a swinging door.

Cassie looked out over Commencement Bay, although her thoughts still churned and she hardly noticed the beauty before her. She had a distinct feeling that their professional agreement was about to come to an end.

Other than one brief interchange—when he asked how she liked her coffee—all was silent.

After a few minutes, Simon reappeared with two cups of coffee. He handed her one, careful to avoid physical contact, before taking a seat as far away as the room allowed. He stared down at his coffee. "I would like to know what happened back at the mall," he said after a tense moment.

"Okay." It wasn't as if they could ignore the episode. "Which part do you want to discuss?"

"What were those tears about?"

Now Cassie stared into her coffee. "My father," she began, then shook her head. "The last child in line."

"The little girl who was by herself?"

"Yes. She came to Santa because…" The lump in her throat made it necessary to pause and swallow before she could continue. "She didn't want toys or clothes or gifts, she…she wanted her daddy back."

"Ah." Simon's eyes softened with understanding and what looked like sympathy. "She reminded you of yourself at that age. You said as much, didn't you?"

Cassie nodded. "My father left during the holidays. So he

not only broke our hearts, he made sure Christmas would never be the same."

"He sounds like a real jewel of a human being," Simon said disdainfully.

But Cassie didn't wish her father ill. He'd paid for his mistakes; in his late sixties now, he was essentially alone. While she liked to think she'd put all the bitterness behind her, she didn't really have a relationship with him, nor did she seek one. Every so often, Pete made the effort to contact her, but they had nothing in common, nothing to talk about, nothing to share. The conversation typically lasted a few minutes. Invariably Cassie felt sad afterward.

"I don't want you to assume I'm the kind of woman who breaks into tears at the drop of a hat. I… It was like seeing myself all those years ago. Like feeling pain so raw it tore my heart out." Her voice quavered and she tried to conceal it by sipping coffee.

"Pain and the memory of pain—which often amounts to the same thing—don't really go away," Simon said. "That's why we have to learn to assimilate it."

She nodded.

Simon didn't say anything else for some time. "I believe it would be best if we…"

He stopped speaking, which made Cassie look at him.

"That kiss," he murmured, shifting his weight.

Seeing Simon ill at ease was so unusual she couldn't help enjoying it, although that was probably unkind of her. At least it was a distraction from her own painful past. "Yes, the kiss."

He frowned. "I want to assure you I don't make a habit of kissing my clients."

She instinctively recognized that as the truth.

"Weeping women don't generally affect me like that, either. I don't have any excuse and I wish to apologize."

His gaze held hers and she couldn't doubt the sincerity of his words. "I was as much at fault as you," she felt obliged to admit. "I—"

"I will refund your money," he said, cutting her off.

It was what she'd been afraid of. "But why?"

"I stepped over the line. This is the only way I can rectify the...incident."

Cassie bit her lip. She conceded that the kiss shouldn't have happened. But that wasn't a good reason to ruin everything. "Will I still meet John?" she asked, then held her breath, almost afraid of what he'd say. She was practically gasping for air by the time he replied.

"Considering that I was the one who initiated the...incident, I feel honor-bound to hold up my part of the bargain."

"If that's the case, then that kiss just cost you thirty thousand dollars."

He didn't look any too pleased with himself, but merely shrugged. "So be it. This was a lesson well learned."

"I don't feel I can let you do that." Tempting as it was for Cassie to accept, fair was fair. She hadn't exactly pushed him away. In fact, she'd welcomed his kiss, welcomed his comfort.

"I am not in the habit of arguing with my clients."

"Or with anyone, it seems."

He blinked as if it took him a moment to comprehend what she'd said. "Or with anyone," he agreed.

She sighed. "I appreciate the offer, Simon, really I do, but you weren't the only one who learned a lesson. How about if we both forget it ever happened and just move forward?"

"Fine," he said curtly. "I would like your promise that you'll never mention our kiss again. Can you do that?"

She nodded. "Yes. Of course."

"Good. I'll undertake to do the same thing."

She mimed zipping her lips closed. "It's gone, forgotten, cast into the deepest part of the ocean." The thought flashed into her mind that the ocean was filled with treasures—treasures no one even knew were there. When it happened, Simon's kiss had felt like treasure, unexpected and...beautiful.

"My plan for the third task is to have you cook Christmas dinner," he reminded her.

Cassie raised her hand. "Yes, I wanted to talk to you about that."

"What about it?"

She might as well be blunt. "Like I told you before, I don't have the best neighbors."

"What precisely is the problem?"

Cassie sat up straighter. The Simon she recognized was back. He wasn't interested in listening to any excuses—except that in this instance excuses were necessary. Cassie couldn't possibly invite her neighbors to Christmas dinner. She didn't really know these people, and what she did know unnerved her.

"Out with it, Cassie. I don't have all day."

Hiding her smile would have been impossible.

"What's that silly grin for?" he demanded in the gruff voice she'd grown accustomed to.

"You. You're back!"

"I never left."

"But you did," she said. "A few minutes ago, while we were discussing—you know, what we promised never to mention again—you seemed...almost human."

His left brow rose, mocking her. "*Almost,* you say?"

"Yes—and I rather liked it."

"Don't get used to it."

"Oh, not to worry. I won't." She set her coffee aside and sat on her hands. "Anyway, continue."

"We were discussing your third task."

"I feel you should know that one of my neighbors, Mrs. Mullinex, is a thief."

"She has a police record?"

"I... No, I don't think so. But who knows? Anyone who'd purposely take my newspaper..."

"Your *newspaper?*"

"Yes, that's what she's been stealing for the last few months." Then, stricken by an attack of conscience, Cassie went on to explain. "To be honest, Mrs. Mullinex does return it, but she clips out the coupons. Then, a couple of weeks back, she went so far as to take the Sunday edition, and get this—she likes to do the Sunday *New York Times* crossword puzzle. *My* crossword puzzle." She narrowed her eyes. "I wouldn't have to invite her, would I?"

"Oh, yes."

"And Mr. Oliver?"

"What's wrong with Mr. Oliver?"

Cassie had no qualms about detailing her other neighbor's faults. "First, he's rude. More than once, Mr. Oliver has deliberately allowed the elevator doors to close on me." She wagged her index finger at Simon. "I'm positive he could see me, too. I saw that gleam in his eyes. The Sunday before last he left me standing there, loaded down with groceries, and he *enjoyed* it."

"I...see." Once more he seemed unimpressed by her tales of woe.

"Then there's the guy whose condo's next to mine. I don't know his name and I don't want to. He plays his music so loud it shakes my whole kitchen. It's horrible music, too. Rap and heavy metal." She paused. "Now here's the interesting part."

"I can hardly wait."

Simon might be making fun of her, but Cassie forged on. "I saw him in the hallway for the first time this week. All along I'd assumed that whoever he was, he must be college age. This guy was *old*. He had to be sixty if he was a day."

Having laid out her case, Cassie felt certain that Simon would understand why she wouldn't want to go to all that effort for these people. "So you'll reconsider?" she asked him.

"Reconsider what?"

"Giving me a different third task. Surely even you can see it would be impossible to put on a festive dinner for my neighbors."

"No, after hearing this, I believe the third task will be perfect."

CHAPTER ELEVEN

Simon says: The perfect neighbor is the one who's never home.

"You mean you *won't* reconsider?" Cassie sputtered. Simon was being totally unreasonable.

"Did you or did you not agree to host this dinner?"

"Well, yes," she admitted with some reluctance, "but that was before I realized I'd be obliged to fly through the air with my underwear showing." A little guilt on his part might not be amiss.

"A small wardrobe malfunction."

He said it with a straight face and Cassie stared at him, wondering if this was meant to be a joke. "I suppose you could call it that."

"At least you didn't have a television audience."

She rolled her eyes. "Yeah, that makes it better."

"Regardless, you are still required to complete a third task."

Cassie made a face. "You're a cruel man, Dr. Dodson."

"You were well aware of the conditions of our agreement before you signed the contract. However…"

"Yes?" Hope filled her.

"However, I believe it might be advantageous if you served this dinner *prior* to Christmas. In other words, not on Christmas Day itself as I originally specified."

"Advantageous how?"

"If you agree to this new stipulation, I'll arrange for you to meet John before the twenty-fifth."

"Oh." Cassie had her suspicions. "And when did you make this decision?" She wasn't fooled; Simon wanted her gone and on her way to marital bliss so he wouldn't have to deal with her anymore.

"Why the dirty look? I would think you'd be grateful."

"I'd be a whole lot more grateful if I didn't distrust your motives."

Simon watched her steadily. "And what is wrong with my motives?"

Irritated, Cassie stood. She wasn't sure why his latest suggestion upset her—the opposite *should* be true. It should thrill her, since she'd be that much closer to meeting John. But it didn't. She walked over to the picture window. "You want me out of your life," she mumbled, her back to him.

"I didn't say that."

"You didn't need to."

"Listen, Cassie, and this is important. Don't fall in love with me. I'm not good husband material. Furthermore—"

"Oh, please," she snapped. "You're in greater danger of falling for me!"

"Don't flatter yourself." He went into the kitchen with their coffee cups. When he came back, she guessed it was time to leave. Her clue was that he'd put on his coat and scarf.

On the return trip to the mall, there was silence between them, no music, not even the radio. When they arrived, Cassie told him where to drop her off. Simon pulled up behind her parked car.

"Please let me know when you intend to serve the Christmas meal," he said.

"Can I get back to you?"

He kept his hands on the steering wheel and gazed straight ahead. "Fine. But remember that all three tasks must be completed to my satisfaction. So far, you've done well."

Was that praise? From the high and mighty Simon Dodson? She could hardly believe it. He *must* have an ulterior motive, no matter how much he claimed otherwise. Although, now that she considered it, he hadn't exactly denied her accusation. "I'll call you later in the week with the date."

"Good. I thought you'd come around."

She opened the passenger door, then climbed out and banged it shut. *"Good,"* she mimicked. Seeing someone waiting eagerly for her parking space, Cassie hurriedly got into her car and backed out.

On the drive home she did her best to analyze why someone she disliked could affect her so profoundly. It troubled her that she'd enjoyed Simon's touch and his kiss, that she felt invigorated by his—occasionally annoying—conversation.

Not until the following Wednesday was Cassie able to work out a date that was agreeable to all her neighbors, as well as Angie and Shawn. Dinner was scheduled for the Sunday before Christmas.

To her credit, Mrs. Mullinex seemed pleased by the invitation and offered to bring her special pickled brussels sprouts. Her mother's recipe, she said. Cassie declined, saying she'd take care of everything.

Mr. Oliver gave a one-word answer. "Why?"

"It's just an invitation to dinner," Cassie said. "I'm doing all the cooking and…and it seemed neighborly to have a Christmas celebration." The explanation struck her as a bit lame, but she could hardly tell him her *real* reason.

"Who else are you inviting?"

She told him.

"I suppose I could come," he said and closed the door. He made it sound as if he was doing her a favor. In retrospect, maybe he was.

The rap-music man was harder to catch. She rang his doorbell several times, then pounded hard, but either he didn't want to answer or he was so deaf he couldn't hear her. In the end she slipped a note under his door.

He responded in kind, placing a message under her door that said he'd be delighted to join her for dinner. He signed it *Bob,* which seemed a rather inoffensive name for someone who listened to such belligerent music.

Now that the arrangements were made, Cassie was ready to contact Simon. She knew he kept evening hours a couple of days a week for the benefit of working clients, and this was one of those days.

"He's not in the office," Ms. Snelling informed her. "I don't see your name on the appointment list."

"He asked me to call." Or maybe she'd volunteered; Cassie couldn't remember.

"I see. Do you wish to leave a message for him?"

"No." Cassie was emphatic about that. She preferred to speak to him personally. In her opinion, it was time that he learned the art of compromise. She was going to ask for one small concession, and if Simon had any common sense at all, he'd agree.

"Can you tell me when he'll be available?"

"Oh, dear, I'm afraid I can't. Dr. Dodson is home sick with the flu."

Simon was sick? Cassie felt immediate sympathy. "How long has he been out?"

"Two days, and when he phoned in, he sounded absolutely dreadful."

"Poor man." Cassie hung up and went about her business. Her apartment looked Christmassy, thanks primarily to her brother's tree. She'd draped it with merrily twinkling lights that brought a festive quality to the dark evening. Cassie had added a trio of angels to the fireplace mantel. A lovely wreath hung on the inside, rather than the outside, of her door because she didn't trust her neighbors (one in particular) not to steal it.

Even with Christmas music playing in the background and cookbooks strewn across the kitchen counter, all Cassie could think about was Simon, sick and in bed. He was alone. He'd never mentioned family. She didn't know about friends, either. As far as she could tell, there was no one to check up on him. If she'd had a special recipe for chicken noodle soup she would've made him a pot of it.

Then it came to her—why *not* make him some soup? Medicinal soup for a friend. Simon might not consider her a friend, but Cassie couldn't ignore the fact that he might need someone. She began paging through her cookbooks....

She didn't fool herself into believing Simon would appreciate the effort. But even knowing he'd probably resent her dropping off the soup wasn't enough to change her mind.

"You're going to a lot of trouble for him," Angie told her the next morning at work when Cassie brought in a full quart of her concoction.

"That's true," she said, finding space in the lunchroom fridge for her plastic container.

"Why would you care? He's such a difficult man. I bet he'll bite your head off for making him get out of bed to answer the door."

Cassie nodded.

"How do you know where he lives, anyway?"

Rather than launch into the whole complicated tale, she said, "It's a long story. I'll save it for when we have more time."

"I'm holding you to that."

Fortunately, two colleagues joined them for lunch, so Cassie was spared the necessity of telling Angie what had happened on Saturday, when she'd been an elf. After work she called Simon's office and learned he was still sick. Her decision made, Cassie drove to Tacoma. She had no problem locating the neighborhood but had to drive around numerous streets before she found his house.

By then, it was completely dark and the rain fell in sheets. Racing from the car to his front door, carrying her quart container, she shook the moisture out of her hair before she rang his doorbell. When no one answered, she was tempted to leave the soup on his porch and drive away.

Just as she turned to do exactly that, the door opened and Simon stood there in his housecoat and slippers. He looked even worse than she might have imagined, with a pale face, rumpled hair and rheumy eyes. Her sympathy was instantly aroused and it was all she could do not to reach out and test his brow for fever.

"Cassie?"

She hadn't planned what she'd say, and now her tongue seemed to twist itself into knots. "I heard you were sick.... I—I brought you some homemade chicken noodle soup."

He stared at her as if he wasn't sure whether he was hallucinating.

"How are you feeling?" she asked, although the answer was obvious.

"Terrible." He stepped aside, silently inviting her into the house.

Cassie hadn't expected that. In fact, she'd been sure that he'd be angry. She'd expected him to growl and demand that she leave.

"I can't stay long. Like I said, I wanted to drop off the soup and tell you the turkey dinner's set for Sunday."

Simon covered his mouth and coughed. It resembled a dog's barking and seemed to rack his entire body. She wondered if he had pneumonia.

"Have you seen a doctor?" she asked urgently.

"I'll be fine. Don't fuss, Cassie."

"Someone should. Now, lie down and I'll heat up this soup." Taking charge, she walked past him and into his kitchen, which to her shock was untidy. Dishes littered the counter and pots were stacked in the sink. She could see that he'd made an effort to straighten up but had either grown too tired or was too sick to continue.

Before she started heating the soup, she placed the dirty dishes in the dishwasher and turned it on. Her soup warmed on the stove as she cleaned up the kitchen. Simon had disappeared and now returned dressed in slacks and a sweater. He'd apparently showered, because his hair was wet and combed.

"This is thoughtful of you." He actually sounded grateful.

Dishcloth in hand, Cassie regarded him suspiciously. "You mean to say you're not angry?"

"Why would I be angry?"

"I'm invading your privacy."

He acknowledged that with a slight tilt of his head.

The soup began to boil and Cassie removed the pan from the burner, poured some in a bowl and set it on the kitchen table with a spoon.

While Simon had his soup, she made them both cups of strong, hot tea, then sat across from him at the table. She declined his suggestion of soup, since she was too nervous to eat.

"This might surprise you, but I quite like you when you're sick."

He set the spoon next to his bowl and studied her warily. "I beg your pardon?"

That must have sounded strange. "You're more human when you're vulnerable." He didn't respond.

Cassie was gratified to see that he finished the entire bowlful of soup.

"Shall we have our tea in the living room?" she asked, noting that the television was on, the volume low.

Simon nodded. "I've watched more television in the past three days than the previous three years."

"Oh, *Jeopardy!*'s just starting. That's my favorite game

show," she said, sitting on the couch. Simon sat beside her, a careful distance away—not too close and not too far.

He picked up the remote and turned up the volume. The thirty minutes passed quickly. She couldn't resist shouting out answers—"What is the Battle of Gettysburg?" "Who are Sacco and Vanzetti?" "What is silver nitrate?" She was pleased that she was almost always right, although she noticed that Simon didn't participate at all. He must be feeling very ill.

"I should leave," she said after Final Jeopardy ("Who was St. Nicholas?") and started to stand.

Simon reached for her hand. "Stay a while longer, if you don't mind."

"I don't..." The sudden surge of tenderness she felt shocked her. What shocked her even more was that his hand continued to hold hers. His touch was light, but sometime during the next thirty minutes he intertwined their fingers. It was hard to concentrate on the rerun of *Frasier*—a Christmas episode she'd already seen—when her whole body was focused on his hand holding hers. Innocent enough on the surface, his action was highly sensual in its effect. She felt his touch in every part of her, in every sensitized nerve, every cell. She needed all her self-control not to turn into his arms and beg him to kiss her.

"My brother might be at the dinner," she said, hoping she didn't sound as breathless as she felt.

"I'd enjoy meeting him."

"You would? Angie might be able to come, too."

"Angie?"

"My best friend. You met her—and rejected her."

"Ah, yes, I remember her now."

"I wish you'd given her a chance," Cassie murmured.

"I couldn't. She was in love with someone and refused to admit it."

"How do you know?" she asked.

"It's my job. That's the point of such a detailed questionnaire. I explore people's responses and I read between the lines." He looked at her sternly, their hands still linked. "You know I can't discuss this with you."

"Oh." Her mouth had gone dry. If Simon could read others so well, she wondered if he was aware of the intense sensation she was experiencing. Did he feel it, too?

"Will you come for dinner?" she asked. This was the concession she'd intended to request. She wasn't quite sure why. She'd told herself it was so he'd be able to judge the way she handled the third task, which would expedite her introduction to John. But now...

He didn't answer.

"Please?"

He rubbed his thumb along hers and it was all Cassie could do not to faint. Her eyes drifted shut.

"I'll be there," he finally agreed.

"Thank you."

The argument between Frasier and Niles on the TV seemed to fade into the background. "I should go," she said.

"Yes," he said in a whisper. "You should." He released her and she clenched her fist to keep from grabbing his hand again.

"I'll see you at three o'clock on Sunday," she said hoarsely, staggering to her feet.

He nodded.

He didn't walk her to the door.

CHAPTER TWELVE

Simon says: The perfect match lights a lasting fire.

Cassie pored over every cookbook she owned. They were all full of wonderful recipes. Even more encouraging, the instructions didn't seem too difficult. She had her menu set for this all-important dinner: roast turkey with a traditional stuffing, mashed potatoes and gravy, fresh green beans with butter and sliced almonds, two different salads and three kinds of pie, apple, pumpkin and pecan. Her grocery list was two pages long.

Angie had offered to help with the shopping; she'd also volunteered to set the table. This was by far the most elaborate meal Cassie had ever undertaken.

Her brother, too, seemed eager to help. Luckily, Shawn was in town for a benefit and he'd promised to hand-etter the place cards. He said he'd also do small drawings on each, which were sure to be highly collectible—if any of her neighbors recognized her brother as the famous mural artist. Well, even if they didn't, they were bound to like the personal touch.

Reading over the stuffing recipe one last time, Cassie rested her elbows on the kitchen counter.

Unfortunately, her mind kept wandering from the page. She hadn't seen Simon since she'd visited him in his home. He'd fully recovered from his bout with the flu and gone back to work.

Cassie knew that because she'd phoned and chatted briefly with his assistant who'd told her Simon was indeed in the office. But when Ms. Snelling asked if Cassie wished to speak to him, she'd declined and hurriedly got off the phone.

Simon hadn't called to thank her for the soup, not that she expected him to. He was coming to dinner on Sunday and she almost dreaded seeing him; at the same time, she could hardly wait.

She hardly thought of John—John the engineer, John the perfect man—anymore. Only Simon seemed to inhabit her mind. And her heart?

Something was very wrong.

The doorbell rang and Cassie left her kitchen. Angie breezed into the room as though floating on air. This wasn't unusual these days. Her friend was in love. Angie seemed like a different person; nothing upset her, nothing annoyed her. In fact, she glowed with happiness. And yet she remained secretive about this new man in her life. Still, Cassie had begun to have her suspicions. In retrospect, the night of her solitary tree-decorating should have been a giveaway.

"You ready?" Angie asked.

"Shawn phoned earlier," Cassie said and carefully watched her friend's expression.

Angie revealed nothing.

"Oh, he's in town?"

"My brother seems to have a fair amount of business in the Pacific Northwest lately," Cassie said, playing along. "He said he was here for some benefit, but if you ask me, the one who's benefiting is my brother."

Angie turned away and walked into the kitchen. She set down her purse, then removed her coat and draped it over the back of a kitchen chair. "This is your menu for tomorrow?" she said, still avoiding eye contact. She studied the paper on which Cassie had written her menu ideas. "Three different pies seems a bit ambitious, don't you think?"

"I wanted there to be choices." It didn't escape Cassie's notice how quickly Angie had diverted the subject from Shawn.

"Simon agreed to come, right?"

Switching the topic to Simon was a clever move. "Yes." Before she could expand or hint further about Shawn, the doorbell chimed again. Cassie opened the door to her brother, who hugged her enthusiastically. His eyes gleamed with a merriment that was due to more than the season, Cassie thought. When he saw Angie his expression sobered. He greeted her politely, even rather distantly.

"This dinner is becoming quite the affair," Shawn said, handing her the place cards. The artwork—small watercolors, all individual, of Christmas trees and bells and stars—was beautiful.

"Thanks!" Cassie kissed his cheek. "Okay, you two, sit down," she ordered. She indicated the sofa. "Before you say anything, I want you to know that I arranged for you to be here at the same time."

Shawn and Angie took opposite sides of the sofa while

Cassie stood directly in front of them, her arms crossed. "You aren't fooling me, you know. I suspected the two of you were seeing each other."

"We wanted to tell you," Angie blurted out. "Well, I did, but Shawn felt we should wait."

"We weren't sure this was going anywhere," Shawn explained, glancing at Angie.

"We wanted to keep it to ourselves for a while," Angie said in a small voice, glancing back at Shawn.

"If you're upset, blame me," Shawn said, quick to defend Angie.

"Why wouldn't you want me to know?" Cassie asked, directing the question to both of them. "I'm happy for you!"

"It just kind of happened."

"We dated for a while a year ago after we met at your birthday party, and it didn't work out," Shawn said.

"For him, maybe, but it worked for me. I fell in love with Shawn." Angie looked down at her hands, which were neatly folded in her lap.

"Oh, my goodness!" Cassie brought one hand to her mouth. "Simon wouldn't take you on as a client because you were in love with someone else. That someone was my brother, wasn't it?"

Angie's ears turned red as she nodded. "Shawn and I went out last year, like he said, and just when everything seemed to be going well… I didn't hear from him."

"I was traveling a lot," he said. "A relationship's hard when I'm on the road so much. Besides, I was falling for Angie and it scared me. I'd dated plenty of women but I didn't feel about them the way I did about Angie—and I panicked."

"I was distraught when we broke up," Angie whispered. "I wanted to tell you, but Shawn—"

"You never said a word." Cassie was embarrassed that she'd been so oblivious. "Before *or* after you called it quits."

Angie shrugged apologetically.

"I like my privacy," Shawn said. "You know that."

Cassie couldn't help being a little hurt. "For crying out loud, I'm your sister."

"I'm sorry." Shawn did appear regretful. "Neither of us meant to offend you or anything."

"After we broke it off, I tried to move on," Angie said. "Which is why I agreed when my mother wanted me to meet the matchmaker."

"I made an effort to get over Angie, too," Shawn confessed, smiling at her, "but I couldn't get her out of my mind."

"Then we met again just before Thanksgiving."

"Here," Angie clarified. They both nodded.

"And I realized how much I'd missed Angie," he went on, "and how foolish I'd been to let our relationship end."

"And *I* realized that Simon was right and despite everything, I was still in love with Shawn."

They slid closer on the couch and Shawn took Angie's hand. They stared into each other's eyes.

Cassie wanted to kick them both for being so foolish, for not understanding what they had the first time around. They deserved a second kick for keeping it a secret from her.

"We've been so happy," Angie told her, "and I was afraid that if we said anything, you'd feel left out."

"Left out? If I feel left out it's because you guys—two of

Cassie had difficulty wiping the grin off her face. Shawn and Angie were perfect together. She wondered why she hadn't thought of it before—or noticed what was going on. Angie would probably move away from Seattle once they were married, which was the only disadvantage to an otherwise ideal situation.

All of a sudden it became crucial to talk to Simon. She had his office number and as she suspected he had an answering service.

"Would you please ask Mr. Dodson to return my call? It's...an emergency."

She didn't have to wait long for him to call back. When his name flashed across caller ID, Cassie exhaled a huge sigh of relief.

"Simon?" she said.

"Yes."

Cassie smiled at his gruff, unfriendly tone. She felt better already.

"There's been a change in our dinner plans."

"That's why you phoned?"

"Yes. My brother and Angie won't be attending."

"That's your emergency?'

"This might not be earth-shattering to you but—"

"Cassie..."

"I knew they were secretly involved, or at least I guessed they were. It's wonderful for them. They make a fabulous couple. I couldn't be happier, even if it means I'm going to lose my best friend."

Her outburst was followed by a short silence. "I don't quite understand why you called me. And I suggest you

the most important people in my life—didn't let m
something as big as this!"

"We did plan to tell you," Angie said.

"And when would that have been?"

"After the big dinner party."

Cassie laughed. "So that's why it was so easy to conv
you to make an appearance."

Shawn nodded. "Now that you know, we don't have
show up, do we? Angie and I have better things to do tha
attend this crazy dinner party of yours."

"Shawn," Angie chastised.

The hopeful expression on his face was enough to make
Cassie laugh. "No, you two are excused. Angie, you don't
need to help with the shopping."

"I'll come if you want," Angie said.

She would, too, but Cassie could see that she'd rather be
alone with Shawn than spend the day in a crowded grocery store.

"I'll be fine. Do something productive with your time,
though—like shopping for an engagement ring."

Angie blushed again and Shawn cleared his throat. "As
it happens, I have a ring picked out."

"You do?" Angie asked with tears in her voice.

"I'm not letting you get away from me again," Shawn
said. "There's still plenty to discuss, but I can't see—"

"Yes."

"Yes, what?" he asked.

"Yes, I'll marry you and, yes, there's a lot still to be decided. But there's no obstacle the two of us can't overcome."

They left a few minutes later, so in love they couldn't
keep their hands off each other.

think of it as gaining a sister-in-law," he advised wryly, "not losing a friend."

"Yes, that's true, but she'll leave Seattle and the lab.... Anyway," she said in a more cheerful voice, "I wanted to let you know you were right about her being in love."

"Of course I was right. Did you seriously doubt it?"

"Well, perhaps not." She paused. "I shouldn't have called. You must consider me a nuisance."

"We can agree on that," he murmured.

"I know you regret taking me on as a client and I apologize for being such a pest."

"I've dealt with worse clients."

Funny how reassuring Cassie found even that faint encouragement.

He exhaled slowly. "You're upset. Is it because of your friend and your brother? Anything that upsets the status quo—even a good thing like this—takes time to accept."

Cassie wasn't sure why she'd felt such an overwhelming urge to hear his voice. His certainty was comforting, she supposed. He always had an answer, a reason, a solution.

"How can I help?" he asked, his tone almost gentle.

"I... I don't know."

"I have an idea," he said, his voice brightening.

"What?"

"I'll tell you something else about John."

"John?"

"The man I've matched you with."

"Oh. Yes." The man she'd paid thirty thousand dollars to meet. He'd completely slipped her mind.

"Okay," he said. "Let me think about it."

"What were you doing?" She felt guilty at the thought of interrupting him. "Before I called."

"What was I doing?" he repeated. "Why do you ask?"

"If I'm being too much of a bother, I'll hang up." She viewed him as someone who operated with purpose. Someone whose day was filled with constant demands. He had too many responsibilities to be interrupted by such mundane matters as her doubts and insecurities.

"I'm watching a college football game."

"You watch football?" He couldn't have shocked her more had he said he was on an aircraft headed for the moon. Practically every day Simon surprised her with how...*human* he was.

"Why would you find that unusual?"

"I didn't think football would interest you. It's so...so normal."

He laughed. "I am normal, Cassie. I'm like every other man."

"No, you aren't," she insisted. "You aren't like any other man I've ever known, and now I'm seeing this whole other side of you and it's confusing."

He muttered something under his breath; it sounded as if he'd said he was confused himself, but Cassie couldn't be sure of that.

"About John," he said, changing the subject.

"I don't want to hear about John right now."

"Maybe you should. It'll adjust your focus."

"No, thanks. I'll be meeting him soon, won't I?"

"I can arrange the meeting for Monday afternoon if you like. When I last spoke to him about scheduling a face-to-

face, John was ecstatic. He's *very* eager to make your acquaintance."

"Oh."

"He called it an early Christmas gift."

"Oh, yes, Christmas."

Silence stretched between them.

"I'll get to your condo a few minutes early," Simon said,
filling the empty space. "I have your address. From your
application—and the check."

The thirty-thousand–dollar check...

"See you then," he added.

"Yes, for dinner." Not until she'd hung up her phone,
did she wonder why he wanted to come early.

CHAPTER THIRTEEN

Cassie was up half the night baking pies and getting everything ready for her final task. Her alarm went off at six on Sunday morning. She staggered from her bed, got the turkey out of the refrigerator and nearly dropped it on the kitchen floor. Who knew twenty pounds would be so heavy?

Because she'd methodically planned every detail of the dinner preparations, she was right on schedule. She stuffed the turkey and it was in the oven and roasting nicely an hour later. She started on the salads next. The dining room table was set with a crisp white linen cloth. There were sprigs of holly beside each place card for a festive accent. She'd arranged every detail with the hope of impressing Simon. She'd dressed in a red-and-black velvet pantsuit and taken care with her makeup. For a final holiday touch she wore a ring with a large red stone.

He arrived a full hour before her guests were due, carrying a huge, perfect poinsettia for the centerpiece.

He handed it to her almost as if he was grateful to be rid of it.

"How lovely," she said delightedly. "Thank you."

She put the poinsettia on the table and stepped back to examine it.

"I love it, Simon." Rising onto the tips of her toes, she kissed his cheek.

He was frowning when she stepped back. "That was inappropriate," he said disapprovingly.

She didn't point out that he'd kissed her a few weeks ago. But to prove how wrong he was, she kissed his cheek a second time.

However, when she started to move away, Simon clasped her by the shoulders and pulled her into his embrace. Then he lowered his mouth to hers. Before she could account for her response, she threw her arms around his neck and kissed him back.

They both seemed to realize at precisely the same moment what they'd done. They leaped apart; Simon shoved his hands in his pockets, while Cassie turned around in an effort to regain her composure.

As they faced each other again, Cassie made a sweeping gesture toward the table, hoping to bring some levity to the situation. "Well, what do you think?" she asked.

He nodded. "You've done a wonderful job."

"Would you like to see the turkey?" she asked.

"If you wish."

"I do. You're the one who told me I had to do this... and in retrospect I'm glad you did." She led him into the kitchen, grabbed one of her oven mitts and opened the door. She basted the turkey and noted with pride how crisp and brown it looked. According to her calculations, it would be finished in forty minutes. Simon could remove it from the oven and it would sit for an additional fifteen minutes before being carved.

"Very nice," he said, when she closed the oven door. "Smells delicious, too."

"Have I surprised you?" she asked and knew she had, which was what she'd hoped.

He smiled. "I admit that you're one surprise after another." Which was exactly the thought she'd so recently had about him....

She managed to restrain herself from dancing a small, gleeful jig.

She poured Simon a glass of eggnog while they waited for the rest of her company. "Store-bought," she confessed as she joined him in the living room. They sat on opposite ends of the sofa.

That wasn't the only similarity to the way Shawn and Angie had behaved the previous day. Like her brother and her friend, Simon and Cassie hardly looked at each other. Neither seemed inclined toward conversation, either.

"I was thinking..." Cassie began.

"It seems to me..." Simon said.

They both stopped, then Simon gestured toward her to speak.

"No, you first," she insisted.

"Please," he said.

Cassie didn't get a chance because the doorbell rang just then. Eager to break the unexplained tension between them, she hurried to answer. As she might have guessed, Mrs. Mullinex arrived first. She stood in the hallway dressed in her finest. For the first time in Cassie's memory, her hair wasn't in curlers. In fact, this was the first time she'd seen her neighbor's hair, period. It was…curly.

"This is so nice of you," the older woman chirped. Her eyes flew instantly to Simon and widened with womanly appreciation.

"This is…" Cassie wasn't sure how to introduce him. "Simon. My friend. Simon Dodson, Mrs. Mullinex."

"How do you do?" her neighbor cooed sweetly. "Please call me Phyllis."

"Phyllis," Cassie repeated. She'd lived in the building for three years and hadn't been aware of Mrs. Mullinex's first name, which didn't appear on the mailbox, not even as an initial. Her neighbor had never seen fit to share it with Cassie.

"I didn't realize Cassie had a male friend," Mrs. Mullinex said ever so coyly. "She is a sly one."

Cassie excused herself and disappeared inside the kitchen while she prepared the hors d'oeuvres. She'd leave Simon to fend for himself. When she heard the two of them chatting amicably, Cassie sighed. Simon possessed a few social graces, after all—but none that he was willing to display for *her* benefit.

Mr. Oliver showed up next. "The Seahawks game starts at four. This isn't going to take longer than that, is it?" he asked as he barreled past her and into the condo. He looked around and when he saw Phyllis Mullinex, a frown darkened his face.

"Mr. Oliver," Mrs. Mullinex greeted him stiffly.

"Phyllis."

They glared at each other like alley cats with hackles raised, each waiting for the other to make the first move.

"So...you two know each other," Cassie commented, watching them carefully.

"No," said Mrs. Mullinex.

"Oh, yes, we know each other very well," Mr. Oliver countered. "Would you mind if I turned the TV on?" he asked as he claimed the most comfortable chair. Not waiting for a response, he reached for the remote, leaned forward and pressed the on button. The television screen lit up and he immediately found the station he wanted. It featured another football game—not the Seahawks.

"I'd like to introduce my friend Dr. Simon Dodson," Cassie said, speaking loudly enough to be heard above the roar of the sports announcer.

Mr. Oliver acknowledged Simon with a disinterested nod of his head.

Her doorbell rang again. Grateful for an excuse to escape, Cassie rushed forward to answer. Bob, the rap aficionado from next door, stood on the other side. He'd apparently gone to some effort with his appearance; he'd greased his graying hair back from his forehead and donned a fresh pair of jeans and a sweater. He grinned when he saw her and handed her a lone rose.

"Welcome," Cassie said and brought him into the room.

When he saw the others, Bob's face fell. "You didn't say there'd be anyone else here," he said.

"Oh...sorry. I assumed you knew."

"So, dinner isn't just for the two of us?"

"Ah...no. I'm sure you've met Mrs. Mullinex and Mr. Oliver," Cassie said, motioning toward her guests.

"No, and I don't particularly care to," he grumbled.

"This is my friend Dr. Simon Dodson."

Bob's frown deepened. "You have a…friend?"

"Well, yes, sort of." The last thing she needed was for Bob to think she was interested in his attentions. If avoiding *that* trap meant stretching the truth, then so be it.

The oven timer went off, and Cassie took the opportunity to leave and close the kitchen door behind her. After all her hard work, this meal was going to be a disaster. None of these people liked one another.

Simon followed her into the kitchen. "Should the turkey come out yet?" he asked.

"Yes," she said distractedly as he slipped his hands into her Santa-face oven mitts.

"Simon," she pleaded. "What are we going to do?"

"About what?"

"Can't you see?" she cried. "Mrs. Mullinex and Mr. Oliver can barely stand to look at each other, and Bob thought this dinner was going to be a private affair between him and me."

"It'll be fine," he said soothingly.

Cassie sincerely doubted that.

Simon lifted the turkey out of the oven and set it on top of the stove.

Cassie thanked him. "According to my cookbook, the turkey should sit for no less than fifteen minutes before being carved."

"Do you need help with anything else?"

"No." She'd seen to everything before the guests were due. "I just have to get the food into the serving dishes."

Bowls lined the counter. Cassie was pleased with her organizational abilities. The potatoes were cooked and ready to be mashed. Green beans simmered on the stovetop. She drained off the liquid, added the melted butter and almonds and placed them in the bowl she'd chosen.

Simon returned to the living room with the others.

Then, picking up the bowl in which she planned to put the stuffing, she noticed something wrong. For a moment, all Cassie could do was stare at her hand.

No! Oh, dear. Now what?

Putting down the bowl, she opened the door slightly and peered out of the kitchen. "Simon," she called in a deceptively casual voice. "Would you come in here for a minute?"

He gave her an odd look but did as she requested.

The instant he set foot in the kitchen, she took his arms and pulled him all the way in. "Houston, we have a problem," she said in an urgent whisper.

"What kind of problem?"

"A very big one." Splaying her fingers, she held out her hand. "My ring is missing."

"Your ring."

"Yes, my ring."

He seemed unconcerned. "I'm sure it's around here somewhere. Can't you look for it later?"

"No."

"And why not?" he asked.

"Because the last time I saw it, I was stuffing the turkey."

"In other words…"

"Yes. In other words it's inside the bird."

"You're positive?"

"No, but where else would it be?"

Simon rolled his eyes toward the ceiling.

"What am I going to do?" A dozen scenarios played in her mind, none of them the least bit amusing. If someone bit into it and broke a tooth… "I'll be sued!" she said hoarsely, covering her eyes. "Someone might choke on it. My neighbors don't deserve to die, even if my newspapers do turn up missing now and then."

"Dish the stuffing into the bowl. You might find it."

"Okay, okay."

"And don't panic."

"Easy for you to say," she muttered as she transferred stuffing into the bowl, inspecting each spoonful closely.

"Mrs. Mullinex is a sweet lady," he was saying. "I don't know why you think she'd want to cause you any trouble."

"And Mr. Oliver?"

"He probably wouldn't even notice if he bit into the ring, especially if you left the football game on."

"And Bob?"

"He'd assume you were proposing marriage."

"Very funny."

"Oh, Cassie, I just—"

Mrs. Mullinex stuck her head into the kitchen. "Anything I can do, dear?"

"Ah, no, thanks. Everything's fine," Cassie assured her.

"Simon, come back and sit with me," the older woman wheedled.

Simon turned away from the counter and offered Mrs. Mullinex his arm, then threw Cassie a look that told her she was on her own.

A lot of help *he'd* been.

No sooner had Simon left than the door opened again. This time it was Bob.

"So," he said, leaning against the kitchen counter. "It's just the two of us now."

"Yes, well…" Cassie inserted the spoon inside the turkey to finish taking out the stuffing, but with Bob watching every move, she couldn't make a huge production of plowing through it, searching for her ring.

"I've always loved stuffing."

"Oh, me, too, but I'm not sure this turned out that well. I was thinking I wouldn't serve it."

"Let me taste." Before she could protest, he took her spoon and helped himself to a sample. After blowing on it, he popped it into his mouth. He smiled widely in approval. "This is fabulous! The best I've ever tasted."

"You're just being kind."

"Not at all. Here, I'll take it out for you."

"No," she cried and made an effort to stop him, but to no avail. Bob carried the bowl into the dining area.

When she followed with the salads, she saw that he'd taken a forkful to Mrs. Mullinex. "Cassie says the stuffing didn't turn out to her liking. I disagree. What do you think?"

Mrs. Mullinex gave it a dainty taste. "Perfection," she said. "You're being modest, Cassie."

Mr. Oliver stood. "What's a turkey dinner without stuffing?"

"I didn't want to ruin anyone's diet," Cassie said, searching for an excuse, any excuse, to get the stuffing off the table.

Mr. Oliver raised his hand. "I'm on a low-carb diet myself."

"Then you won't want any of the stuffing," Cassie said thankfully.

"I thought I'd make an exception, this being Christmas and all."

"Oh…"

"Let's all help," Mrs. Mullinex suggested cheerfully. "We can bring out the rest of the serving dishes. We shouldn't leave all the work to Cassie."

Cassie sent a pleading glance in Simon's direction. He, however, was looking elsewhere.

CHAPTER FOURTEEN

Simon says: A good matchmaker stays in the background, just like Santa's little helper, then swoops in at the opportune moment.

Cassie couldn't swallow a single bite as she carefully studied her guests enjoying their turkey with all the trimmings. Every time she saw a forkful of stuffing heading toward someone's mouth she had to restrain herself from leaping to her feet and yanking it away.

Simon revealed no such concern. Mrs. Mullinex had him engaged in a lengthy conversation. Judging by the attention he paid her, anyone would think she was the wittiest, prettiest woman on the face of the earth. Every once in a while, the older woman released a girlish trill that sounded, to Cassie's somewhat jaundiced ear, like a songbird strangling on too much seed.

"Mighty fine dinner," Bob told Cassie, eyeing her with far more appreciation than his meal.

"Thank you." She quickly looked away and offered Mr. Oliver more beans. More salad. More anything.

"Do you always cook like this?" Mr. Oliver asked. Before she could answer, he continued. "You probably have plenty of leftovers. No need to let 'em go to waste."

"That'd be a shame," Bob threw in. "I'd be happy to come over and help you finish them a few times a week."

Cassie felt it was important to set *him* straight right away. "Since I work and there's only me to cook for, I generally don't go to this much trouble." *Generally—like never!*

Bob glanced at Mr. Oliver, whose plate was heaped high with large portions of mashed potatoes and gravy. "I thought you said you were watching your weight?"

"Low-carb's the only way to go." He reached across the table for the butter, which he slathered on a roll.

"Cassie, dear," Mrs. Mullinex said in the same high-pitched bird voice she'd used since meeting Simon. "It's been such a long time since I made gravy. Does yours always have these lumps in it?"

Cassie stiffened her shoulders at the frightening thought that the ring might have slipped into the gravy. Then she realized her neighbor was denigrating her gravy-making skills, although she wasn't sure why. Her gravy was flawless, and if there were any lumps, which there weren't, it was a fluke. "No, I added them for your benefit," she answered in an equally saccharine voice.

Simon's gaze narrowed.

"Oh." Mrs. Mullinex blinked as if gauging whether or not to be offended.

"I'm joking, Mrs. Mullinex," Cassie said, feeling slightly guilty. "I apologize if there are lumps in the gravy."

"You can put lumps in my gravy anytime you want,"

Bob told her. He winked at her, then jiggled his eyebrows. Disgusting! The man was old enough to be her father.

"I believe I'll have some more of that stuffing," Simon said.

Cassie sprang from her chair and grabbed hold of the bowl. "I was going to take it back to the kitchen."

"Gimme that when you're finished," Mr. Oliver said, grinning broadly.

"Ah…" Cassie looked helplessly at Simon, who gently pried the bowl from her hands. "I'm not sure there's enough."

"There's plenty for everyone," Simon said and took a huge spoonful before passing it across the table to Mr. Oliver. "Let me hand it around."

"Doesn't anyone want to save room for pie?" Cassie asked brightly. She described each one, highlighting the fine qualities of the apple, pumpkin and pecan fillings.

"I don't know if I dare," Mrs. Mullinex trilled. "One must watch one's waistline." She paused, gazing around as if waiting for someone to tell her she needn't worry about such things.

Cassie volunteered in the hope that if her neighbor accepted the pie, she'd skip the extra stuffing, which, to her horror, was being passed around the table. "Why, Mrs. Mullinex, you have a very good figure."

"Pleasingly plump," Bob seconded.

The smile faded from the other woman's face. "Plump?"

"*Pleasingly* plump," Cassie said. "That's another way of saying—"

"I'm fat," Mrs. Mullinex cut in, frowning now.

"I like to be direct," Mr. Oliver said, glaring at the older woman. "Plump is plump, no matter how you try to fancy it up."

"Leave it to you to insult me, Harry," she snapped.

"You always were quick to take offense," Mr. Oliver snapped back. "A man makes a simple comment and you jump all over him and ruin a perfectly fine friendship."

"Ah..." Cassie raised her index finger, trying to get a comment in before the confrontation broke into a full-fledged argument.

"I don't know how anyone could even imply that you're overweight," Simon said, pouring everyone a little more wine.

Cassie managed a smile at his smooth handling of what was rapidly becoming an awkward situation. It also gave her an opportunity to make off with the stuffing unobserved.

"I'll put on a pot of coffee," Cassie said, jumping up from the table. She grabbed the stuffing bowl and practically ran into the kitchen, convinced she was about to have a nervous breakdown. Once inside, she leaned against the wall and breathed deeply, wanting nothing more than this dinner to be over.

When she returned, Simon had collected the dinner plates. Cassie reached for the gravy boat and stared down at it. Lumps, indeed! She couldn't find a single one!

Thankfully, after coffee and dessert, Cassie started to relax. Again Mrs. Mullinex damned her with faint praise regarding the pie, but by then Cassie didn't care. Besides, she had to agree—the apples were unevenly sliced.

"Don't you have anything good to say?" Mr. Oliver muttered. "I thought the pies were great. All of 'em."

"Excellent meal," Bob told her and tried to take her hand.

Cassie snatched it away before he had the chance. As far as she was concerned, the man should be arrested.

"I'll have you know, *Mr.* Oliver, I've paid Cassie several compliments," Mrs. Mullinex said righteously.

If that was the case, they'd flown right over Cassie's head.

By the time she saw her last neighbor to the door, Cassie was exhausted. As soon as Bob left—with obvious reluctance—she collapsed into a chair.

"You look a bit out of sorts," Simon commented.

"You think?" The man had mastered the art of understatement.

He grinned and sat on the sofa across from her. "Actually, the meal went well."

"You have got to be kidding. It was a disaster!"

"You're being too hard on yourself. You did an admirable job, and while it might not seem that your neighbors fully appreciated what you did, I believe they had an enjoyable afternoon."

She gave him a weak smile. "I don't know if I should be glad the ring didn't show up or not."

"Is it valuable?"

"Not really. I bought it in Hawaii a few years back. I hate to lose it, though." She raised her shoulders in a shrug. "But if it hasn't turned up by now, I doubt it ever will. For all I know, it might be in Mr. Oliver's digestive system."

"I'm sure it's not."

"What makes you say that?"

Reaching inside his suit pocket, Simon pulled out the ring, displaying it proudly between index finger and thumb. "Is this the ring you misplaced?"

Speechless, all Cassie could do was stare at him. Once

the shock wore off, she lunged forward and grabbed the ring. "You're telling me you found it?"

"I did."

"Where?"

"On the kitchen counter. You must've taken it off and forgotten. I tried to get your attention in the kitchen and then at dinner but you ignored me."

"I didn't take it off." Cassie would've remembered that.

"Then it must have fallen off before you stuffed the turkey."

Cassie held the ring in one cupped hand, her relief overwhelming. Then, slowly, her suspicions started to rise. "Exactly when did you find this?"

"Just before Phyllis came into the kitchen. As I said, I tried to tell you but you were too flustered to notice."

"Phyllis?" she echoed. "Mrs. Mullinex is now Phyllis to you?"

"She's a delightful mature woman."

"Hmm. Then again, she isn't stealing *your* newspapers."

"I suggest you purchase her a subscription for Christmas."

"I'll think about it," Cassie muttered. Then, remembering the ring, she glared at him. "That was cruel and unusual punishment, letting me worry that someone was going to swallow this ring."

"I *tried* to tell you I'd found it," Simon said in his own defense. "Why else do you think I was passing the stuffing around?"

Well, there was that. "I'm too tired to argue with you." She stretched her legs out and let her hands dangle at her sides. Unable to prevent it, she yawned.

Taking that as his cue to leave, Simon stood. "I'd better go."

Cassie realized with a start that she wanted him to stay. "Don't go yet," she urged.

"Do you want help with the cleanup?"

"No."

"A drink or more coffee?"

She shook her head. "There's a football game on," she said.

Cassie could see he was tempted. Smiling up at him, she hoped that was enough incentive to get him to change his mind.

"I should get home," he finally said.

"Why?"

"I just should. And don't forget I'll be seeing you tomorrow," he reminded her.

"Tomorrow?"

"In my office. Late afternoon."

She couldn't recall an appointment, but if they had one, she'd certainly keep it.

"John will be there."

Oh, my goodness. Cassie had forgotten she was supposed to meet John. "Cancel it," she said hurriedly.

Simon frowned.

"I'm not ready to meet John."

"You've completed your three tasks to my satisfaction. I don't understand why you're hesitating. You've worked hard and waited for quite a while, and so has John. I hate to disappoint him."

Cassie's head was spinning with doubt and fear. "I need to talk to you first."

"Talk to me now," he said, none too patiently.

"I can't—I'm tired, and besides, I... I need to think."

He continued to frown, and she could see he wasn't happy with her. He left soon after.

Cassie sat on the sofa for at least an hour, trying to make sense of her relationship with Simon. Her feelings for him and her original expectations of John were scrambled in her mind. Eventually, when her whole life felt like a hopeless tangle, she called Angie.

Thankfully her friend was home.

"I need help," Cassie whispered.

"Cassie?" Angie said. "What's wrong?"

"I've done something foolish."

"What?"

She said the words out loud for the very first time. "I've fallen in love with Simon."

CHAPTER FIFTEEN

Simon says: There's a perfect match for you; it just isn't me.

By the time Cassie reached Simon's office, she'd worked everything out. She'd rehearsed her speech all day. Her one hope was that Simon would own up to the fact that he shared her feelings.

His assistant greeted her warmly. "Hello, Ms. Beaumont. It's good to see you again."

"You, too, Ms. Snelling. Oh, nice tree."

That was the extent of the Christmas decorating in Simon's office—a small Norfolk pine on the credenza, draped with tiny white lights. Simple, classy, elegant.

Given her previous experiences visiting his office, Cassie automatically took a seat and picked up a magazine.

"Dr. Dodson will see you now."

"Already?"

"Yes, he told me I was to bring you into his office as soon as you arrived."

Cassie set the magazine aside and stood. It was now or

never. The only thing left to do was forge ahead and pray they could discuss this with openness and honesty.

Ms. Snelling held the door for her. "Ms. Beaumont," she said, announcing Cassie.

As he had at their first meeting, Simon sat behind his desk, studying a periodical. He glanced up, acknowledging her with a nod, then resumed reading.

Cassie took a seat, crossed her legs, uncrossed them, then folded her hands as she waited. She knew Simon now and was familiar with his ways.

When he did finally look up, Cassie could see that he was on edge. She wondered if he'd managed to sleep after he'd left her apartment and suspected he'd tossed and turned, the same as she had.

"You said you wanted to speak to me." His voice was expressionless.

"Yes, please."

He checked his watch. "You have ten minutes."

That dictatorial approach didn't fool her. He wasn't going to intimidate her, nor was he going to scare her into being silent.

"Ten minutes," she said softly. "I doubt it'll take that long."

He leaned back and Cassie leaned forward. "If you'll re-call, it was my friend Angie who suggested I make an appointment with you."

He indicated with a slight nod that he remembered.

"You turned her down, right?"

"Yes." He sounded bored. "You know very well I did."

"For an excellent reason," she said, "as you and I are both aware."

He checked his watch again, as if to point out that the minutes were ticking away.

"Even though you rejected her, Angie thought highly enough of your skills as a matchmaker to recommend you to me."

"I know my business, Cassie."

"You won't get any argument from me." She grinned and looked down at her hands, surprised by how calm and controlled she sounded. While her heart continued to beat at an accelerated rate, she remained outwardly collected. "At first I thought the idea of those three tasks was ridiculous, but I complied. In fact, I was willing to do just about anything to prove my value as a wife."

Once more he glanced at his watch.

"I understand now why you chose the tasks you did. Each one served a specific purpose. You knew all the facts I could list on a sheet of paper, and as a psychologist you could discern a great deal from that, but you didn't know the real me." She'd given much thought to his motives. "You didn't know my heart."

"Yes, well..."

"You wanted to find out how I interact with strangers as a volunteer. You wanted to see how well I deal with children and then you were interested in my homemaking skills."

"Practical aspects of any good marriage. But these tasks also told me that you have compassion and flexibility and a sense of humor."

She bowed her head to hide her pleasure at his words.

"John is looking for a woman who's willing to have children with him. A woman who enjoys socializing and wants to be part of a community. You are all those things."

He'd introduced the subject of John, so she'd better get that out of the way right now. "Oh, yes. John, the match you chose on my behalf. I do hope you cancelled the appointment."

"Per your request I did. However, I feel you should know John was extremely disappointed, as I expected he would be."

"I would've been, too, if I'd been waiting to meet my perfect match. Or as you'd probably say, my most *suitable* match," she said with a grin.

"And you aren't?" Simon challenged.

"No, unfortunately I've already made his acquaintance."

Simon's eyes narrowed. "Before you say anything else, I want you to think this through very carefully."

"I have," she said.

"I beg to differ." Simon spoke in the same unfriendly tones she'd heard at the beginning of their relationship.

"I brought up Angie's name for a specific reason. You knew after reading her answers to your questionnaire, and during your initial meeting, that she was in love with someone else." She paused. "As I told you on Saturday, that someone happens to be my brother. As I also told you, I was impressed by your insight in recognizing her feelings for Shawn so easily."

"As I've repeatedly said, I'm good at my job."

"You knew it would be wrong to introduce her to another man when she loved my brother."

"Yes."

"It would be just as wrong to introduce me to John when I'm in love with...you."

Simon briefly closed his eyes, then stood. "I've said it

before and I'll say it again. Don't do this, Cassie. I'm off-limits."

"I can't keep still. I wish I could, but I can't."

He reclaimed his seat. Looking exasperated, he informed her, "This happens far more often than you realize. I've lost count of the number of women who believe they've fallen in love with me."

"I'm sure that's true." Simon was an attractive man. He had a strong sensual appeal and would turn heads wherever he went. She didn't assume for an instant that she was the only woman ever to fall for him.

"The thing you seem to forget is that you've paid thirty thousand dollars to meet the man I've chosen as your match."

Cassie hadn't forgotten.

"I held up my part of the bargain," he said.

"Yes, you did."

"I've deposited the check and it's cleared your bank."

She nodded.

"If you voluntarily decide not to meet your match, you should know there'll be no refund."

"I didn't think there would be."

"If you walk away now, without meeting John, you'll forfeit your money." He said it again, as if he felt it necessary to remind her of what was at risk.

"I'm aware of that."

"It would be foolish for you to do this."

"I've been called a fool for lesser things," she said calmly.

He shook his head. "I wouldn't have expected you to be an unreasonable woman."

"Really?" She smiled, just a little.

He looked pointedly at his watch. "Your time's about up. Is there anything else you'd care to say...in closing?"

This last part was said with emphasis, as though he was eager to usher her out the door.

"I'm almost finished," she told him.

He sighed.

"I'm not telling you how I feel so you can laugh at me, Simon."

His gaze held hers. "I would never do that," he said, then added, "any more than I did with the other women."

She tried to disguise a smile. "Nor do I wish to be humiliated."

He agreed with a nod.

"I have reason to believe you share my feelings."

"You—"

"Do you kiss other female clients?" she asked, interrupting him.

He was silent.

"I didn't think so. How many have you taken to your home?"

"None," he admitted from between clenched teeth.

"That's what I thought," she said. To her relief, he was being honest.

"I've never had a woman...a client break down in tears and turn to me for comfort. Yes, I stepped over the line. I regretted it immediately and, if you recall, I apologized."

"You did."

"I realized it was a mistake to allow any client access to my personal life after you showed up at my home later with the soup. I should never have invited you inside."

"Why did you?"

He refused to meet her eyes. "I'd been ill for several days and my resistance was weak."

"Resistance to me?"

"No," he countered sharply, "resistance to impropriety."

"Ah." So that was the excuse he'd chosen.

"Afterward, I was afraid you might have read more into that evening than was warranted, and I see now that you have. I'm sorry I didn't address the subject earlier. I wish I had. As I feared, you've got the wrong impression."

"I see."

"It would be best if we could forget that evening entirely, put it out of our minds."

"I'm sorry," she said. "I can't forget that night. I can't make myself regret it, either. It was after our evening together that I knew, Simon. I'd fallen in love with you."

Simon met her look unflinchingly and yielded no emotion. "Please don't continue. This is embarrassing for you *and* for me."

"I have one other comment," she said, striving to remain unemotional. "Actually, it's more of a question than a comment."

"Then out with it, and let this matter be laid to rest."

She thanked him with a brief nod. "I can accept that a distraught female weeping on your shoulder might have caused you to offer comfort in a way you normally wouldn't."

"Thank you. I appreciate your understanding."

"I can even accept the fact that your resistance was low when I dropped by your home that evening."

Once more he nodded.

"But how do you account for the way you kissed me on Sunday?"

"Sunday?" he repeated. The color seemed to drain from his face.

"Can you tell me what prompted that kiss?" she asked.

He didn't answer for a long moment. "I have no excuse," he finally said.

"I'm not looking for excuses, Simon, I'm looking for honesty. It hasn't been easy to lay out my heart for you. If I've misread the situation, then I apologize. In that case, I'll walk out your door right now and you'll never hear from me again."

"That would…be a shame."

"Yes, it would," she agreed, hope seeping in for the first time since she'd entered his office.

"You've paid me a lot of money and I'd feel bad if you allowed this opportunity to slip by. John is awaiting an introduction, and I hate to disappoint him."

Cassie closed her eyes, struggling to hold on to her poise. After a moment, she opened them and met his look head-on. "I'm not meeting John or any other man you deem the right mate for me. Or my 'suitable' mate or whatever word you want to use. I've already found him and it's you."

Simon didn't acknowledge that comment in any way.

"*Have* I misread your feelings, Simon?" she asked softly.

He refused to answer.

Reluctantly she stood; she'd gone past her allotted ten minutes. "I won't embarrass you further—or myself for that matter. But before I go, I have one simple request."

"Fine," he said tersely.

"Look me in the eyes and tell me you don't love me. Do that and I'll leave and never trouble you again."

"I'm not playing word games with you, Cassie."

"This isn't a game. It's my life, my future—our future."

He squinted up at the ceiling. "Why do women have such a flair for the dramatic? I suppose you're going to spend the rest of your life pining away for me."

"No, I won't," she told him. "I love you and it's up to you to accept or reject that love. It'll hurt me, but I know I'll get over you in time. In every likelihood I'll marry someone else one day and perhaps even have children. Rest assured that if you reject me, I won't leap off a bridge."

"That's a relief."

She moved away from the chair, her heart pounding so hard she was astonished it didn't echo through the room. She gave him ample opportunity to stop her.

He didn't.

With her hand on the door, she turned back to look at Simon one last time. He sat at his desk, reading. She wasn't fooled. He might not admit it, but he loved her.

"Merry Christmas, Simon."

He glanced up and his eyes flared as though he was surprised to see her still in the room. "Oh. Merry Christmas."

"Goodbye."

She didn't wait for a response. Head held high, she marched out the door. Once on the other side, she closed her eyes, almost collapsing to the floor as a wave of deep loss hit her.

Ms. Snelling's chair scraped as she stood. "Oh, dear. Are you all right, Ms. Beaumont? You look like you're about to faint."

"I—I'm okay," she stammered. "Thank you...." she added politely.

It was exactly as Cassie had feared. Simon Dodson, professional matchmaker, was an expert at finding love for everyone except himself.

CHAPTER SIXTEEN

"Hold the elevator!" Cassie shouted, rushing across the condo foyer on Wednesday afternoon. When she saw that the lone occupant was Mr. Oliver, she automatically slowed her steps. No need to rush; he'd take sadistic delight in letting the doors shut in her face. To her amazement, he thrust out his arm and stopped them from closing.

Cassie hardly knew what to think. "Thank you," she managed as she hurried into the elevator, loaded down with her mail, the newspaper, her purse and a couple of last-minute Christmas purchases.

The newspaper.

She hadn't even realized Mrs. Mullinex hadn't "borrowed" it since their dinner together. That was progress.

"My pleasure," Mr. Oliver said as the elevator doors glided shut. "Can't thank you enough for the great dinner."

It seemed wrong to confess that if it hadn't been for Simon she would never have thought to invite Mr. Oliver.

Try as she might, she couldn't get Simon out of her mind. She'd given it her best shot, told him how she felt and done what she could to convince him that he shared her feelings. But she hadn't expected the strength of his conviction in denying his love for her. Nor could she understand why he fought it so hard.

What bothered her most was his inability to admit to her face that he didn't love her. If he had, she might have believed him. However, for reasons she'd likely never know, he refused to accept her love.

"Nice young man…"

"I'm sorry," Cassie said. "I didn't catch what you said?"

"That Simon of yours. He's a fine young man. You've chosen well."

"I…thank you," she whispered. No need to explain that he wasn't "hers," or that she wouldn't be seeing him again. Cassie had been sincere when she'd told him she wouldn't pine away for the rest of her life. He'd made his decision and she'd made hers.

The elevator stopped, and Mr. Oliver held the door for her to exit first. When they stepped into the hallway, Mrs. Mullinex opened her condo door and, seeing the two of them, waved cheerfully. Cassie noticed that the other woman's eyes immediately went to Harry Oliver.

"Oh, what perfect timing," Phyllis said. Her hair was brushed into soft waves and she looked lovely.

"Good afternoon, Harry," she purred.

"Hello, Phyllis."

Cassie hid a satisfied grin. Apparently there'd been a breakthrough in that relationship. Wonderful!

"I was hoping to see you," she said, smiling shyly at Harry. "I thought I'd invite my dearest friends over for eggnog on Christmas Eve. I do hope you can join me." As if she realized she'd directed the invitation solely to Mr. Oliver, she turned to Cassie. "I'd like it if you could come, too."

"Why…thank you, I'd be honored." Cassie's brother and Angie had invited her to spend Christmas Day with Angie's family. They'd been generous to include her, and Cassie had gratefully accepted.

"I wonder…" Phyllis began. "If you'd like to invite your young man, please do. That Simon is quite the charmer."

She nodded. "I'll mention it if I talk to him between now and Christmas Eve." That was highly improbable, but again she didn't feel it was necessary to go into details.

"Why wouldn't you be talking to him?" Mrs. Mullinex pressed. "'Tis the season and he's your sweetheart."

Cassie glanced away. "Actually, he isn't."

"You don't mean that!"

"They might've had a spat," Harry suggested.

"In that case, dear, I urge you to settle it before Christmas." She looked at Harry and blushed. "Don't let too much time elapse before you set things right."

Harry stepped closer to Phyllis. "I couldn't agree with you more."

Rather than tell them there was nothing to settle, Cassie just thanked them for their advice.

They made an arrangement to meet, and Cassie let herself into her condo. The festive cheer of the season greeted her, and for a moment all she could do was stand and stare at her Christmas tree and the other decorations, at the Christmas cards lined up on her mantel and the pile of wrapped gifts. She struggled to ignore her heavy heart.

As she tossed the mail on the kitchen counter, Simon's bold handwriting, slanted across a business-size envelope, instantly caught her attention. She grabbed it with both hands. Two or three minutes must have passed before she mustered the courage to tear it open.

With her pulse hammering in her ears, she pulled out a refund check for the total amount of his fee. The check was wrapped in a single sheet of white paper. When she unfolded the sheet, she found it blank.

He'd made the check out to her and in the memo line, he'd written one word: *refund*. She had always assumed he'd keep the money. Perhaps this was the only way he had of relieving his conscience. The only way of saying he had regrets, too. Not knowing just what she'd do with it, Cassie propped the check against the base of a blooming poinsettia—the very one he'd given her. She'd need to think about her response.

She could refuse to cash it out of pure stubbornness. That seemed foolish. When she'd paid Simon, she'd explained that the funds had come from a special savings account, which she'd set up to pay for her wedding. Perhaps he was saying he wanted her to have that wedding.

No, she mused, shaking her head. She couldn't second-guess him, couldn't drive herself insane trying to analyze his motives.

The phone rang and, still absorbed in her thoughts, Cassie picked it up. "Hello," she murmured.

"Hello." The male voice was unfamiliar. "My name is John Fitzsimmons and I was given your number by a... mutual friend."

"What can I do for you, John?" she asked, suspicion springing to life.

"Well... I was hoping we could meet for coffee." He sounded nervous.

"What friend?"

"Ah…"

"Is it Simon?" she asked. It hadn't taken her long to catch on. The matchmaker in him was incapable of letting this go. He'd found the man he believed to be her ideal match. Obviously, Simon was hoping to assuage his guilt by making sure she had the opportunity to meet John—an opportunity she'd already declined.

"Simon suggested it might be better if I implied it was someone else, but I'm not much good at prevarication."

"I'm not, either."

John chuckled. "He said you backed out at the last minute."

"I did," she confirmed.

"I know it's none of my business, but would you mind telling me why?"

Cassie bit her lip and debated how wise it would be to reveal the truth, then decided she owed him that. "I apologize because I realize I let you down, but…unfortunately I fell in love with someone else."

"Oh." She heard a world of disappointment in that one word. He didn't say anything for a moment. "Did you tell Simon this?"

"Yes, I was in his office on Monday." Could that have been just forty-eight hours ago? It seemed far longer; it seemed like a lifetime.

John hesitated again. "Then I don't understand why Simon was so insistent that I call you."

Cassie, however, was completely aware of his motivation. "I'm afraid…well, the man I fell in love with is Simon."

"Oh." There was a wealth of meaning in his short response. "I guess it would be safe to say he doesn't return your feelings?"

Cassie believed he did. "Apparently not," she said softly, hoping the pain she felt wasn't obvious.

"I guess that explains why he urged me to contact you."

She disagreed, but didn't voice her opinion.

"I realize you...like Simon, but seeing that he doesn't feel the same way, it might help if we met. Simon spoke highly of you on several occasions and I thought the two of us might have a lot in common."

"What did he say about me?" she asked.

"Well..." He drew out the word. "He said that you're thoughtful and caring of others."

Despite herself, Cassie smiled. Simon had chosen to forget her negative attitude toward her neighbors and how she'd done everything she could to get out of hosting the pre-Christmas dinner party.

"He said you're wonderful with children."

"He did?" She closed her eyes and remembered the sad little girl who'd come to visit Santa. All that child wanted for Christmas was for her father to come home. Even the hardest heart would've been affected by such a request.

"He also said how generous you are to others."

Cassie wasn't sure that was true.

"And he told me you're one of the most beautiful clients he's ever had the pleasure of working with. He said your beauty is special because it's internal as well as external."

"That was kind of him." Simon would cringe if he heard her say that. He didn't receive compliments gladly.

"Actually, Simon couldn't say enough good things about

you. He urged me to ask you out and not to take no for an answer. You will meet me, won't you?"

She probably should but couldn't dredge up any enthusiasm for even a casual meeting. She needed time to deal with her complicated feelings for Simon. Her love was as strong now as when she'd stepped into his office two days earlier, and yet it was useless to believe he'd change his mind.

"I don't know," she said honestly.

"What would it hurt?" John asked. "All I'm suggesting is that the two of us have coffee together."

He had a point, but she hesitated. "It's, uh, nice that you'd still like to meet, especially since you know how I feel about Simon."

"I do. From everything Simon had to say, it sounds as if we're a perfect match. Or—" and she could hear the smile in his voice "—the most suitable one."

That might've been true a few weeks ago, but it wasn't anymore. She loved Simon.

"I think perhaps we should drop it for now," she said.

To her surprise, John laughed. "Simon told me you'd say that, but he also said I should be persistent."

Cassie straightened and a chill went down her spine. "Did he?"

"Yes. In fact, he said I shouldn't listen to any arguments. He went so far as to say he's introduced dozens of couples over the past few years and in all that time he's never met two people who were a better fit for each other than you and me."

Cassie had to restrain a laugh. Simon was doing his utmost to push her into the arms of another man, and his determination only served to confirm that she'd been right all along.

But telling John this would be touchy. "Why do you suppose he praised me so much?" she asked him.

"Well…"

"I suppose you've noticed that Simon isn't really one for flattery."

"Yeah."

"When I first met him, I wasn't sure what to think."

"Me neither," he said.

"He seemed way too dictatorial."

"I hear a lot of people have the same feeling. The friend who told me about Simon and his matchmaking business said I shouldn't take offense at his gruff manner."

"Did his attitude change?" she asked. "Did he start to react to you in a different way?"

"Not really. Why?"

"He did with me."

"Oh. That's the reason you asked why he had so many wonderful things to say about you, isn't it?"

"Yes."

"So you think he's in love with you, too?"

"I do."

John sighed. "Seems funny, doesn't it, that a matchmaker would have such a hard time admitting he's in love."

Cassie wasn't exactly laughing. "In any other circumstances, you and I would probably have gotten along famously—and maybe even decided to marry."

"Maybe," he concurred. "Who's to know."

"Thank you for calling, John. I want nothing but the very best for you."

"Thanks." He paused and she could hear Elvis Presley's "Blue Christmas" in the background. "I guess this means you're definitely not going out with me."

"That's true."

"Okay."

"Bye." She started to hang up when John stopped her.

"Yes?" she said.

"Cassie, I was wondering if you'd take my phone number—in case you have a change of heart."

"It's in my phone, John. I have it."

"You won't lose it, will you?"

"No, I won't lose it," she promised. "Merry Christmas, now."

Late the following day, Christmas Eve, Cassie was grateful for Mrs. Mullinex's invitation. She hated the idea of spending the evening alone.

Although she wasn't Catholic, she thought she might attend midnight mass at the cathedral after that. The beauty of the service and the music would lift her heart and infuse her with holiday spirit.

The small get-together at Mrs. Mullinex's was congenial, with Harry and Phyllis exchanging fond smiles over their fruitcake and eggnog. Love seemed to be blossoming all around her. First Shawn and Angie, and now her two cantankerous neighbors.

She toasted her newfound friends and after a respectable length of time made her excuses. They all hugged and wished each other a Merry Christmas, and she did the same.

As she left she saw a male figure heading toward the elevator. From behind he resembled Simon. He was about to step through the elevator doors when she called his name.

"Simon?"

He turned abruptly, a frown darkening his face.

"What are you doing here?" she asked.

"Why did you turn John Fitzsimmons down?"

"I think you know," she said calmly.

"You're a stubborn woman."

"You mean you've only noticed that now?" She unlocked her door and entered the apartment.

After a moment's hesitation, Simon followed her inside.

CHAPTER SEVENTEEN

Simon says: The perfect Christmas is the one I spend with you.

Simon strode into Cassie's apartment but couldn't seem to stop moving, from door to window and back again.

Cassie wished she dared to throw her arms around him and halt his frantic pacing.

"Why wouldn't you agree to at least meet John?" The anger seemed to radiate from him.

"Simon, you know why. I'm in love with you."

His eyes slammed shut and he clenched his jaw. "I don't want your love."

"So you said." That didn't change the way she felt, though.

"What harm would it have done to meet John?"

"None, I suppose," she said with a shrug. "But I felt I would've been doing him a disservice."

It was as though he hadn't heard her. "In other words, despite your assurances that you're willing to move on with your life, you refuse to do so," he challenged.

Cassie sat on her sofa while Simon continued pacing.

She tracked his movements with her eyes. "Don't worry. I'll date other men—when I'm ready."

He whirled around and glared at her.

Cassie felt it was her turn to pose a few questions. "Why are you fighting this?" she asked, looking up at him. "And... why are you here at all?"

"I had to talk to you about John." Simon shook his head. "Don't you realize marrying *me* would be a disaster?"

"Really?" It didn't escape her notice that he hadn't denied anything—and that he'd brought up marriage. Evidently the subject had been on his mind, which was encouraging. "Why's that?"

Simon abruptly stood still. "I suspect I'm not telling you anything you don't know. I'm not...comfortable with emotions on a personal level. I prefer to analyze and guide other people's emotional lives. I have a hard time admitting this, but I've always steered clear of the intensity, the giving up of control...." He sounded so unlike the confident, self-assured man she'd come to know, and his vulnerability made him even more appealing.

"I hate this confusion," he muttered. "I'm good at helping my clients sort through their feelings, good at writing about them—but not good at experiencing them. It makes me...miserable."

"I've been pretty miserable myself," Cassie said.

"Then we should both find ways of dealing with these emotions because I'm not changing my mind."

"So you've said."

"I mean it, Cassie."

She wasn't going to argue. "Yes, I know."

He stared at her, eyebrows raised. "Don't be so agreeable. I'm not used to it, and I don't know how to react when you're amenable to everything I say."

She nodded.

"See? That's what I mean." He pointed accusingly at her. "Listen. I know what kind of man makes a good husband—and I'm not it."

Cassie had to smile. "That's something I *don't* agree with. You've shown me truths about myself. Let me do the same for you."

Simon shook his head as if that possibility was beyond him.

Cassie wasn't about to let him assume he was incapable of love when she knew otherwise.

She stood and walked purposefully toward him. He was still pacing, so she caught his hand. Her fingers curled around his and he turned back to stare at her. Not giving him a chance to object, she leaned forward and placed her mouth on his.

Simon slipped one hand around the back of her head and kissed her with a hunger that thrilled her.

"We'll start with teaching you to accept my love," she whispered when he broke off the lengthy kiss.

Again he briefly closed his eyes.

"Love is one thing," he muttered. "But you want children. I don't know about children except in theory. I'm not good with them," he said. "They cry and make messes in their diapers and drool."

"That they do."

"I don't understand why people willingly submit themselves to the uncertainty and stress of raising children." He splayed his fingers through his hair.

Even as he spoke she heard the longing in his voice. Despite his claims to the contrary he desired a family, just like most people did. Just like *she* did. Unable to resist a moment longer, she slid her arms around his waist and hugged him close. He resisted at first and attempted to break free.

Cassie held tight. Smiling up at him, she stood on the tips of her toes, rested her hands on his shoulders and pressed her mouth to his. It was only a matter of seconds before he became fully involved in the kiss.

When her legs were about to give way, Simon tore his mouth from hers and stepped back, still holding on to her, which was a good thing. Otherwise Cassie would have collapsed in a heap on the floor.

He wagged a warning finger at her. "No more of that."

"Sorry." She felt she should probably apologize but giggled instead. "I couldn't help myself. Oh, Simon, you're right. I do want children—your children. We'll have very special babies."

His expression was wry. "They won't cry and make messes and—"

"Of course they will," she said, nudging him.

"Like I already said, I have no skills in this area."

"But I don't, either. We'll learn together, the way other parents do."

She wasn't sure if she'd convinced him or not because he continued to stare at her.

Then, as if he'd noticed the Christmas decorations for the first time, he frowned and said, "When you came to me, you talked about a perfect Christmas."

She nodded.

"I'm not big on Christmas."

"I think that's kind of a weak argument," she told him. "Seeing how every assignment you gave me had to do with the holidays."

"Only because there's a surfeit of them at this time of year."

"True, but there are plenty of others and you *chose* the Christmas-related tasks."

"You've found some hidden meaning in that?"

"Yes. It's obvious to me that you enjoy the holidays."

When he started to protest, she held up a hand.

"Let me amend that. You enjoy watching other people enjoy Christmas. You understand why it's important to them, the same way you understand—in theory—why love and marriage and children are important. If you don't like Christmas, it's because you're alone. You don't have any-one to share it with. But, Simon, that's about to change."

"Aren't you making assumptions you have no business making?"

"Is this really so difficult?" she asked.

"Yes," he groaned.

Cassie gently laid her head against his chest and sighed meaningfully.

His sigh echoed hers. "Oh, I give up. You knew I'd fallen in love with you." He drew her toward him and rested his chin on her head.

"I *hoped* so."

"I do love you, Cassie."

"And I love you."

He leaned down and shattered what remained of her composure with a single kiss.

"You seriously want to marry me?" he whispered.

EPILOGUE

From: Cassie
Sent: Thursday, December 1, 5:35 p.m.
To: Mom; Pete; Shawn&Angie; Phyllis&Harry; Amanda Snelling; Bob; JohnFitz
Cc: Simon
Subject: Dinner on Christmas Eve—Save the Date!

Hi, Everyone,

I know what a busy time of year this is, so wanted to send our invitation now. I'm not even going to *try* to fancy it up.

Here goes: You are all invited to dinner with Cassie and Simon on Christmas Eve. Come at 7. Our house. Significant others welcome! Bring a favorite Christmas memory to share! RSVP.

Not to be a bossypants, but the sooner you can let me know, the better. Look forward to catching up with everyone!

Cassie (and, of course, Simon)

From: Shawn&Angie
Sent: Thursday, December 1, 5:45 p.m.
To: Cassie; Mom; Pete; Phyllis&Harry; Amanda Snelling; Bob; JohnFitz

Cc: Simon
Subject: RE: Dinner on Christmas Eve—Save the Date!

Hi, Cassie and Simon,
Thanks for this! Shawn and I will be delighted to attend. We're flying out of Portland and into SeaTac on the 23rd, staying with my mom and dad.

What's on the menu? Let me know what we can bring.

I'll bet you can guess my favorite Christmas memory (and yes, it involved your charming brother, Shawn!)

Angie

From: Cassie
Sent: Thursday, December 1, 6:30 p.m.
To: Shawn&Angie
Subject: RE: Dinner on Christmas Eve—Save the Date!

Thanks, Angie. Email and phone calls and texting are great, but I am *so* looking forward to seeing you two in person! As for dinner, just bring yourselves. I'm making the same thing I did for my famous Christmas dinner two years ago—my third task, remember? Turkey, stuffing (and I'll try not to lose my wedding ring in the stuffing!), mashed potatoes, gravy, green beans with almonds, salads. And a selection of pies for dessert. Plus a nice Washington State wine, which Simon will select. (With both of us being pregnant, you and I will have to skip that this year.)

Let's talk soon!
C

From: Mom
Sent: Thursday, December 1, 6:32 p.m.

To: Cassie; Shawn&Angie; Simon
Subject: RE: Dinner on Christmas Eve—Save the Date!

Darlings, I'm so sorry but we won't be able to leave Hawaii this Christmas, after all. Joseph and I have guests coming from New Zealand.

Cassie and Shawn (and Simon and Angie)—I'll talk to you Christmas Day. I want you all to come for a midwinter holiday in Honolulu, well before the babies arrive. That's my Christmas gift to you. Confirm ASAP!!!

Meanwhile, say hello to your father for me.

Much love,
Mom

From: Cassie
Sent: Thursday, December 1, 6:39 p.m.
To: Mom
Cc: Shawn&Angie; Simon
Subject: RE: Dinner on Christmas Eve—Save the Date!

Hawaii? Oh, Mom, what a great gift. Sun, sand, palm trees...

I called Simon (he's working late) to check with him, and we're thrilled to accept. I hope Shawn and Angie will be able to come, too. We were thinking end of January. (Does that work for you, too?)

We'll miss you and Joseph this Christmas but seeing you in January will make up for it, especially in Hawaii! We'll book the tickets this week.

Love,
Cass

From: Shawn&Angie
Sent: Monday, December 12, 7:42 p.m.

To: Cassie
Subject: RE: Dinner on Christmas Eve—Save the Date!

Works for us, too. Shawn will email your mother tonight. Late Jan. should be fine, since I'm due in April and your Simon, Jr. (or whatever you decide to call him) won't make his appearance until May. Which reminds me: make sure you let us know when the two of you settle on a name. Shawn hates it that I refuse to find out if we're having a boy or a girl, but as you know, I've always enjoyed a bit of suspense!

Here's something else to keep you guessing. I'm *making* your Christmas present. Yes, me, Angie, the science geek. I told you I took knitting classes, right? Well, I'm knitting something wonderful for you. I've already made a baby Santa hat for your little guy to wear next Christmas! Aren't you proud of me, knitting and all?

Did I tell you we've narrowed down the names? Julia, Katherine, Savannah or Kristin. And for a boy, Luke or Karl.

One more thing—Shawn's going to paint name cards for you again (like he did two years ago). The theme this time will be...a surprise.

Ange

From: Amanda Snelling
Sent: Friday, December 2, 9:02 a.m.
To: Cassie
Cc: Simon
Subject: RE: Dinner on Christmas Eve—Save the Date!

Hello, Cassie,
My husband, Robert, and I accept your invitation with pleasure.

I've mentioned this to Simon but knowing him, he'll probably forget to mention it, so I thought I should let you know myself.

Please tell us what we can bring. Robert's very good when it comes to choosing wine.

Look forward to seeing you.

Amanda

Amanda Snelling

Assistant to Simon Dodson

From: Pete

Sent: Friday, December 2, 12:15 p.m.

To: Cassie

Cc: Shawn&Angie

Subject: RE: Dinner on Christmas Eve—Save the Date!

Cassie, thanks for the invite. I'll be there if I can. OK if I let you know closer to the date?

Pete

P.S. Is your mother planning to attend?

From: Cassie

Sent: Monday, December 13, 12:15 p.m.

To: Pete

Cc: Shawn&Angie

Subject: RE: Dinner on Christmas Eve—Save the Date!

Pete/Dad,

Fine, but could you confirm by December 21st?

And no, Mom's got a friend visiting from New Zealand and can't make it.

Please feel free to bring a companion if you want to—just let me know!

Cass

From: Phyllis&Harry
Sent: Friday, December 2, 4:30 p.m.
To: Cassie
Subject: RE: Dinner on Christmas Eve—Save the Date!

Dearest Cassie,
Harry and I would be *thrilled* to come for dinner. Thank you so much for thinking of us!

I'll bring my famous apple pie. And did I tell you Harry's making wine these days? He'll bring a bottle or two. (It's not too bad, especially if you've already had a few glasses of something else to—how shall I put it—dull your palate.)

By the way, what's a five-letter word for "perfect"? I'm working on today's crossword.

Love,
Phyllis

From: Cassie
Sent: Friday, December 2, 4:41 p.m.
To: Phyllis&Harry
Subject: RE: Dinner on Christmas Eve—Save the Date!

Hi, Phyllis,
How could anyone refuse your apple pie? By all means, bring one and thank Harry for the offer of wine, but Simon and Amanda's husband, Robert, are taking care of that. Your special pie is more than enough. My mouth is watering already.

5-letter word for "perfect"? Hmm. What about "ideal"? Does that work?

Cassie

From: Phyllis&Harry
Sent: Friday, December 2, 4:43 p.m.
To: Cassie
Subject: RE: Dinner on Christmas Eve—Save the Date!

That's perfect!

From: Bob
Sent: Friday, December 2, 9:16 p.m.
To: Cassie
Subject: RE: Dinner on Christmas Eve—Save the Date!

Hey Cassie—
Sounds cool. I'll volunteer to bring the music. I have a great rap CD of the Xmas classics. You haven't heard anything until you've heard "Not So Silent Night."

Your friend and former neighbor,
Bob

From: Cassie
Sent: Friday, December 2, 4:41 p.m.
To: Bob
Subject: RE: Dinner on Christmas Eve—Save the Date!

Hi, Bob—
Thanks for the offer but just bring yourself.

Cassie

From: JohnFitz
Sent: Friday, December 2, 2011, 5:20 p.m.

To: Cassie
Cc: Simon
Subject: RE: Dinner on Christmas Eve—Save the Date!

Cassie & Simon,
Christa and I would love to join you for dinner on the 24th. We had a lovely time with you last weekend and hope to return the favor soon.

By the way, I have news... Christa and I have set the date for the wedding next summer. You two and the baby will definitely be invited. After all, Simon, you introduced us! Come to think of it, Cassie, Simon did a good job matching up the two of us—but not to each other! Kind of ironic, isn't it? I couldn't be happier, and I know you feel the same way.

Just to be on the safe side, let me check—no one will be required to complete any tasks before we're allowed to eat our dinner, right?

John

From: Cassie
Sent: Friday, December 2, 5:32 p.m.
To: JohnFitz
Cc: Simon
Subject: RE: Dinner on Christmas Eve—Save the Date!

John, don't worry! The only thing required will be your presence. By the way, congratulations to you and Christa. I think this is a perfect match—and I'm so glad we've all become friends....

Cassie

From: Simon
Sent: Friday, December 2, 5:39 p.m.

To: Cassie
Subject: Dinner TONIGHT—Save the Date!

C—plan on dressing up. I'm taking you somewhere special tonight. I want to escort my wife—my *pregnant* wife—out on the town for a pre-Christmas treat! Reservation's at 7:30. Sorry for the short notice! I'll pick you up at the house around 7.

S

From: Cassie
Sent: Friday, December 2, 5:45 p.m.
To: Simon
Subject: RE: Dinner TONIGHT—Save the Date!

Simon, dinner tonight would be perfect. *You're* perfect. I'll be there, waiting for you, with bells on. And speaking of bells, I'm bringing a bunch of ten-dollar bills so I can give one to every charity bell-ringer we come across!

All my love,
Cassie

★ ★ ★ ★ ★

CASSIE'S IDEAS FOR THE PERFECT CHRISTMAS PARTY

I love Christmas, and I love giving Christmas parties, especially parties for friends or family in my home. I particularly like organizing the party in a way that lets less fortunate people in my community benefit from the celebration, too.

Whether you're planning a party for a traditional family, or for a family of friends, here are some ideas to make the occasion special and memorable:

* Establish a fun dress code: ask each woman to wear her most outrageous Christmas sweater, each man, his wildest, craziest Christmas tie. Have your guests vote for the winning sweater and tie. Take a photo of the winners for posterity! (Another idea: the winners are in charge of the Perfect Christmas Party for the following year.)

* Start the party by having your guests make paper snowflakes—all you'll need is white paper, scissors, some glue. Hang the ornaments around your house or apartment.

* Check with your local homeless shelter or church and select a group or a family to receive food and decorations that you and your guests will provide. Make arrangements to deliver the goods immediately after your party, whether that's on Christmas Eve or another day during the holidays.

  o A good way to handle this type of party: you prepare the main course (for example, cook two turkeys, hams or casseroles), then ask each of your guests (or couples) to bring two disposable containers of their favorite dish, one to serve at the party, one for the needy family or group.

  o Give your guests a list of things your beneficiary group needs—socks, warm hats, mittens—and suggest that they make or bring one of these items to the party. Set up a wrapping station, complete with paper and ribbon.

  o Set up an ornament-making station (simple glass balls, old jewelry, ribbon, scrap yarn, sequins, etc.) and ask each of your guests to make one to give to your beneficiary group.

* If children are among your guests, ask each parent to bring the child's favorite Christmas book. Take turns reading these books to the children.

* Purchase inexpensive Christmas stockings (check the local dollar store), or make some if you're crafty. Ask each guest to make, wrap and bring something for everyone at the party, but set a dollar limit. (Two dollars? Three?) Give examples, such as home-baked cookies

or candy, hot chocolate mix in a jar. Encourage them to let creativity be their guide.

* Create a custom Christmas puzzle by making a collage of photos of your guests. You can search online for sites that make personalized custom puzzles. Divide the puzzle pieces so that each guest will have the same number. When the guests arrive, give them each a small bag or festively wrapped box containing their puzzle pieces. Set up a puzzle station so all the guests can fit their pieces into the whole. In the case of a party attended by friends, the puzzle will represent all the lives brought together in friendship, the total greater than the assortment of individuals. Also include in each guest's gift bag a Christmas-themed question to answer during dinner. Examples: What is your first Christmas memory? What is your favorite Christmas gift of all time? What, for you, constitutes the perfect Christmas?

* Out of white card stock, create a Christmas bingo game, using such iconic images as a pine tree, wreath, ornament, candy cane, etc. for the squares. Have peppermint candies on hand to use for place holders. As prizes, give away Christmas music CDs, packages of homemade candy or cookies—use your imagination!

At the end of your party, gather up the food and gifts for your chosen family or group and deliver them, serenading them with Christmas carols before you depart.

Sigh. *In my humble opinion,* the perfect Christmas party! I love Christmas—and *Debbie Macomber's Christmas Cookbook* proves it. (As if you didn't already know!)

This beautiful cookbook has recipes for Christmas morning breakfast or brunch, appetizers for a get-together with colleagues, family or friends, Christmas dinner, desserts (yes, a whole chapter), cooking with kids and a lot more. As well, the recipes are interspersed with decorating tips, gifts to make (edible and otherwise), wrapping ideas and all kinds of other Christmas-related things. I've opened every chapter with personal reminiscences and references to my various Christmas stories.

In the chapter "Christmas and Christmas Eve Dinner," I talk about *The Perfect Christmas*—since, of course, one of Cassie's tasks is to create the perfect dinner for her neighbors. And since she chooses to replicate that dinner two years later, in the story's new epilogue....

I've included six recipes from my cookbook:

* ★ Christmas Eggnog

* ★ Crock-Pot Chicken Chili

* ★ Five-Minute Cranberry Walnut Cobbler

* ★ Ice Krispie Snowmen

* ★ Many Bean Soup Mix

* ★ Cream Scones with Dried Figs and Cherries

These are all easy to follow and easy to make—and they're guaranteed to delight everyone who tries them.

I hope they'll whet your appetite for *Debbie Macomber's Christmas Cookbook* and the fabulous recipes inside!

Debbie Macomber

Debbie Macomber's Christmas Cookbook is available in stores and from online retailers.

Christmas Eve Eggnog

This classic eggnog recipe calls for warming the egg yolks to assure a decadent, delicious yet safe drink for your party guests. (Except, of course, for children!)

Serves about 12

6 large eggs, separated
1 cup granulated sugar
3 cups whole milk
1 vanilla bean, split lengthwise
Salt
½ cup brandy
1 cup heavy cream
Garnishes: Ground nutmeg, chocolate shavings, cinnamon sticks

1. Place a large bowl in a larger bowl of ice water; set aside.

2. In a medium bowl, whisk egg yolks and ½ cup of the sugar until thick, for about 2 minutes.

3. In a medium saucepan over medium-low heat, bring milk, vanilla bean, and pinch of salt to a simmer. Remove from heat; whisk 1 cup of this hot milk mixture into the yolks. Slowly pour yolk-milk mixture into milk remaining in saucepan. Place pan over medium heat; cook, stirring constantly with a wooden spoon,

until mixture reaches 160°F and is thick enough to coat the back of spoon.

4. Strain eggnog base through a fine-mesh sieve into bowl in ice bath. Let cool for about 20 minutes, stirring occasionally. Cover and refrigerate until chilled, for about 1 hour.

5. Whisk brandy and cream into chilled eggnog. In large bowl using an electric mixer on high speed, beat egg whites until soft peaks form. Add remaining ½ cup sugar; beat on high until stiff peaks form. Gently fold whites into eggnog until blended. Cover, refrigerate for several hours or overnight, or until cold. Pour into a pitcher to serve. Garnish servings as desired.

TIP:
Vanilla beans are the dried seedpods of the vanilla plant. To use, slice the long pods open lengthwise to expose the tiny seeds inside.

Crock-Pot Chicken Chili

Serve this creamy, slightly spicy stew with fresh warmed flour tortillas or tortilla chips.

Serves 8

1 pound dried Great Northern or cannellini beans, soaked overnight

3 cups reduced-sodium chicken broth, warmed

1 large onion, chopped

3 garlic cloves, minced

1 jalapeño pepper, minced

1 tablespoon plus 1 teaspoon chili powder

2 teaspoons ground cumin

Salt and black pepper

1 pound (about 3 cups, chopped) cooked chicken or turkey meat

1 box (10 ounces) frozen corn kernels

2 cups shredded Monterey Jack cheese

1 tablespoon fresh lime juice

Garnishes: Sour cream, chopped fresh cilantro, salsa, chopped scallions

1. Combine beans and warm broth in a large slow cooker; let sit for 10 minutes. Stir in onion, garlic, jalapeño, chili powder, cumin, salt and pepper. Cover and cook on low heat for 10 hours, or until beans are tender.

2. Stir in chicken, corn and cheese. Cook for 10 minutes, until chicken and corn are warmed through and cheese

is melted. Add lime juice and season to taste with salt and pepper. Garnish as desired.

> **TIP:**
> Crock-Pot cooking times can vary widely depending on your machine. Be sure to cook this until the beans are tender but not mushy.

Five-Minute
Cranberry Walnut Cobbler

This homey dessert is so easy to make and so sweetly sat-isfying that you will make it again and again. Serve warm with whipped cream if you are feeling decadent.

Serves 8

2½ cups fresh or frozen cranberries

¾ cup chopped walnuts

½ cup plus ¾ cup granulated sugar

2 large eggs

12 tablespoons (1½ sticks) unsalted butter, melted

¼ teaspoon almond extract

1 cup all-purpose flour

Pinch salt

1. Preheat oven to 350°F. In a 9-inch pie pan, combine cranberries, walnuts and ½ cup of the sugar; toss until coated.

2. In a medium bowl, whisk eggs, melted butter, remain-ing sugar and almond extract until blended. Fold in flour and salt until combined. Pour the batter over the

cranberry mixture. Bake for 40 minutes, until crust is golden and fruit bubbles. Transfer to a wire rack to cool.

TIP:
No cranberries? No problem. Substitute blue-berries or strawberries, but cut the sugar added to the fruit in half.

Ice Krispie Snowmen

No snow? No problem. Bring winter fun indoors with these sweet snowmen that kids can make and decorate themselves.

Makes 6

4 tablespoons (½ stick) unsalted butter, plus more for pan
1 bag (10 ounces) mini marshmallows
5 cups crispy rice cereal
1½ cups sweetened shredded coconut
Prepared vanilla icing, as needed
Decorations: Mini chocolate chips, candy corn, black gumdrops, peppermint patties, colorful fruit leather

1. Line a baking sheet with parchment or waxed paper. Place butter and marshmallows in a glass bowl; microwave in 30-second intervals, until fully melted, stirring often. Place cereal in a large bowl; fold in marshmallow mixture until coated.

2. Place coconut in a medium deep bowl. Butter your hands lightly. Scoop up a spoonful of the mixture and drop into coconut. Using your hands, roll each mound in coconut, pressing into a tight ball as you roll. Make 18 balls: 6 large, 6 medium and 6 small. Using a dab of icing to stick balls together, form 6 snowmen. Set the snowmen upright on prepared baking sheet.

3. Decorate snowmen as desired. Some ideas: chocolate chips for eyes, tip of candy corn for nose, gumdrop placed atop mint patty for hat. Cut a strip of fruit leather for scarf. Use icing to "glue" candy onto snowmen.

Many Bean Soup Mix

Here's a gift that's good for everyone on your list. Who doesn't crave a cup of warm, homemade soup on a cold winter's night?

Makes 1 gift jar

½ cup dried yellow split peas
⅓ cup dried green split peas
⅓ cup dried red lentils
¼ cup instant minced onion
⅓ cup dried green beans
½ teaspoon ground cumin
½ teaspoon garlic powder

Layer all ingredients, in order listed, in a 1-pint glass jar. Store tightly covered at room temperature up to 2 months.

On gift tag write recipe for soup as follows:

Many Bean Soup

1 tablespoon olive oil

2 carrots, peeled and sliced

2 celery stalks, thinly sliced

Salt and black pepper

1 meaty ham hock

8 cups reduced-sodium chicken broth

1. Warm oil in a medium heavy saucepan or Dutch oven over medium heat. Add carrots and celery; season with salt and pepper. Cook for 5 minutes, stirring. Add ham hock, Many Bean Soup Mix and broth; bring to a boil. Reduce heat; bring to a simmer. Cover and simmer for 2 hours, until beans are tender, stirring occasionally.

2. Remove ham hock from pot; slice ham from bone. Trim excess fat from ham; cut into small pieces. Add ham to soup; cook until warmed through.

TIP:
Many large supermarkets or health food stores allow you to buy beans out of bins, so you only need to purchase the amount you need.

Cream Scones with Dried Figs and Cherries

Making these in the food processor means the dough comes together in minutes. These are not very sweet—feel free to increase the sugar if desired.

Makes 8

2 cups all-purpose flour
¼ cup granulated sugar, plus additional for sprinkling
1 tablespoon baking powder
½ teaspoon salt
12 tablespoons (1½ sticks) unsalted butter, cut into chunks
2 large eggs
½ cup heavy cream
¾ cup dried cherries or cranberries
½ cup dried figs, chopped
1 egg, beaten with 1 tablespoon cream, for wash

1. Preheat oven to 375°F. Line a baking sheet with parchment paper.

2. In a food processor, pulse flour, sugar, baking powder and salt until combined. Add butter chunks; pulse until mixture resembles fine crumbs. In a glass measuring cup, whisk eggs and cream until well blended;

add to batter and pulse until just combined. Pulse in dried cherries and figs.

3. Scrape dough out onto a lightly floured surface. Knead dough just enough to assure ingredients are combined. Using floured hands, shape dough into a ¾-inch-thick round. Using a sharp knife, cut round into 8 wedges. Transfer to prepared baking sheet. Brush scones with egg wash; sprinkle with sugar.

4. Bake for 20 to 25 minutes, until golden and firm to the touch. Transfer to a wire rack to cool.

TIP:
For all quick breads, for a moist and tender crumb, take care to stir the batter until just blended.

Can This Be
Christmas?

For my dear friend Betty and her Judge

Many years of happiness, my friend

To the new Mr. and Mrs. Jim Roper

CHAPTER ONE

I'll Be Home for Christmas

A robust version of "Little Drummer Boy" played in the background as Len Dawber glanced at his watch—for at least the tenth time in five minutes. He looked around the depot impatiently, hardly noticing the Christmas decorations on the windows and walls—the cardboard Santa's sleigh, the drooping garland and blinking lights.

Len was waiting with a herd of other holiday travelers to board the train that would take him to Boston. The snowstorm that had started the previous evening meant his early-morning flight out of Bangor, Maine, had been canceled and the airport closed. Although the airlines couldn't be blamed for the weather, they'd done everything possible to arrange transportation out of Maine. Len suspected more than a few strings had been pulled to get seats on the already full midmorning train. Maybe some of the original passengers canceled, he thought with faint hope.

Because, unfortunately, that crowded train was his only chance of making it to Boston in time to connect with his flight home for Christmas.

Len got to his feet, relinquishing his place on the hard

station bench to a tired-looking man. He walked quickly to the door and stepped outside. He lifted his gaze toward the sky. Huge flakes of snow swirled in the wind, obscuring his view. His shoulder muscles tensed with frustration until he could no longer remain still. This was exactly what he'd feared would happen when he'd awakened that morning. Even then the clouds had been dark and ominous, threatening his plans and his dreams of a reunion with Amy.

Despite the snow that stung his eyes and dampened his hair, Len began to pace back and forth along the platform, peering down the tracks every few seconds. No train yet. Damn it! Stuck in New England on Christmas Eve.

This was supposed to be the season of joy, but there was little evidence of that in the faces around him. Most people were burdened with luggage and armfuls of Christmas packages. Some of the gift wrap was torn, the bows limp and tattered. The children, sensing their parents' anxiety, were cranky and restless. The younger ones whined and clung to their mothers.

Worry weighed on Len's heart. He *had* to catch the Boston flight, otherwise he wouldn't make it home to Rawhide, Texas, today. He'd miss his date with Amy and the family's Christmas Eve celebration. Part of his precious leave would be squandered because of the snowstorm.

There was another reason he yearned for home. Len didn't intend this to be an ordinary Christmas. No, this Christmas would be one of the best in his entire life. It had everything to do with Amy—and the engagement ring burning a hole in his uniform pocket.

Len had enlisted in the navy following high-school graduation and taken his submarine training in New London,

Connecticut. Afterward, he'd been assigned to the sub base in Bangor, Maine. He thoroughly enjoyed life on the East Coast, so different from anything he'd known in Texas, and wondered if Amy would like it, too....

Len was proud to serve his country and seriously considered making the navy his career, but that decision depended on a number of things. Amy's answer, for one.

A real drawback of military life was this separation from his family. On his most recent trip home last September, he'd come to realize how much he loved Amy Brent. In the weeks since, he'd decided to ask her to marry him. They planned to be together that very night, Christmas Eve—the most wonderful night of the year. Once they were alone, away from family and friends, Len intended to propose.

He loved Amy; he had no doubts about that. He wasn't a man who gave his heart easily, and he'd made sure, in his own mind at least, that marriage was what he truly wanted. In the weeks since their last meeting, he'd come to see that loving her was for real and for always.

They hadn't talked about marriage, not the way some couples did, but he was confident she loved him, too. He paused for a moment and held in a sigh as the doubts came at him, thick as the falling snow. Lately Len had noticed that Amy seemed less like her normal self. They hadn't talked much, not with him saving to buy the diamond. And it was difficult for Amy to call him at the base. So they'd exchanged letters—light newsy letters with little mention of feelings. He had to admit he found their letters enjoyable to read—and even to write—and the cost of stamps was a lot more manageable than some of his phone bills had been. The truth was, he couldn't afford to spend money on long-distance calls anymore, not the way he had in previous months. His airfare home hadn't been cheap, either.

It wasn't as if he'd put off traveling until the last minute, which Amy seemed to suspect. He'd been on duty until the wee hours of this morning; he'd explained all that in a letter he'd mailed earlier in the week, when he'd sent her his flight information. Although Amy hadn't come right out and said it, he knew she'd been disappointed he couldn't arrive earlier, but that was navy life.

He hadn't received a letter from her in ten days, which was unusual. Then again, perhaps not. After all, they'd be seeing each other soon. Amy and his parents were scheduled to pick him up in Dallas, and together they'd drive home to Rawhide. He closed his eyes and pictured their reunion, hoping the mental image would help calm his jangled nerves. It did soothe him, but not for long.

He had to get home for Christmas. He just had to.

This was Cathy Norris's first Christmas without Ron, and she refused to spend it in Maine. She'd buried her husband of forty-one years that October; her grief hadn't even begun to abate. The thought of waking up Christmas morning without him had prompted her to accept her daughter's invitation. She'd be joining Madeline and her young family in Boston for the holidays.

Cathy had postponed the decision until last week for a number of reasons. To begin with, she wasn't a good traveler and tended to stay close to home. Ron, on the other hand, had adored adventure and loved trekking through the woods and camping and fishing with his friends. Cathy was more of a homebody. She'd never flown or taken the train by herself before—but then, she was learning, now, to do a great many unfamiliar things on her own. In the past Ron had always been with her, seeing to their tickets, their luggage and any unforeseen problems. He had been such a dear husband, so thoughtful and generous.

The battle with cancer had been waged for a year. Ron had put up a gallant fight, but in the end he'd been ready to die, far more ready than she was to let him go. Trivial as it seemed now, she realized that subconsciously she'd wanted him to live until after the holidays.

Naturally she'd never said anything. How could she, when such a request was purely selfish? It wasn't as if Ron could choose when he would die. Nevertheless, she'd clung to him emotionally far longer than she should have—until she'd painfully acknowledged that her fears were denying her husband a peaceful exit from life. Then with an agony that had all but crippled her, she'd kissed him one final time. Holding his limp hand between her own, she'd sat by his bedside, loving him with her entire being, and waited until he'd breathed his last.

Ron's death clouded what would otherwise have been her favorite month of the year. She found it devastating to be around others celebrating the season while she struggled to shake her all-consuming grief. She'd accepted Madeline's invitation as part of a concerted effort to survive the season of peace and goodwill.

Charting a new course for herself at this age was more of a challenge than she wanted. Life, however, had seen fit to make her a widow one month, then thrust her into the holiday season the next.

She was doing her best, trying to cope with her grief,

finding the courage to smile now and again for her children's sake. They realized how difficult the holidays were for her of course, but her daughters were grieving, too.

This snowstorm had been an unwelcome hitch in her careful plans. Madeline had urged her to come sooner, but Cathy had foolishly resisted, not wanting to overstay her welcome. She'd agreed to visit until the twenty-seventh. Ron had always said that company, like fish, began to smell after three days.

"Mom," Madeline had said when she'd phoned early that morning, "I heard on the news there's a huge snowstorm headed your way."

"I'm afraid it arrived last night." The wind had moaned audibly outside her window as she spoke.

"What are you going to do?" Madeline, her youngest, tended to worry; unfortunately she'd inherited that trait from her mother.

"Do?" Cathy repeated as if a fierce winter blizzard was of little concern. "I'm taking the train to Boston to join you, Brian and the children for Christmas. What else is there to do?"

"But how will you get to the station?"

Cathy had already worked that out. "I've phoned for a taxi."

"But, Mom—"

"I'm sure everything will be fine," Cathy said firmly, hoping she sounded confident even though she was an emotional wreck. She felt as though her life was caving in around her. Stuck in Bangor over Christmas, grieving for Ron—that would have been more than Cathy could handle. If spending the holiday with family meant taking her chances in the middle of a snowstorm, then so be it.

The first hurdle had been successfully breached. Listening to Andy Williams crooning a Christmas ballad, Cathy stood in line at the Bangor train depot, along with half the town, it seemed. The taxi fare had been exorbitant, but at least she was here, safe and sound. She'd packed light, leaving plenty of room in her suitcase for gifts for her two youngest granddaughters. Shopping had been a chore this year, so she'd decided simply to give Madeline and Brian a check and leave it at that, but she couldn't give money to her grandchildren. They were much too young for that. The best gifts she could think to bring them were books, plus a toy each.

Madeline had consented to let Lindsay and Angela, aged three and five, open their presents that evening following church services. Then the children could climb onto Cathy's lap and she'd read them to sleep. The thought of holding her grandchildren close helped ease the ache in her heart.

Everything would be all right now that she was at the depot, she reassured herself. Soon she'd be with her family. The train might be late, but it would get there eventually.

All her worries had been for nothing.

Matthew McHugh hated Christmas. And he didn't have a problem expressing that opinion. As for the season of goodwill—what a laugh. Especially now, when he was stuck in an overcrowded train depot, waiting for the next train to Boston where he'd catch the flight into LAX. The timing of this snowstorm had been impeccable. Every seat in the station was taken, and people who weren't sitting nervously paced the confined area, waiting for the train, which was already fifteen minutes late. Some, like that guy in the navy uniform, were even prowling the platform—as though *that* would make the train come any faster.

Christmas Eve, and the airports, train depots and bus stations were jammed. Everyone was in a rush to get somewhere, him included. As a sales rep for a Los Angeles–based software company, Matt was a seasoned traveler. And he figured anyone who spent a lot of time in airports would agree: Christmas was the worst. Crying babies, little old ladies, cranky kids—he'd endured it all. Most of it with ill grace.

His boss, Ruth Shroeder, who'd been promoted over him, had handed him this assignment early in the week. She'd purposely sent him to the other side of the country just so he'd know *she* was in charge. Rub his face in it, so to speak. This could easily have been a wasted trip; no one bought computer software three days before Christmas. Fortunately he'd outfoxed her and made the sale. By rights, he should be celebrating, but he experienced little satisfaction and no sense of triumph.

Ruth had been expecting him to make a fuss, demand that the assignment go to one of the junior sales reps. Matt had merely smiled and reached for the plane tickets. He'd sold the software, but was left feeling that although he'd won the battle, he was destined to lose the war.

And a whole lot more.

Pam, his wife of fifteen years, hadn't been the least bit understanding about this trip. If ever he'd needed her support it was now, but all she'd done was add to his burden. "Christmas, Matt? You're leaving three days before Christmas?"

What irritated him most was her complete and total lack of appreciation for his feelings. It wasn't like he'd *asked* for this trip or wanted to be away from the family. The fact that Pam had chosen the evening of his departure to start an argument revealed how little she recognized the stress he'd been under since the promotions were announced.

"I already said it couldn't be helped," he'd explained calmly as he packed his bag. His words were devoid of emotion, although plenty of it simmered just below the surface. He carefully placed an extra shirt in his bag.

Pam had gone strangely quiet.

"I'll be home Christmas Eve in time for dinner," he'd promised, not meeting her eyes. "My flight gets into LAX at four, so I'll be back here by six." He spoke briskly, reassuringly.

Silence.

"Come on, Pam, you have to know I don't like this any better than you do," he said, and forcefully jerked the zipper on his garment bag closed.

"You're going to miss Jimmy in the school play."

He was sorry about that, but there were worse things in life than not seeing his six-year-old son as an elf. "I've already talked to him about it, and Jimmy understands." Even if his wife didn't.

"What was he supposed to say?" Pam demanded.

Matt's shrug was philosophical.

"You were away when Rachel had the lead in the Sunday-school program, too."

Matt frowned, trying to remember missing that. "Rachel was in a Sunday-school program?"

"Three years ago... I see you've already forgotten. It

broke her heart, but I notice you've conveniently let it slip your mind."

Matt had heard enough. He folded his garment bag over his arm and reached for his coat and briefcase.

"You don't have anything else to say?" Pam cried as she stormed after him.

"So you can shovel more guilt at me? Do you want me to confess I'm a rotten father? Okay, fine." His voice gained volume. "Matthew McHugh is a rotten father."

Pam blinked back tears. Matt longed to hold her, but they'd gone too far for that.

"You aren't a bad father," she said after a moment, and his heart softened. A fight now was the last thing either of them needed. He was about to tell her so when she continued. "It's as a husband that you've completely failed."

Matt swore under his breath. Any tenderness he'd felt earlier shattered.

"You're leaving me to deal with Christmas, the shopping, dinners, everything. I can't take it anymore."

"Take it?" he shouted. "Do you know how many women would love to be able to stay home with their families? You have it easy compared to working mothers who're out there competing in a man's world. If you think shopping and cooking dinner is too much for you, then—"

Pam's expression grew mutinous. "My not working was a decision we made together! I can't believe you're throwing that in my face now. If you're saying you want me to get a job, fine, consider it done."

Matt's fist tightened around his briefcase handle. That wasn't what he wanted, and Pam knew it.

"All I'm saying is I could use a little support."

"It wouldn't hurt you to support me, either," she snapped. They glared at each other, neither willing to give in.

"Have a good time," she said flippantly. "Just go. I'll do what I always do and make excuses for you with the children and your parents. I'll be at the school for Jimmy, so don't worry—not that you ever have."

If Matt heard about this stupid Christmas pageant one more time, he'd blow a fuse. Rather than continue the argument, he headed out the door. "I'll call you in the morning."

"Don't bother," she exploded, and slammed the door in his wake.

Matt had taken his wife at her word and hadn't phoned once in the past three days. It was the first time in fifteen years on the road that he hadn't called his family. Pam had the number of his hotel, and she hadn't made the effort to call him, either. They'd argued before, all couples did, but they'd never allowed a disagreement to go on this long.

Now as he stood in the crowded depot, waiting for the train to arrive, Matt was both tired and bored. For a man who'd purposely avoided any contact with his wife, he was in an all-fired hurry to get home.

This should be the happiest Christmas of Kelly Berry's life. After a ten-year struggle she and Nick were first-time parents. She liked to joke that her labor had lasted five years. That was how long they'd been on the adoption waiting list. Five years, two months and seventeen days, to be exact. Then the call had finally come, and twenty hours later they'd brought their daughter home from the hospital.

In less than a day, their entire existence had been turned

upside down. After the long frustrating years of waiting, they were parents at last.

This would be their first trip home to Macon, Georgia, since they'd signed the adoption papers. Brittany Ann Berry's grandparents were eager to meet her.

The infant fussed in her arms and let loose with a piercing cry that cut into Neil Diamond's rendition of "Jingle Bells." A businessman scowled at them; Nick, muttering under his breath, grabbed the diaper bag. Doing the best she could, Kelly gently placed the baby over her shoulder and rubbed her tiny back.

"She's all right," Kelly said, smiling to reassure her husband while he rummaged through the diaper bag in search of the pacifier.

As Nick sat upright, he dragged one hand down his face, already showing signs of stress. They hadn't so much as left the train depot and already their nerves were shot. Despite their eagerness to be parents, the adjustment was a difficult one. Nick had proved to be a nervous father. Kelly wasn't all that adept at parenthood herself. She smiled again at Nick, accepting the pacifier. Everything would be easier once Brittany slept through the night, she was sure of that.

Her two older sisters were much better at this mothering business than she was. Never had Kelly missed her family more; never had the need to talk out her fears and doubts been more pressing.

This flight home was an extravagance Nick and Kelly could ill afford. Then the storm had blown in, with all its complications, and they'd been rerouted to Boston by train.

A whistle sang from the distance, and the sound of it was as beautiful as church bells.

The train was coming, just like the man at the ticket counter had promised. She listened to the announcement listing the destinations between here and Boston as people stood and reached for their bags. Nick automatically started gathering the baby paraphernalia.

They were headed home, each and every one of them. A little snow wasn't going to stand in their way.

CHAPTER TWO

"I Wonder as I Wander"

The train filled up quickly, and Len was fortunate to find a seat next to a grandmotherly woman who pulled out her knitting the moment she'd made herself comfortable. Mesmerized, he watched her fingers expertly weave the yarn, mentally counting stitches in an effort to keep his mind off the time and how long it was taking his fellow passengers to get settled.

The nervousness in the pit of his stomach began to ease as the conductor, an elderly white-haired gentleman, shuffled slowly down the aisle, checking tickets.

"Will we reach Boston before noon?" That question came from the woman with the baby seated across from him.

Len was grateful she'd asked; he was looking for answers himself.

"Hard to say with the snow and all."

"But it has to," she groaned, again voicing his own concerns. "We'll never catch our flight otherwise."

"I heard the airports are closed between Bangor and Boston," he said amiably. He scratched the side of his white head as if that would aid his concentration. "The train's running, though, and you can rest assured we'll do our best to see you make it to Boston in time."

His words reassured more than the young couple with the baby. Len's anxious heart rested a little easier, too. Glancing at the older woman in the seat next to him, he decided some conversation might help distract him.

"Are you catching a flight in Boston?"

"Oh, no," she said, tugging on the red yarn. "My daughter and her family live in Boston. I'm joining them for Christmas. Where are you headed?"

"Rawhide, Texas," Len said, letting his pride in his state show through his words.

"Texas," she repeated, not missing a stitch. "Ron and I visited Texas once. Ron wanted to see the Alamo. He's my husband…was my husband. He died this October."

"I'm sorry."

"So am I," she murmured with such utter sadness that Len had to look away. She recovered quickly and continued. "It's mind-boggling that people can fly across this country in only a few hours, isn't it?"

It was a fact that impressed Len, too, but he was more grateful than astonished. He felt even more appreciative when the whistle pierced the chatter going on about him. Almost immediately the train started to move, then quickly gained speed. Everyone aboard seemed to give a collective sigh of relief.

Len and the widow chatted amicably for several minutes and eventually exchanged names. Cathy asked him a couple of questions, about Texas and the navy, and he asked her a few. After a while, their conversation died down and they returned to their own thoughts.

The train traveled at a slow but steady pace for an hour or so. The unrelenting snow whirled around them, but the passengers were warm and cozy. For all the worry this storm had caused earlier, it didn't seem nearly as intimidating from inside the train. Relaxed, Len stretched out his legs, confident that with a little luck, he'd connect with the flight out of Logan International.

The train stopped now and then at depots on the way. Each stop resulted in a quick exchange of passengers. Len noticed that the storm appeared to have changed people's holiday plans; far more exited the train than entered. The brief stops lasted no more than ten minutes, and soon there were a number of vacant seats in the passenger car. Before long Len heard the conductor say they'd be crossing into New Hampshire.

Len figured you could fit all of these tiny New England states inside Texas. He'd seen cattle ranches that were larger than Rhode Island! The thought produced a pang of homesickness. The song sure got it right—there's no place like home for the holidays. His life belonged to the navy now, but he was a Texas boy through and through.

"Do you have someone at home waiting for you?" Cathy asked him.

"My family," Len told her, and added, prematurely, "and my fiancée." Saying the words produced a happiness in him that refused to be squelched.

"How nice for you."

"Very nice," he said. Then thinking it might help ease

his mind, he opened the side zipper of his carry-on bag and pulled out Amy's most recent letter, dated two weeks earlier.

Dear Len,

I waited until ten for you to phone, then realized it was eleven your time and you probably wouldn't be calling. I was feeling low about it, then received your letter this afternoon. I'm glad you decided to write. You say you're not good at writing letters, but I disagree. This one was very sweet. It's nice to have something to hold in my hand, that I can read again and again, unlike a telephone conversation. While it's always good to hear the sound of your voice, when we hang up, there's nothing left.

Everything's going along fine here at home and at work. For all my complaining about not finding a more glamorous job, I've discovered I actually enjoy being part of the nursing-home staff. The travel agency that didn't hire me is the one to lose out.

Did I tell you what happened last week? Mr. Perkins exposed himself in the middle of a pinochle game. All the ladies were outraged, but I noticed that the sign-up sheet for pinochle this Thursday is full. Mrs. MacPherson lost her teeth, but they were eventually found. (You don't want to know where.) I still have my lunch in Mr. Danbar's room; he seems to enjoy my company, although he hasn't spoken a word in three years. I chatter away and tell him all about you and me and how excited I am that you're coming home for Christmas.

I was pleased that your mother asked me if I wanted

to tag along when she and your dad pick you up at the airport on Christmas Eve. I'll be there, you know I will—which brings me to something else. Something I've been wanting to ask you for a long time.

Do you remember my joke about sailors having a woman in every port? You laughed and reminded me that, as a submariner, you didn't see that many ports above water. Bangor's a long way from Rawhide, though, isn't it? I guess I'm asking you about other women.

Well, I'd better close for now. I'll see you in two weeks and we can talk more then.

Love,
Amy

Len folded the letter and slipped it back inside the envelope. Amy shouldn't need to ask him about other women. He didn't know what had made her so insecure, but he'd noticed the doubt in her voice ever since he returned in September.

The diamond ring should relieve her worries. He smiled just thinking about it. He could hardly wait to see the look on her face.

Cathy set her knitting aside and stared sightlessly out the train window. The snow obliterated everything, not that the scenery interested her. Try as she might, she couldn't stop thinking about Ron.

Other years, she'd been working in her kitchen Christmas Eve day, baking cookies and pies, getting ready for the children and grandchildren to arrive. As a surprise—although it had long since ceased to be one—she'd always baked Ron a lemon meringue pie, his favorite. And he'd always pretend he was stunned that she'd go to all that trouble just for him.

Christmas had been the holiday her husband loved most. He was like a kid, decorating the outside of the house with strand upon strand of colorful lights. Last year he'd outdone all his previous efforts, as if he'd known even then that he wouldn't be here this Christmas.

She remembered how, every year, Ron had wanted to put up the tree right after Thanksgiving. She was lucky if she could hold him off until it was officially December.

It took them an entire day to decorate the tree. Not that they ever chose such a large one. Trimming their Christmas tree was a ritual that involved telling each other stories about past Christmases, recalling where each decoration came from—whether it was made by one of the girls or bought on vacation somewhere or given to them by a friend. It wasn't just ornaments, baubles of glass and wood and yarn, that hung from the evergreen branches but memories. They still had several from when they were first married, back in 1957. And about ten years ago, Cathy had cross-stitched small frame ornaments with pictures of everyone in the family. It'd taken her months and Ron was as proud of those tiny frames as if he'd done the work himself.

Memories... Cathy couldn't face them this Christmas. All she could do was hope they brought her comfort in the uncertain future.

Since he'd retired from the local telephone company four years ago, Ron had used his spare time puttering around his wood shop, building toys for the grandchildren. Troy and Peter had been thrilled with the race cars he'd fashioned from blocks of wood. Ron had taken such pride in those small cars. Angela and Lindsay had adored the dollhouse he'd carefully designed and built for them. The end table he'd started for Cathy remained in his wood shop unfinished. He'd longed to complete it, but the chemotherapy had drained away his strength, and in the months that followed, it was enough for him just to make it through the day.

Ron wouldn't be pleased with her, Cathy mused. She'd made only a token effort to decorate this year. No tree, no lights on the house. She'd set out a few things—a crèche on the fireplace mantel and the two cotton snowmen Madeline had made as a craft project years ago when she was in Girl Scouts.

Actually Cathy couldn't see the point of doing more. Not when it hurt so much. And not when she'd be leaving, anyway. She did manage to bake Madeline's favorite shortbread cookies, but that had been the only real baking she'd done.

Resting her head against the seat, Cathy closed her eyes. She tried to let the sound of the train lull her to sleep, but memories refused to leave her alone, flashing through her mind in quick succession. The sights and sounds of the holidays in happier times. Large family dinners, the house filled with the scents of mincemeat pies and sage dressing. Music, too; there was always plenty of music.

Madeline played the piano and Gloria, their oldest, had been gifted with a wonderful voice. Father and daughter had sung Christmas carols together, their voices blending beautifully. At least one of their three daughters had made it home for the holidays every year. But Gloria couldn't afford the airfare so soon after the funeral, and Jeannie was living in New York now and it was hard for her to take time off from her job, especially when she'd already asked for two weeks in order to be with her father at the end. Madeline would have come, Cathy guessed, if she'd asked, but she'd never do that.

Dear God, she prayed, *just get me through the next three days.*

Matthew McHugh's patience was shot. The cranky baby from the station was in the same car and hadn't stopped fussing yet. Matthew's head throbbed with the beginnings of a killer headache. His argument with Pam played over and over in his mind until it was so distorted he didn't know what to think anymore.

If Pam was upset about his being gone this close to Christmas, he could only imagine what she'd say when he arrived home hours later than scheduled.

He could picture it now. His parents, Pam and the kids, all waiting for him to pull into the driveway so they could eat dinner. When he did walk in the house, they'd glare at him as though he'd stayed away just to inconvenience them. He'd seen it happen before. As though he were somehow personally responsible for weather conditions and canceled flights.

As for Pam's complaining about having to do all the shopping and cooking herself, he didn't understand it. If she preferred, they could order one of those take-out Christmas dinners from the local diner. She didn't need to do all this work if she didn't want to. The choice was hers. He couldn't care less if the jellied salad was homemade or came out of a container. Pam was putting pressure on herself.

The same thing applied to inviting his parents for Christmas Eve dinner. He wasn't the one who'd asked them. That had been Pam's doing. His mom and dad lived less than an hour away; they could stop by the house anytime they wanted. To make a big deal out of having a meal together on Christmas Eve was ridiculous to him, especially if Pam was going to bitch about it.

The baby cried again. Matt clenched his fists and tried to hold on to his patience. The infant wasn't the only irritation, either. A little girl, five or so, was standing on the seat in front of his, staring at him.

"What's your name?" she asked.

"Scrooge."

"My name's Kate."

"Shouldn't you be sitting down, Kate?" he asked pointedly, hoping the kid's mother heard him and took action. She didn't.

"It's going to be Christmas tomorrow," she said, ignoring his question.

"So I hear." He attempted to look busy, too busy to be bothered.

The kid didn't take the hint.

"Santa Claus is coming to Grandma's house."

"Wonderful." His voice was thick with sarcasm. "Don't you know it's impolite to stare?"

"No." The kid flashed him an easy smile. "I can read."

"Good for you."

"Do you want me to read you *How the Grinch Stole Christmas?* It's my favorite book."

"No."

An elderly black couple sat across the aisle from him. The woman scowled disapprovingly, her censure at his attitude toward the kid obvious. "Why don't you read to her?" Matt suggested, motioning to the woman. "I've got work to do."

"You're working?" shrieked Kate-the-pest.

"Yes," came his curt reply, "or trying to." He couldn't get any blunter than that.

"Can I read you my story?" Kate asked the biddy across the aisle from him. Matt flashed the old woman a grin. Served her right. Let *her* deal with the kid. All Matt wanted was a few moments' peace and quiet while he mulled over what was going to happen once he got home.

Some kind of commotion went on in front of him. The little girl whimpered, and he felt a sense of righteousness. Kate's mother had apparently put her foot down when the kid tried to climb out of her seat. Good, now maybe she'd leave him and everyone else alone. If he'd been smart he would have pretended he was asleep like the man sitting next to him.

"Mom said I have to stay in my seat," Kate said, tears glistening as she peered over the cushion at him. All he could see was her watery blue eyes and the top of her head with a fancy red bow.

Matt ignored her.

"Santa's going to bring me a—"

"Listen, kid, I don't care what Santa's bringing you. I've got work to do and I don't have time to chat with you. Now kindly turn around and stop bothering me."

Kate frowned at him, then plunked herself back in her seat and started crying.

Several people condemned him with their eyes, not that it concerned Matt. If they wanted to entertain the kid, fine, but he wanted no part of it. He had more important things on his mind than what Santa was bringing a spoiled little brat with no manners.

★ ★ ★

The train had been stopped for about five minutes. "Where are we now?" Kelly asked, gently rocking Brittany in her arms. The baby had fussed the entire time they'd been on the train. Nothing Kelly did calmed her. She wasn't hungry; her diaper was clean. Kelly wondered if she might be teething. A mother was supposed to know these things, but Kelly could only speculate.

It helped that the train was becoming less crowded. With the storm, people seemed to be short-tempered and impatient. The guy who looked like a salesman was the worst; in fact, he was downright rude. She felt sorry for Kate and her mother. Kelly appreciated what it must be like traveling alone with a youngster. She'd never be able to do this without Nick. Frankly, she didn't know how anyone could travel with a baby and no one to help. An infant required so much *stuff*. It took hours just to organize and pack it all.

"According to the sign, we're in Abbott, New Hampshire," Nick informed her.

Kelly glanced out the window, through the still-falling snow. "Oh, Nick, look! This is one of those old-fashioned stations." The redbrick depot had a raised platform with several benches tucked protectively against the side, shielded from the snow by the roof's overhang. A ticket window faced the tracks and another window with many small panes looked into the waiting room.

"Hmm," Nick said, not showing any real interest.

"It's so quaint."

He didn't comment.

"I didn't know they had any of these depots left anymore. Do you think we could get off and look around a bit?"

She captured his attention with that. "You're joking, right?"

"We wouldn't have to take everything with us."

"The baby shouldn't be out in the cold."

Her enthusiasm faded. "Of course...she shouldn't."

The conductor walked down the center aisle and nodded pleasantly in Kelly's direction.

"That's a lovely old depot," she said.

"One of the last original stations in Rutherford County," he said with a glint of pride. "Built around 1880. Real pretty inside, too, with a potbellied stove and hardwood benches. They don't make 'em like this anymore."

"They sure don't," Kelly said, smiling.

"Shouldn't we be pulling out soon?" the man in the navy uniform asked, glancing at his watch.

"Anytime now," the conductor promised. "Nothing to worry about on this fine day. Snow or no snow, we're going to get you folks to Boston."

CHAPTER THREE

"Have Yourself a Merry Little Christmas"

"It's been twenty minutes," Len said, straining to see what had caused the delay. Cupping his face with his hands, he pressed against the window and squinted at the station. The snow had grown heavier and nearly obliterated the building from view. The train had been sitting outside the depot in Abbott twice as long as it had at any previous stop. Apparently the powers-that-be didn't fully grasp the time constraints he and several other passengers were under to reach Logan International. Too much was at stake if he missed his flight.

"I'm sure everything will be all right," Cathy assured him, but he noticed that she was knitting at a frantic pace. She jerked hard on the yarn a couple of times, then had to stop and rework stitches, apparently because of a mistake.

Len saw that he wasn't the only one who seemed concerned. The cranky businessman got out of his seat and walked to the end of the compartment. He leaned over to peer out the window at the rear of the train car, as if that would tell him something he didn't already know.

"Someone's coming," he announced in a voice that said

he wasn't going to be easily pacified. He wanted answers, and so did Len. Under normal circumstances Len was a patient man, but this was Christmas Eve and he had an engagement ring in his pocket.

The wind howled and snow blew into the compartment as the elderly conductor opened the door. He stepped quickly inside, then made his way to the front. "Folks, if I could have your attention a moment…"

Even before the man spoke, Len's gut told him it wasn't good news.

"We've got a problem on the line ahead."

"What kind of problem?" the sales rep demanded.

"Track's out."

A chorus of mumbles and raised voices followed.

The conductor raised his hands and the passengers fell silent. "We're doing the best we can."

"How long will it take to get it fixed?" The shout came from a long-haired guy at the front of the car. With his leather headband and fringed jacket, he resembled an overgrown hippie. He sat with a woman whose appearance complemented his—straight center-parted hair that reached the middle of her back and a long flower-sprigged dress under her heavy coat.

The conductor's face revealed doubt. "Couple of hours, possibly longer. Can't really say for sure."

"Hours!" Len exploded.

"We have a plane to catch," the young father cried, his anger spilling into outrage.

"The airlines arranged for us to be on the train for *this?*"

the businessman shouted, not bothering to disguise his disgust. "We were better off waiting out the storm in Bangor."

"I'm sorry, but—"

"Does this podunk town have a car-rental agency?" someone asked. Len couldn't see who.

"Not right here. There's one in town, but with the storm, I'd strongly recommend none of you..."

Len didn't stick around to hear the rest. As best he could figure, he was less than sixty miles from Boston. If he could rent a car, there was a chance he might still make it to the airport on time. Moving faster than he would've thought possible, Len reached for his bag and raced off the train.

The moment he jumped onto the depot platform, a sudden blast of cold jolted him. He hunched his shoulders and kept his face down as he struggled against the icy wind to open the door. Not surprisingly, the inside of the depot was as quaint as the outside, with long rows of hardwood benches and a potbellied stove.

The stationmaster looked up as people started to flood inside. Apparently he handled the sale of tickets and whatever was available to buy—a few snack items, magazines, postcards and such. Three phones were positioned against the far wall. One bore an Out of Order sign.

A long, straggling line had already formed in front of the two working phones. Len counted ten people ahead of him and figured he had a fair chance of getting a vehicle until he remembered a friend telling him you needed to be twenty-five to rent one. His hopes sagged yet again. He was a year too young. Discouraged, he dropped out of line.

His nerves twisting, he sat on a hard wooden bench away

from the others. It was hopeless. Useless to try. Even if the train had arrived anywhere close to its scheduled time, there was no guarantee he'd actually have a seat on the plane. Because of the storm, the airline had tried to get him on another flight leaving four hours later. But he was flying standby, which meant the only way he would get on board was if someone didn't show.

The reservation clerk had been understanding and claimed it wasn't as unlikely as it sounded. According to her, there were generally one or two seats available and he was at the top of the list. It had all sounded promising—and now this.

Cathy Norris sat down on the bench next to him. "I guess I should call my daughter," she said.

Len didn't know if she was speaking to him or not. "I suppose I should phone home, too."

The line for the phones had dwindled to five people. Len rejoined the group and impatiently waited his turn. It seemed to take forever before he was finally able to use the phone. He thought about contacting his parents, but he'd already spoken to them once that day.

Placing the charges on a calling card, he dialed Amy's number and prayed she was at home.

"Hello."

His relief at the sound of her soft drawl was enough to make him want to weep. "Hello, Amy Sue."

"Len?" Her voice rose with happy excitement. "Where are you?" Not giving him time to answer, she continued, "Your mother phoned earlier and said your flight had been canceled. Are you in Boston?"

"Abbott, New Hampshire."

"New Hampshire? Len, for mercy's sake, what are you doing there?"

"I wish I knew. The airline put us on a train."

"Your mother told me about the storm and how they closed the airport and everything," she said. He was distracted by the people lining up behind him, but her voice sounded…sad, almost as if she knew in advance what he was about to tell her.

"There's something wrong with the tracks. It's going to take a couple of hours to repair, so there's no telling what time I'll get to Boston."

"Oh, Len." Her voice was more breath than sound. "You're not going to make it home for Christmas, are you?"

He opened his mouth to insist otherwise, but the truth was, he no longer knew. "I want to, but…"

He could feel Amy's disappointment vibrate through the telephone wire. It was agony to be so far away and not able to hold her. "I'll do whatever I can to get to the airport on time, but there's no guarantee. You know I'd do anything to be with you right now, don't you?"

She didn't answer.

"Amy?" Talking with a lineup of people waiting to use the phone was a little inhibiting.

"I'll get in touch with your parents and let them know," she whispered, and her voice broke.

"I'll call you as soon as I hear anything," he said. Then, despite a dozen people eavesdropping on his conversation, he added, "I love you, Amy."

Unfortunately the line was already dead.

★ ★ ★

He should phone home, Matt decided, and even waited his turn in the long line that formed outside the telephone booth. He was three people away when he suddenly changed his mind. He had no idea why; then again, maybe he did.

It went without saying that Pam would be furious. He could hear her lambaste him now, and frankly, he wasn't in the mood for it.

He crossed to one of the vacant benches and sat down. These old seats might look picturesque, but they were a far sight from being comfortable. He shifted his position a number of times, crossed and uncrossed his legs.

As bad luck would have it, the couple with the baby sat directly opposite him. Matt didn't understand it. He seemed to attract the very people who irritated him most. Thankfully the infant was peacefully asleep in her mother's arms.

Matt studied the baby, remembering his own children at that age and how happy he and Pam had been in the early years of their marriage. That time seemed distant now. His dissatisfaction with his job didn't help. He felt as if he was struggling against everything that should make life good—his family, his marriage, his work. As if he stood waist-deep in the middle of a fast-flowing stream, fighting the current.

His wife had no comprehension of the stress he experienced day in and day out. According to her, he went out of his way to make her life miserable. Lately all she did was complain. If he went on the road, she complained; if he was home, she found fault with that, too.

The thought had come to him more than once these past few days that maybe they'd be better off living apart. He hadn't voiced it, but it was there in the back of his mind. Unhappy as she was, Pam must be entertaining these same thoughts. He couldn't remember the last time they'd honestly enjoyed each other's company.

Restless now, he stood and walked about. The depot had filled up, and there wasn't room enough for everyone to sit. The stationmaster was on the phone, and Matt watched the old man's facial expressions, hoping to get a hint of what was happening.

The man removed his black hat, frowned, then nodded. Matt couldn't read anything into that. He waited until the old guy had replaced the receiver. No announcement. Apparently there wasn't anything new to report. Matt checked his watch and groaned.

Thinking he might be more comfortable back on the train, he hurried outside, rushing through the bone-chilling wind and snow to the security of the train itself. The conductor and other staff had disappeared, Matt didn't know where. Probably all snug in the comfort of some friend's home. Not so for the passengers. The wind and snow nearly blinded him. He wasn't on board more than twenty minutes when the young father hurried inside and reached for a diaper bag tucked under the seat.

"Your first kid?" Matt asked, bored and miserable. A few minutes of conversation might help pass the time. The answer was fairly obvious. He was no expert when it came to infants, but it was clear to him that this couple was far too high-strung about parenthood. To his way of thinking, once these two relaxed, their baby would, too.

The man nodded, then sat down abruptly. "I had no idea it would be like this."

"Nothing's the same after you have kids," Matt said. The train, now that it'd shut down, wasn't heated, and the piercing cold had quickly permeated the interior.

"Do you have kids?"

"Two," Matt said, and despite his mood, he grinned. "Matt McHugh." He held out his hand.

"Nick Berry."

"This isn't exactly how I expected to spend Christmas Eve."

"Me, neither," Nick said. He lifted his shoulders and rubbed his bare hands. "If it was up to me, we'd never have left Bangor, but Kelly's parents haven't seen the baby yet."

Matt grunted in understanding.

"I'd better get back inside," Nick said. "Kelly's waiting."

"I might as well go in with you." It was obvious that he wouldn't be able to stay on the train much longer. He'd come for peace and quiet and found it not worth the price of having to sit alone in the cold. The temperature wasn't the only source of discomfort; he didn't like the turn his thoughts had taken. He didn't want a divorce, but he could see that was the direction he and Pam were headed.

Matt and Nick sprinted back into the depot just as the stationmaster walked to the center of the room. Nick rejoined his wife and handed her the diaper bag.

"Folks," the old man said, raising his arms to attract their attention. "My name's Clayton Kemper and I'm here to give you as much information as I can about the situation."

"How much longer is this going to take?" the long-haired guy demanded.

"Yeah," someone else shouted. "When do we get out of here?"

"Now, folks, that's something I can't predict. The problem involves more than the storm. The tracks are out."

His words were followed by low dissatisfied murmurs.

"I realize you're anxious to be on your way, seeing it's Christmas Eve and all. But no one can tell us just how long it'll be before the repairs are finished. Our first estimate was two hours, but the repair crew ran into difficulties."

The murmurs rose in volume. "We need answers," Matt said loudly, his fists clenched. "Some of us are booked on flights."

Clayton Kemper held up his hands. "I'm sorry, folks, I really am, but like I said before, there's just no way of predicting this sort of thing. It could be another hour...or it could be till morning."

"Morning!" The grumbling erupted into a flurry of angry shouts.

"What about hotel rooms?" an older man asked, placing a protective arm around the woman beside him.

Matt watched Nick glance at his wife as he stepped forward. "That's a good question. Should we think about getting a hotel room?" It went without saying that a young family would be far more comfortable in one. "And what's available here?"

"There's a hotel in town and a couple of motels that should have a few rooms left. I can call and they'll send their shuttle vans for anyone who wants to be picked up.

Same goes for the car rental agency. But—" Mr. Kemper rubbed the side of his jaw "—I can't tell you what would be best. When the repairs are finished, the train's pulling out. We won't have time to call all over town and round people up. If you're here, you go. If not, you'll need to wait for the next train."

Matt weighed his options and decided to wait it out. He was probably being too optimistic, but he'd rather take his chances at the depot. His choice wasn't the popular one. The majority of those on the train decided to get hotel rooms. Within ten minutes, the depot had emptied, leaving twenty or so hardy souls willing to brave the rest of the afternoon.

"What about you two?" Matt asked Nick, glancing at the younger man's wife and baby. He'd expected Nick to be among the first to seek more comfortable accommodations.

"Kelly thinks we should stay."

"It could be a long hard afternoon," Matt felt obliged to remind him. Later, when Nick and his wife changed their minds, there likely wouldn't be any rooms left.

Matt's gaze went to the telephones. He probably should phone Pam, but the prospect brought him no pleasure. He'd wait until he had a few more pertinent details. No use upsetting her this soon. She had four hours yet before she needed to know he wasn't on his scheduled flight. In this instance ignorance was bliss.

"Mother... Oh dear, this isn't working out the way I'd hoped." Madeline's distress rang over the wire.

Cathy's thoughts echoed her daughter. She pressed the telephone to her ear. "I don't want you to worry."

"I have every right to worry," Madeline snapped. "I should have come up there and gotten you myself."

"Nonsense." As far as Cathy was concerned, that would only have made matters worse. The last thing she wanted was to take her daughter away from her family on Christmas Eve.

"But Daddy would—" Madeline abruptly cut off the rest of what she was about to say.

"I'm perfectly fine."

"You're in the middle of a snowstorm on Christmas Eve. You're stuck without family, alone in some train depot in a dinky town in New Hampshire. You are not fine, Mother."

Alone. The word leaped out of her daughter's mouth and hit Cathy hard. Hard enough that she took an involuntary step backward. Alone. That was how she'd felt since Ron's death. It seemed as though she wandered from day to day without purpose, linked to no one, lost, confused. And consumed by a grief so painful it virtually incapacitated her. All she had was the promise that time would eventually ease this ache in her heart.

"The entire situation is horrible," Madeline continued.

"What would you have me do? Scream and shout? Yell at the stationmaster who's done nothing but be as helpful and kind as possible? Is that what you want?"

Her question was followed by Madeline's soft unhappy sigh.

"I feel so incredibly guilty," her daughter confessed after a moment.

"Why in heaven's name should you feel anything of the

sort?" It was ludicrous that Madeline was blaming herself for these unfortunate circumstances.

"But, Mother, you're with strangers, instead of family, and I'd hoped—"

"Now stop," Cathy said in her sternest voice. "None of this is your fault. In any case, I'm here in Abbott and perfectly content. I brought my knitting with me and there are plenty of others for company."

"But it's Christmas Eve," Madeline protested.

Cathy closed her eyes and inhaled sharply. "Do you honestly believe any Christmas will ever be the same for me without your father?"

"Oh, Mom." Her daughter's voice fell. "Don't mention Daddy, please. It's so hard without him."

"But life goes on," Cathy said, doing her best to sound brave and optimistic.

"I'd wanted to make everything better for you."

"You have," Cathy told her gently. "I couldn't have stayed at the house alone. I'd rather be in this depot with strangers than spending Christmas with memories I'm not ready to face. And sometime tonight or tomorrow, I'll be with all of you. Now let's stop before we both embarrass ourselves."

"You'll phone as soon as the tracks are repaired?"

"The minute I hear, you'll be the first to know."

"Brian and I and the girls will come down to the depot for you."

"Fine, sweetheart. Now don't you worry, okay?"

Madeline hesitated, then whispered, "I love you, Mom."

"I love you, too. Now promise me you won't fret."

"I'll try."

"Good." After a few words of farewell, Cathy replaced the receiver and returned to her seat. The depot was warm, thanks to the small stove. Those who'd stayed had taken up residence on the hardwood benches. As Cathy reached for her knitting, she battled back a fresh wave of depression.

Madeline was right. It was a dreadful situation, being stuck in a train depot this day of all the days in the year. She glanced around at the others. They appeared just as miserable as she.

Could this really be Christmas?

CHAPTER FOUR

"The Most Wonderful Day of the Year"

"Hi." A little girl with pigtails and a charming toothless smile sauntered up to Cathy.

"Hello," Cathy said in a friendly voice. Not including the baby, two children remained in the depot. A girl and a boy. The girl bounced about the room like a red rubber ball, but the boy remained glued to his parents' sides.

"What are you doing?" the child asked, slipping onto the wooden bench next to her.

"Knitting. This is a sweater for my granddaughter. She's about your age."

"I'm five."

"So is Lindsay."

"I can read. The kindergarten teacher told Mommy I'm advanced for my age."

"That's wonderful. I'll bet your mother and father are very proud of you." Cathy smiled at the youngster while her fingers continued to work the colorful yarn.

The little girl's head drooped slightly. "My mommy and daddy are divorced now."

Cathy felt the child's confusion and pain. "That's too bad."

She nodded, looking wise beyond her years. "We're going to spend Christmas with my grandma Gibson in Boston."

"Kate." A frazzled young woman approached the little girl. "I hope you weren't bothering this lady."

"Not at all," Cathy assured her.

"My grandma said Santa was coming tonight and bringing me lots of presents." Kate's sweet face lit up with excitement. "Santa'll still come, won't he, even if the train is late?"

"Of course he will," the child's mother told her in a tone that suggested this wasn't the first time she'd reassured her daughter.

"He'll find us even in the storm?"

"He has Rudolph's nose to guide his sleigh, remember?"

Kate nodded.

Cathy let her knitting rest in her lap.

"Can I read to you?" the youngster asked, her eyes huge. "Please?"

"Why, I can't think of anything I'd enjoy more." Cathy could, but it was clear the restless child needed something to take her mind off the situation, and she was happy to listen. Having grandchildren, she could well appreciate the difficulty of keeping a five-year-old entertained in conditions such as these.

Kate raced for her backpack and returned a moment later with her precious book.

"Thank you," Kate's mother whispered. "I'm Elise Jones."

"Hello, Elise. Cathy Norris."

Kate scooted onto the bench between Cathy and her mother and eagerly opened the book. She placed her finger on the first word and started reading aloud with a fluency that suggested this was a much-read and much-loved story.

Cathy smiled down on the little girl. Soon all this frustration and delay would be over. Mr. Kemper would come out from behind his desk and announce that the tracks had been repaired and they'd be on their way. In a few hours she'd be with Madeline and her family, all of this behind her. Somehow, listening to Kate read soothed her, made her feel that today's problems were tolerable. Inconvenient but definitely tolerable.

Kate's voice slowly faded and her eyes closed. She slumped over, her head against Cathy's side. Seconds later the book slipped from her lap and onto the floor.

"Oh, thank heaven, she's going to take a nap, after all," Elise whispered, getting carefully to her feet. She lifted Kate's small legs onto the bench and tucked a spare sweater beneath her head.

"Children can be quite a handful," Cathy murmured, remembering the first time she and Ron had watched their two granddaughters for an entire day while Madeline and Brian attended an investment workshop. The kids had been picked up by four that afternoon, but she and Ron went to bed before eight o'clock, exhausted.

"Being a single mother is no piece of cake," Elise told her. "When Greg and I divorced, I didn't have a clue what would happen. Then he lost his job and had to manage on his unemployment check. He just started working again—but he's so far behind on everything. Now he's having trouble making the child-support payments on time, which only complicates things." Embarrassed, she looked away as if she regretted what she'd said. "We wouldn't have Christmas if it wasn't for my mother. I certainly can't afford gifts this year."

The pain that flashed in the younger woman's eyes couldn't be hidden. Cathy realized that, in many ways, Elise's divorce had been as devastating as a death. Feeling a kinship with her, she reached over and squeezed her hand.

Elise recovered quickly, then said with forced enthusiasm, "I've always wanted to know how to knit."

"Would you like me to teach you?" Cathy asked, seizing upon the idea. She'd successfully taught her own three daughters and carried an extra set of needles in her knitting bag. Now was ideal, seeing as they had nothing but time on their hands and Kate was sleeping.

"Now?" Elise asked, flustered. "I mean, I'd love to, but are you sure it isn't too much trouble?"

"Of course not. I've found knitting calms my nerves, especially these past few months since my husband died."

"I'm sorry about your husband," Elise said, real sympathy in her voice.

"Yes, I am, too. I miss him dreadfully." With a sense of purpose Cathy reached for her spare needles. "Would you like to start now?"

Elise nodded. "Why not?"

Cathy pulled out a ball of yarn. "Then let me show you how to cast on stitches. It isn't the least bit difficult."

Len had trouble not watching the clock. They'd been in Abbott a total of four hours, with no further word regarding their situation. The stationmaster, Clayton Kemper, had turned out to be a kindhearted soul. He'd made a fresh pot of coffee and offered it to anyone who wanted a cup, free of charge.

Len had declined. Stressed as he was, the last thing he needed was caffeine. Plenty of others took advantage of Kemper's generosity, though. They were a motley group, Len noted. The widow, dressed in her gray wool coat with her knitting and her sad but friendly smile. The divorced mother and her little girl. The grumpy sales rep. The young couple with the baby, the hippie and his wife, the elderly black couple plus an assortment of others.

Kemper walked by with the coffeepot on a tray. "You sure I can't interest you in a cup, young man?"

"I'm sure."

"I found a deck of cards. How about that?"

Len nodded eagerly. "That'd be great." Cards would be a welcome way to pass the time. He sometimes played solitaire and enjoyed two or three different versions of the game. At the mention of cards, the sales rep, who sat close by, looked up from his laptop. Maybe Len could talk two or three of the others into a game of pinochle or poker.

"You play pinochle?" he asked Matt.

"And canasta, hearts, bridge—whatever you want."

"I wouldn't mind playing," Nick volunteered.

"Come to think of it, I've got an old card table in the back room," Kemper said when he returned with the cards. "And a couple of chairs, too, if you need 'em. I should have thought of this earlier. You folks must be bored out of your minds."

A fourth man joined them, and with a little rearranging they soon had the table set up. That was followed by the sound of cards being shuffled and the occasional scrape of a chair as they settled down to a friendly game of pinochle.

Kelly Berry's arms ached from holding the baby. The carrier seat was still on the train, and she hadn't asked Nick to bring it in. He'd already gone outside once and seemed reluctant to venture into the storm again. Besides, he was busy playing cards.

Kelly wondered, not for the first time, if they'd *ever* adjust to parenthood. The whole experience was so…different from what she'd expected. Desperately longing for a child of their own, they'd dreamed and hungered to the point that Kelly felt their marriage would be incomplete without a family. Now, after three months with a fussy, colicky infant, she was ready to admit her spirits were the lowest they'd been in years.

She'd always believed a baby would bring her and Nick closer together. The baby would be a living symbol of their love and commitment to each other, the culmination of their marriage. Instead, Brittany seemed to have driven a wedge between them. Not long ago their world had revolved entirely around each other; these days, it revolved around Brittany. Caring for the baby demanded all their energy, all their time.

Her arms tightened around her daughter, and a surge of love filled her heart. She and Nick felt overwhelmed because this was so new, Kelly told herself. In a few months everything would be easier—for both of them. While confident of Nick's love, Kelly knew he found it difficult to deal with the changes that had come into their marriage since the adoption.

"Would you like me to hold the baby for a while?" The older woman sat down next to her. "I'm Cathy Norris. You must be exhausted."

"Kelly Berry." She hesitated. "You wouldn't mind?"

"Not at all," Cathy said, taking the sleeping infant from her arms. She gazed down at Brittany and smiled. "She's certainly beautiful, and her little red outfit is delightful."

"Thank you," Kelly said, truly grateful. She'd enjoyed dressing Brittany for the holiday season. She could've spent a fortune if Nick had let her, but her ever-practical husband had been the voice of reason. Not that *he* wasn't guilty of spoiling their daughter.

With an ease that Kelly envied, Cathy Norris held Brittany against her shoulder, gently rubbing her back. Brittany shifted her head to one side and her tiny mouth made small sucking sounds. Once more Kelly's heart stirred with love.

She felt someone's gaze and glanced up to find Nick watching her. When he realized he had her attention, he smiled. His eyes softened as he looked at their daughter.

They *would* be all right, Kelly thought. This was their dream; it was just that after waiting and planning all these years, they hadn't been quite as ready for the reality as they'd assumed.

Clayton Kemper walked out of the station and returned almost immediately, a shovel in his hand. "Good news!" he shouted.

Every head in the room shot up, every face alight with expectation, Kelly's included. Some people were already on their feet, reaching for bags of colorfully wrapped gifts.

"The storm's died down. It's stopped snowing."

"Does that mean we can get out of here any sooner?" Matt McHugh demanded.

"Well, it's bound to help the repair crew."

The happy anticipation sank to the pit of Kelly's stomach. *Oh, please,* she prayed, *don't let us end up spending our first Christmas with Brittany stuck in a train depot. Don't let this be our Christmas.*

CHAPTER FIVE

"O Christmas Tree"

The news that the snow had stopped falling should have cheered Len Dawber, but it didn't. Instead, his mood took an immediate dive. He'd figured that with the storm passing, the train would leave soon. It didn't appear to be the case.

His interest in the card game died and he got up to give his seat to someone else, but no one seemed keen to play anymore. Before long, Nick Berry had the deck of cards and sat alone, flipping through them in a listless game of solitaire.

His frustration mounting, Len approached the counter. Clayton Kemper glanced up. "Can I get you anything?"

"How about some information?" Matt McHugh asked, moving to Len's side. "We've been here six hours. There must be *something* you can tell us by now." He clenched his fist and rested it on the counter. "You've got to realize how impossible this situation is for us."

Kemper shrugged helplessly. "I don't know what to tell you."

"Isn't there someone you could phone?" The plaintive

voice of a woman came from behind them. Len looked over his shoulder and recognized the mother of the little boy, who still clung to her side.

"Find out what you can," Matt insisted. "You owe us that much."

"Surely there's someone you can call," the elderly black man said.

Tension filled the room as more people stood up and started walking about. The baby Cathy Norris held awoke suddenly and shattered the air with a piercing cry. Cathy tried to quiet the infant, but it did no good. The young mother couldn't do any better. The baby's cries clawed at already taut nerves.

"Kindly keep that baby quiet, would you?" Len wasn't sure who'd said that; painful as the baby's shrieking was, he felt a fleeting sympathy for the mother.

"Do something," Nick snapped at his wife.

"I'm trying," Kelly said, glaring back at him with a hurt look.

"I've got to get out of here," Nick said, and stalked outside, letting the door slam in his wake.

"We need information," Len pressed Kemper again.

"At least give us an idea how much longer it could be," Matt added. "In case you've forgotten, it's Christmas Eve."

Kemper was clearly at a loss and for an instant Len felt sympathy for him, too, but he felt even worse for himself. He'd been looking forward to this night for weeks. He wanted it to be the most beautiful and romantic evening of his life. Instead, he'd probably be spending it in this train station somewhere in New Hampshire.

Kemper raised his hands to quiet the murmurs of discontent. "I'll make a few phone calls and see what I can find out."

"You should have done that long before now," Matt said irritably.

Len was in full agreement. This damned waiting had gone on long enough. The minute he had a definite answer, he'd call Amy again. Even if he *didn't* have an answer, he was phoning Amy. He needed to hear the sound of her voice, needed to know this nightmare would soon be over and they'd be together—if not for Christmas, then soon.

Len returned to his seat and Matt followed him. "This isn't exactly my idea of Christmas Eve," the older man muttered, more to himself than his companion.

"I don't think any of us could have anticipated this."

It didn't take Kemper long to connect with someone, Len noticed. The stationmaster was on the phone five minutes. He nodded once in a while, then scowled and wrote something down on a piece of paper. When he'd finished, he walked toward the potbellied stove.

Every eye in the room followed him. "Well," he said, with a deep expressive sigh, "there really isn't any news I can give you."

"No news is good news?" Cathy suggested hopefully.

"No news is no news," Matt McHugh returned tartly.

"You were talking to someone," Len said. "They must've had something to say...."

"Only what I found out earlier, that the break in the line is more serious than was originally determined."

"Isn't there anything you can suggest? How long should we expect to wait? Give us your best estimate. Surely you've seen breakdowns like this before." Len's voice thinned with frustration. He noticed a number of people nodding as he spoke.

"Well," Kemper said thoughtfully, "you're right, I have seen plenty of breakdowns over the years. Each one's different. But we've got a full crew working on this one, despite the fact that it's Christmas Eve."

"That's encouraging, anyway," Elise Jones said. "It isn't like any of us planned to spend the holidays here, you know."

"I know, I know." Kemper looked out over the group and seemed to recognize that he wouldn't be off the hook until he gave these people some kind of answer. "My best guess is sometime after midnight."

"Midnight!" Matt shouted.

He wasn't the only one who reacted with anger. But Len barely reacted at all; he felt as though the wind had been knocked clear out of him. Slowly he sank onto the bench and closed his eyes. He no longer knew if the airline could even get him a seat. Because of the snowstorm he'd missed his original flight. Because of the train's delay, he hadn't made the standby flight, either. Nor could he book another. Not until he could give the airline a time.

This felt like the worst day of his life.

Nick knew he was a fool, snapping at his wife in front of a room full of strangers and then stalking out of the train depot like a two-year-old having a tantrum. He'd caught the shocked look in Kelly's eyes. It was uncharacteristic behavior for him, but he'd just been feeling so...on edge. Then he'd lost control because someone had shouted at Kelly to keep Brittany quiet.

What upset him was that he'd been thinking the same thing himself. He wanted her to do something, anything, to stop Brittany's crying. The baby had been contentedly asleep for a few hours, and he supposed he'd been lulled into a false sense of peace. Then she'd awakened, and it seemed that every ounce of composure he'd managed to scrape together had vanished.

He'd say one thing for his daughter. She had an incredible sense of timing. Why she'd pick that precise moment to start wailing, he'd never know. She was a fragile little thing, but obviously had the lungs of a tuba player.

It had felt as though everyone in the room was glaring at him and Kelly with malice, although in retrospect, he thought his own frustrations had probably made him misread their reactions. Everything in life had come hard for Nick; why should fatherhood be any different? He'd been raised in a series of foster homes and the only reason he'd been able to go on with his schooling was because of a scholarship. He'd graduated while holding down two part-time jobs and now worked as a scientist for a pharmaceutical company. He'd met Kelly when they were both in college. He still considered it a miracle that this beautiful woman loved him. For years now, her love had been the constant in his life, his emotional anchor, his sanctuary.

The intense cold had soaked through his coat. He kicked at the snow, depressed and angry with himself. Kelly deserved a better husband, and Brittany sure as hell needed a more loving father.

He was about to go back inside the station when the door opened and Clayton Kemper walked out.

"You're leaving?" Nick asked, shocked that the station-master would desert them at a time like this.

Clayton Kemper looked more than a little guilty. "My shift was over an hour ago and the missus is wanting me home."

Talk about deserting the ship. "Someone else is coming, right?"

"Oh, sure. Don't you worry. Someone'll be by to check up on you folks, but it might not be for a while." Having said that, he headed down the steps, then glanced back over his shoulder and called, "Merry Christmas."

Nick stared at the man in disbelief. This had to be the worst Christmas of his entire life! Trapped with a cranky newborn and a wife who refused to see reason. If it'd been up to him, the three of them would at least have been in a motel room, comfortable and warm. But Kelly hadn't wanted to leave the station, certain the repairs wouldn't take long. Now it was too late. The guy with the long hair and his wife had already made inquiries. Apparently every hotel for miles around was full.

This optimistic bent of Kelly's had always been a problem. He'd been ready to give up on the fertility clinic long before she agreed. The expense had been horrific, and he didn't mean just the financial aspects. Emotionally Kelly was a wreck two weeks out of every month. Only when he was able to talk her into accepting their situation and applying to an adoption agency had she gotten off the emotional roller coaster.

Nick had almost given up hope himself—and then they received the phone call about Brittany. That five-minute conversation had changed their lives forever.

He found himself grinning at the memory. Kelly was the one who'd been cool and calm while he'd sat there trembling. He'd never experienced any excitement even close to what he'd felt when he learned they finally had a baby.

The first instant he saw Brittany, he'd been swept by a love so powerful it was beyond comprehension. Yet here he was, three months later, acting like a dolt and snapping at his wife in public.

That wasn't his only offense, either. For most of the afternoon, he'd ignored Kelly and the baby, wanting to escape them both. He wasn't proud of himself; he'd ignored their needs, leaving Kelly to care for their daughter on her own while he brooded and behaved like a spoiled child.

With that in mind, he boarded the train, walked down the narrow aisle and got the baby seat down from the storage compartment. Kelly's arms must be tired from holding Brittany. He wished he'd thought of this sooner.

Hauling in a deep breath, he walked back into the station and stomped the snow from his boots. When he looked up, he discovered Kelly staring at him, her lips tight, but her eyes forgiving.

"I'm sorry," he whispered as he sat beside her. He gazed down at Brittany, who gazed back at him, her blue eyes wide and curious. His daughter seemed to recognize him, and she, at least, didn't know enough to realize what a cantankerous fool he'd been the past few hours. He offered her his finger, which she gripped eagerly with her little hand.

"I'm sorry, too," Kelly whispered back, sounding close to tears.

Nick set the baby seat on the floor and placed his arm around his wife's shoulders. She leaned her head against him. "I don't know what came over me," he murmured. "I wish we were anyplace but here."

"Me, too," Kelly said.

"Amy?"

Len felt a surge of relief and unmistakable joy at the sound of her "hello."

"Are you in Boston?" she asked excitedly. "When can you catch a flight home?"

"I'm still in Abbott," Len said, his happiness evaporating quickly with the reality of this long day. He was trapped, a hostage to circumstances beyond his control.

"You're still in Abbott?" Amy sounded ready to weep. "Oh, Len, will you ever get home for Christmas?"

"I don't know," he told her, trying to keep his own hopes alive—and failing. It seemed everything was against him.

"Yes," he said suddenly, emphatically. For a moment he didn't know where this optimism had come from. Then he did. It was his overwhelming need to be with Amy. "I *will* get home for Christmas." He wasn't about to let the storm, the damaged tracks or anything else ruin his leave. "I'll be home for Christmas, Amy. You can count on it."

He could almost feel her spirits rise. "Your girl in Rawhide will be waiting for you, sailor man."

"You're more than my girl in Rawhide," Len said. "You're my one and only girl. Period!"

She said nothing after his declaration. "Do you mean that, Len?" she finally asked.

"With all my heart." He was tempted to tell her about the diamond, but that would ruin his surprise, and he didn't want to propose over the phone. It just didn't seem near good enough. He wanted her to see the love in his eyes and watch her face when she saw the ring.

"Oh, Len," she whispered.

"Listen, would you call my mom and dad and tell them I still don't know when I'll be home?"

"Sure. Listen, since you can't be here, I'll go back to the nursing home tonight and play the piano for everyone. They wanted to sing Christmas carols but couldn't find any staff willing to take time away from their families."

Len loved her all the more for her generous heart.

"I can't see sitting around home and moping," she explained.

"Sing a Christmas carol for me."

"I will," she said, and her voice softened.

There was a beep in his ear and Len knew he had only a couple of minutes left on his calling card.

"Oh, Len," Amy said. "Time's running out."

"Remember, I'll see you as soon as I can," he said, ready to hang up.

"Len, Len…"

"Yes? What is it?"

"Len," she said, her voice catching, "I…love you. I was going to wait until tonight to tell you, but I want you to know right now. You might be in New Hampshire and me here in Rawhide, but that doesn't matter, because you have my heart with you wherever you are."

The line went dead. Len wasn't sure if she'd hung up or if the time had simply expired.

"I love you, too, Amy," he said into the silent phone, knowing she couldn't hear the words. Somehow he was certain she could feel his heart responding to hers. Soon she'd know how very much he loved his Amy Sue.

Len replaced the receiver and turned around to face the room. Everyone seemed in a dour mood.

The door burst open just then and a smiling, lighthearted Clayton Kemper walked in. He glanced around and beamed proudly at the group of weary travelers.

"I was on my way home when I ran across this," he said cheerfully. He stuck his hand out the door and dragged in the sorriest-looking Christmas tree Len had ever seen.

One side of the evergreen was bare, the top had split and two branches spiked in opposite directions, resembling bug antennae.

"The man in the Christmas-tree lot gave it to me for a buck."

"You got overcharged," Matt McHugh muttered. His words were followed by a few short laughs and a general feeling of agreement.

"That may well be," Kemper said, not letting their lack of enthusiasm dampen his spirit. "But it seemed to me that since you folks are stuck here on Christmas Eve, you might as well make the best of it."

"That tree looks like it's in the same shape we're in," Elise Jones said dryly.

"The tree is yours to do with as you wish," Kemper told them. "Merry Christmas to you all."

No one thought to thank him, Len noticed.

The sad little tree stood in the center of the room, bare and forlorn, wounded and ugly. He'd have to go along with Elise. The Christmas tree did resemble them—and their attitude.

Five-year-old Kate Jones walked over to it and stood with her arms akimbo, staring at the limp branches. Then, apparently having come to some sort of decision, she turned to confront the disgruntled group.

"I think it's a beautiful tree," she announced. "It just needs a little help." She removed the red bow from the top of her head and pinned it to the nearest branch.

Despite himself, Len grinned. On closer examination, the kid was right. The tree wasn't nearly as ugly as he'd first thought.

CHAPTER SIX

"Sing We Now of Christmas"

Most everyone ignored the Christmas tree, Cathy Norris mused sadly. Except for Kate… Then Kelly walked over and silently added a rattle. She took her time finding just the right spot for it, choosing to hang it directly in the middle, opposite Kate's hair bow.

Turning to the others, she smiled and said, "Come on, you guys, it's Christmas Eve."

"She's right," Nick said, and joined his wife. He bounced the baby gently in his arms, and Brittany grinned and reached for his bright green muffler. Nick removed it, handed the baby to Kelly and placed the muffler on the tree, stretching it out as if it were the finest decorative strand. He wove it between the lower branches of the fir, the wool fringe dangling like green wool tinsel.

Len surveyed the tree, then stepped up and added his white cap, settling it near the top, where it sat jauntily.

The elderly black man moved forward next and added his tie clasp. He clipped it to the branch in an upright position like a clothespin, stepped back and nodded once, apparently pleased with the effect. "Hey, this tree doesn't look so bad."

Soon others became creative about decorating the Christmas tree. Cathy cut strips of red yarn and with Kate's help draped the strands over as many branches as they could reach.

Even the grumpy salesman pitched in. Cathy saw him with the small pair of scissors on his Swiss Army knife, folding and cutting memos into paper snowflakes, then hanging them on the tree with dental floss. Actually they looked quite attractive against the backdrop of red yarn.

It wasn't long before every branch sprouted some sort of odd decoration. True, it wasn't a traditional Christmas tree, but it seemed to possess amazing powers. The scowls and complaints of moments earlier were now replaced by smiles and animated chatter.

"I think my daughter's right," Elise said, walking over to more closely examine their handiwork. "This is actually a beautiful tree."

The little boy, around three or four, who'd stayed close by his parents the entire day, clapped in delight.

Cathy noticed several smiles.

"I'm hungry," Kate whispered to her mother.

Worrying about their situation as she had for most of the day, Cathy hadn't given any thought to food until the youngster mentioned it. She apparently wasn't the only one.

"What about dinner?" Cathy asked, glancing about the room. It looked as though they'd been left to fend for themselves. Mr. Kemper had said someone would come by to check on them, but so far no one had.

"Nothing's going to be open tonight," Matt McHugh grumbled. "Not on Christmas Eve."

"Especially not with the storm and all earlier," Len put in.

Cathy could feel the mood of the room, so recently elevated, plunge. Already those who'd moved closer to the Christmas tree were sliding away to slump on benches by the walls.

"Now, that does bring up an interesting prospect," Cathy said, speaking to the entire group for the first time. "I'm Cathy Norris, by the way. I'm going to visit my daughter and her family in Boston, and I just happened to bring along four dozen of her favorite shortbread cookies. Somehow, I don't think she'd mind my sharing them with all of you."

She brought out the tin and pried open the lid.

"My wife and I have several oranges," the elderly black man said. "We can share those. Since we're going to be eating together, it's only appropriate that we introduce ourselves. My name's Sam Givens and my wife's Louise."

"Thank you, Sam and Louise," Cathy said. "Anyone else?"

"I'm Matt McHugh. I was given a fruitcake on my last sales call," Matt surprised her by saying. "I would've thrown the damn thing out, but one of my kids likes the stuff. I can cut that up if anyone's interested."

"Well, I'm quite fond of fruitcake," Kelly Berry said.

Although the depot office was locked, the counter was free and Cathy placed the tin of cookies there. Matt took out the fruitcake and sliced it with his Swiss Army knife. Sam Givens brought over the oranges, then peeled and sectioned them.

Elise Jones collected paper towels from the restroom to use as napkins. Soon more and more food appeared. It seemed almost everyone had something to share. A plate of beautifully decorated chocolates. A white cardboard box filled with pink divinity and homemade fudge. Then a tin of peanuts and a bag of pretzels. Len added a package of cinnamon-flavored gum.

A crooked line formed and they all helped themselves, taking bits and pieces of each dish. It wasn't much, but it helped do more than dull the edge of their hunger. It proved, to Cathy at least, that there was hope for them. That banding together they could get through this and even have a good time.

"My mother's serving prime rib right about now," Elise lamented as she took an orange segment and a handful of peanuts.

"And to think she's missing out on Matt McHugh's fruitcake," Cathy said, and was delighted by the responding laugh that echoed down the line. Even Matt chuckled. An hour ago Cathy would have thought that impossible.

"I never thought I'd say this about fruitcake," the young sailor said, saluting Matt with a slice, "but this ain't half-bad."

"What about my peanuts?" the guy with long hair asked. "I spent hours slaving over a hot stove to make those."

Everyone smiled and the silly jokes continued.

"Quiet," Nick said suddenly, jumping to his feet. "I hear something."

"A train?" Matt teased.

"'Do you hear what I hear?'" someone sang.

"I'm serious."

It didn't take Cathy long to pick up the faint sound of voices singing. "Someone's coming," she announced.

"Carolers?" Kelly asked. "On a night like this? For us?"

"No night more perfect," Cathy murmured. Years ago

she and Ron had been members of the church choir. Each holiday season the choir had toured nursing homes and hospitals, giving short performances. They'd been active in their church for a number of years. Unfortunately their attendance had slipped after Ron retired, then stopped completely when he became seriously ill. And afterward…well, afterward Cathy simply didn't have the heart for it.

For the first time since the funeral, she felt the need to return. This insight was like an unexpected gift, and it had come to her at the sound of the carolers' voices.

The door opened and a group of fifteen or so entered the train depot.

"Hello, everyone." A man with a bushy gray mustache and untamed gray hair stepped forward. "I'm Dean Owen. Clayton Kemper's a friend of mine and he mentioned you folks were stranded. This is the teen choir from the Regular Baptist Church. Since we weren't able to get out last night because of the snow, we thought we'd make a few rounds this evening. How's everyone doing?"

"Great."

"As good as can be expected."

"Hangin' in there."

"I love your Christmas tree," one of the girls said. She was about sixteen, with long blond hair in a ponytail and twinkling eyes.

"We decorated it ourselves," Kate said, pointing to her hair bow. "That's mine."

"Would anyone mind if I took a picture?" the girl asked, pulling a digital camera from her coat pocket.

"This is something that's got to be seen to be believed,"

Matt whispered to Cathy. "Actually I wouldn't mind having a copy of it myself."

"Me, too."

"Shall we make it a family photo?" Elise asked.

A chorus of yes's and no's followed, but within a minute the ragtag group had gathered around the tree. Cathy ran a comb through her hair and added a dash of lipstick. Others, too, reviewed their appearance as they assembled for the photograph, jostling each other good-naturedly.

What amazed Cathy were the antics that went on before the picture was taken. They behaved like a group of teenagers themselves. Len held up the V for peace sign behind Nick's head. Even Matt managed a crooked smile. For that matter, so did Cathy. Someone joked and she laughed. That made her realize how long it'd been since she'd allowed herself to be happy. *Too long. Ron wouldn't want that.*

The girl took four snapshots. Before long, she had a list of names and email addresses to send copies of the photo. Cathy's name was there along with everyone else's. She wanted something tangible to remember this eventful day—the oddest Christmas Eve she'd spent in her entire life.

"We thought we'd deliver a bit of cheer," Dean said, once the photo arrangements were finished.

Their coming had done exactly that. The travelers gathered around without anyone's direction, positioning the benches in a way that allowed them all to see the singers.

The choir assembled in three rows of five each and began with "Silent Night," sung in three-part harmony. Cathy had heard the old carol all her life, but never had it sounded more beautiful than it did this evening. Without accompaniment, without embellishment, simple, plain—and incredibly lovely. With the beautiful words came a sense of camaraderie and joy, a sense that this night was truly special.

This *was* a holy night.

"Silent Night" was followed by "The Little Drummer Boy," then "Joy to the World," one carol flowing smoothly into another, ending with "We Wish You a Merry Christmas."

While Cathy and the others applauded loudly, Kate, in a burst of childish enthusiasm, spontaneously rushed forward and hugged Dean's knees. "That was so pretty," she squealed, her delight contagious.

Len jumped to his feet, continuing the applause. Soon the others stood, too, including Cathy.

The small choir seemed overwhelmed by their appreciation.

"This is the first time we ever got a standing ovation," the girl with the camera said, smiling at her friends. "I didn't realize we were that good."

"Sing more," Kate pleaded. "Do you know 'Rudolph the Red-Nosed Reindeer'?"

"Can you sing it with us?" Dean bent down and asked Kate.

The child nodded enthusiastically, and Dean had her stand in front of the choir. "Sing away."

"Join in, everyone," he suggested next, turning to face his small audience.

Cathy and the others didn't need any encouragement. Their voices blended with those of the choir as if they'd sung together for weeks. "Rudolph" led to other Christmas songs—"Silver Bells," "Deck the Halls," and the time passed quickly.

When they finished, the choir members brought out paper cups and thermoses of hot chocolate. No sooner had the hot drink been poured than the station door opened again.

"So Clayton was right." A petite older woman, with a cap of white hair and eyelids painted the brightest shade of blue Cathy had ever seen, entered the room. Two other women filed in after her.

"I'm Greta Barnes," the leader said, "and we're from the Veterans of Foreign Wars Women's Auxiliary."

"We've brought you folks dinner," another woman told them.

"Now you're talking!" Len Dawber shouted. "Sorry, folks, but a slice of fruitcake and a few pretzels didn't quite fill me up."

"Made for a great appetizer, though," Nick said.

"The food's out in the car. Would someone help carry it in?" Greta asked. She didn't have to ask for volunteers a second time. Nick, Matt and Len were up before any of the other men had a chance. A couple of minutes later they were back inside, their arms loaded with boxes.

"It's not much," one of the other women said apologetically as she set a huge pot of soup on the counter. "We didn't get much notice."

"We're grateful for whatever you brought us," Sam assured the women. Louise nodded in agreement.

"Luckily the family had plenty of clam chowder left over," the older of Greta's friends said. "The soup's a Christmas Eve tradition in our house, and I can't help it, I always cook up more than enough."

"Eleanor's soup is the best in the state," Greta declared.

"There's sandwiches, too," the third woman said, unpacking one of the smaller boxes.

"And seeing that no one knows when the repairs on those tracks are going to be finished," the spry older woman added, "we decided to bring along some blankets and pillows."

"All the comforts of home," Matt muttered, but the caustic edge that had laced his comments earlier in the day had vanished.

"I must say you folks are certainly good sports about all this."

Considering that this change in attitude had only recently come about, none of them leaped to their feet to accept credit.

"Like I said earlier," Matt told her, speaking for the group, "we're making the best of it."

"We're very grateful for the pillows and blankets," Cathy put in.

"The food, too," several others said.

The church choir stayed and helped pass around the sandwiches, which were delicious. Cathy ate half a tuna-salad sandwich, then half a turkey one. She was amazed at how big her appetite was. Food, like almost everything since Ron's death, had become a necessity and not an enjoyment.

When the teen choir left, it was with a cheery wave and the promise that everyone who'd asked for a picture would be sure to receive one. With a responsible kindhearted man like Dean Owen as their leader, Cathy was confident it would come about.

The soup and sandwiches disappeared quickly. Three

other men helped pack up the leftovers and carted the boxes out to the car.

"You sure we can't get you anything else?" Greta asked before she headed outside.

"You've done more than enough."

"Thank Mr. Kemper for us," Len said, ready to escort the older women to their vehicle.

With many shouts of "Merry Christmas," everyone waved the Auxiliary ladies goodbye.

Len returned, leaning against the door when it closed. Cathy watched as he paused and glanced about the room. "You know," he said, not speaking to anyone in particular, "I almost feel sorry for all those people who decided to stay in hotels. They've missed out on the best Christmas Eve I can ever remember."

CHAPTER SEVEN

"Santa Claus Is Coming to Town"

The station seemed unnaturally quiet after the choir and the members of the VFW Women's Auxiliary had left. The lively chatter and shared laughter that had filled the room died down to a low hum.

Matt knew he should phone home, that he'd delayed it as long as he dared. With the time difference between the east and west coasts, it wasn't quite four in the afternoon in Los Angeles. The dread that settled over him depleted the sense of well-being he'd experienced over the past few hours.

He didn't look forward to a telephone confrontation with Pam, but as far as he could see there was no avoiding one. He could almost hear her voice, starting low and quickly gaining volume until it reached a shrill, near-hysterical pitch.

He wished things could be different, but he knew she'd start in on him, and then, despite his best efforts, he'd retaliate. Soon their exchange would escalate into a full-blown fight.

His feet felt weighted as he crossed the station to the row of pay phones. He slipped his credit card through the appropriate slot, punched in his home number and waited for the line to connect.

The phone rang twice, three times, then four before the answering machine came on. Bored, he tapped his foot while he listened to the message he'd recorded earlier in the year. When he heard the signal, he was ready. "Pam, it's Matt. I'm sorry about this, but I got caught in the snowstorm that struck Maine yesterday. The flights out of Bangor were canceled, so the airline put me on a train for Boston. Now the train tracks are out and I don't have a clue when I'll be home. As soon as I reach Boston, probably sometime Christmas morning, I'll phone and let you know when to expect me. I'm sorry about this, but it's out of my control. Kiss the kids for me and I'll see you as soon as I can."

The relief that came over him at not getting caught in a verbal battle with his wife was like an unexpected gift. This wasn't how it should be, but he felt powerless to change the dynamics of their marriage. Somewhere along the road the partnership they'd once shared had fallen apart. He wasn't the only one who felt miserable; he knew that. The look in Pam's eyes as he'd walked through the house, suitcase in hand, had told him he wasn't the only one thinking about a separation.

His mood was oppressive by the time he returned to his seat.

"What about Santa?" Matt heard Kate ask her mother.

"Honey, he's still coming to Grandma's house." Kate's mother was busy making up a bed for her daughter. She placed a pillow at one end of the bench and arranged the blanket so the little girl could sleep between its folds.

"But, Mom, I'm *not* at Grandma Gibson's house—I'm *here*. Santa might not know."

Elise apparently needed a minute to think about that. "Grandma will have to tell him."

"But what if Santa decides to try to find me here, instead of leaving my presents with Grandma?"

"Kate, please, can't you just trust that you're going to get your gifts?"

Arms crossed, the child shook her head stubbornly. "No, I can't," she said, her voice as serious as the expression on her face. "You told me Daddy was going to come see me before we left and he didn't."

"Honey, I don't have any control over what your father says and does. I'm sorry he disappointed you."

Her look said it wasn't the first time mother and child had been let down.

Kate started to whimper.

"Sweetheart, please," Elise whispered. She seemed close to breaking down herself. She picked up her daughter and held her close. As she gently rocked the little girl, her eyes shone with unshed tears. "Santa won't forget you."

"Daddy did."

"No, honey, I'm sure he didn't, not really."

"Then why didn't he come like he said?"

"Because…" Elise began, then hesitated and forcefully expelled her breath. "It's complicated."

"Everything's complicated since you and Daddy divorced."

Matt felt like an eavesdropper, yet he couldn't tune out the conversation between mother and child. Part of him yearned to let Kate use his credit card to phone her father, but if he suggested that, Elise would know he'd been listening in.

Hearing Kate cry about being forgotten by her dad left Matt to wonder if this would be his own children's future should he and Pam decide to split up. He didn't want a divorce, never had. But it was obvious they couldn't continue the way they'd been going—belittling each other, arguing, eroding the foundation of their love and commitment.

"Why didn't Daddy come see me like he said he would?" Kate persisted.

Elise took her time answering. "Your daddy was embarrassed."

"Embarrassed?"

"He felt bad."

"About what?"

"Being late helping to pay the bills. He didn't come see you because…well, because I don't think he could afford to buy you anything for Christmas, and he didn't want you to be disappointed in him because he didn't have a gift."

Kate mulled that over for a while, nibbling her bottom lip. "I love him and I didn't have a gift for him, either."

"Your daddy loves you, Kate, that much I know."

"Can I talk to him myself?"

Elise took a deep breath. "You can phone him when we reach Grandma's house, and you can tell him about spending the night in the train depot. He'll want to hear about all your adventures on Christmas Eve."

Matt considered what would happen to his relationship with his children if he and Pam went their separate ways.

The love he felt for Rachel and Jimmy ran deep, and the idea of Pam having to make excuses for him...

His thoughts tumbled to an abrupt halt. That was exactly what Pam had been forced to do the afternoon he'd left for Maine. Jimmy had been counting on him to attend the school Christmas program and, instead, he'd raced off to the airport. Matt's stomach knotted, and he sat back, wiping a hand down his face.

A whispered discussion broke out between the widow and the elderly couple who'd supplied the oranges. Matt had no idea what was going on and, caught up in his own musing, didn't much care.

Not long afterward, he discovered that a few of the senior crowd had decided to take this matter of Christmas for the two children into their own hands.

Cathy walked by Kate, paused suddenly and held one hand to her ear. "Did you hear something?" she asked the youngster.

"Not me," Kate answered.

"I think it's bells."

Elise cupped her ear. "Reindeer feet?"

"Bells," Cathy returned pointedly.

"Yes," Louise piped up. "It's definitely the sound of bells. What could it be?"

They weren't going to get any Academy Award nominations, but they did manage to convince the children.

"I hear bells!" the other child called. "I do, I do." It was the first time the little boy had spoken all day.

Kate sat up straight on her mother's lap. "I hear them, too."

Matt had to admit the two old ladies really had him going; he could almost hear them himself. Then he realized he really *could* hear the jingle of bells.

A knock sounded loudly on the station door. "I'll get it." Sam eagerly stepped to the door. He opened it a couple of inches, nodded a few times and looked over his shoulder. "Do we have a little girl named Kate here and a boy... Charlie?"

"Charles," his mother corrected.

"Kate and Charles," Sam informed the mysterious visitor no one was allowed to see. "As a matter of fact, Kate and Charles *are* here," Sam said loudly. "You do...of course. I'll see to it personally. Now don't you worry, you have plenty of other deliveries to make tonight. You'd best be on your way."

Matt glanced around and noticed that Nick Berry was missing...and he seemed to remember that their baby had a rattle with bells inside.

The room went quiet as Sam closed the door, and the jingling receded. He had a pillowcase in one hand, with a couple of wrapped gifts inside. "That was Santa Claus," he announced. "He heard that Kate and Charles were stuck here on Christmas Eve. Santa wanted them to know he hadn't forgotten them."

"Did he bring my presents?" Kate sprang off her mother's lap and ran toward Sam, still standing near the door.

Charles joined her, gazing up at the man with hopeful eyes.

"Santa wanted me to tell you he left plenty of gifts at your Grandma Gibson's house, Kate, but he didn't want you to worry that he'd missed you, so he dropped this off." He thrust his arm into the pillowcase and produced a wrapped box.

Matt recognized it right away as one he'd seen poking out of Cathy Norris's carry-on bag when she'd removed the tin of cookies.

"I believe this one is for you, Charles," Sam said. The second gift went to the four-year-old. The boy raced back to his parents and dropped to his knees. He tore into the wrapping paper, scattering pieces in all directions. The minute Charles saw the rubber dinosaur, he cried out in delight and hugged it to his chest.

Kate, on the other hand, opened her present with delicate precision, carefully removing the ribbon first and placing it on the tree. Next came the wrapping paper. Matt couldn't figure out how she did it, but she managed to pull off the Christmas wrap without tearing it even once. When she saw the Barbie doll, she looked up at her mother and smiled wonderingly.

"Daddy must have given it to Santa. This is what I told him I wanted."

"I'm sure he did." Elise was gracious enough to concur.

Matt didn't know what had gone wrong in this woman's marriage, but it wasn't difficult to see the pain that divorce had brought into her life. Could bring into his own, if he allowed it to happen.

Cathy and the elderly couple exchanged smiles that their small ploy had worked. Actually Matt was touched by their generosity; they'd obviously given up Christmas presents meant for their own grandchildren.

He wasn't sure what prompted the idea, but he reached for his briefcase. "As a matter of fact, Santa left a few goodies with me, too. Is anyone interested in a sample of the latest software from MicroChip International?"

It didn't take long to discover that a number of people were.

"Are you sure, man?" the ex-hippie asked. "This is worth a good two hundred bucks in the store."

"Five hundred, actually," Matt said. "Consider it compliments of the company."

"We've got extra pictures of the baby, if anyone would like," Nick offered.

"Sure," Len said. "Amy—my fiancée—is crazy about babies." He took one and so did Cathy, Elise and several others.

As had happened earlier with the food, a variety of gifts, some wrapped and others not, started to appear. The joking and laughter continued during the impromptu gift exchange. By the end, everyone had both given and received at least one gift.

Sam, who'd stayed in the background most of the day, stepped forward with a worn Bible in his hand. "This being the night of our Savior's birth," he said, "I thought we might like to listen to the account of the first Christmas."

Most people nodded in silent agreement. Sam pulled out a chair and set it close to their Christmas tree, then perched a pair of glasses on his nose.

The room hushed as he began to read. His rich resonant voice echoed through the depot. Everyone listened with an attentiveness Matt found amazing.

When he'd finished, Sam reverently closed the Bible and

removed his glasses, tucking them into his shirt pocket. "It seems to me that we all have something in common with Mary and Joseph. They, too, were weary travelers and there wasn't any room for them at the inn." He paused and held up one hand. "I checked earlier and every room in this town has been booked for the night."

There were grins and murmurs at his remark. Sam got to his feet and sang the first words of "Silent Night." Everyone joined in, their voices rising in joyful sound. Matt thought he'd never heard anything so achingly beautiful, so...sincere.

As the last line died away, Sam walked over to the wall and turned out the light. The room went dim, but the outside lights cast a warm glow into the station's interior.

"It's nine o'clock," the ex-hippie announced. "I haven't been to bed this early in twenty years, but I'm more than ready to hit the hay."

His wife giggled. The two of them cuddled awkwardly on the hard bench, kissing and whispering.

Matt felt a pang of regret at seeing the closeness they shared, a closeness so sadly lacking in his own marriage. He glanced at his watch, certain that Pam would be home now, probably seething about the brief message he'd left. Nevertheless he wanted to talk to her. No, he corrected himself, he *needed* to talk to her.

Light from the window guided him to the far wall of the station, to the phones. Because it was still early, people continued to talk. He slipped his credit card through the slot and waited for the line to connect.

Pam answered on the first ring. "Hello." Her clipped tone told him she was angry, as he'd expected.

"It's Matt," he said.

"Matt?" She paused. "Matt?" she said again. "Where—"

"Merry Christmas, sweetheart," he whispered.

"How can you 'Merry Christmas' me with the kids screaming in my ear? Your parents are due any minute, and the house is a mess. The cat tipped over the Christmas tree and you're…you're…" She burst into tears.

"Pam," he said softly. "Honey, don't cry."

"I can't help it! I suppose you're in some posh hotel, ogling the cocktail waitress, while I'm here—"

"I'm not in any hotel."

"Then where are you?"

"A hundred-year-old train depot with…" Now it was his turn to pause. "With friends who were strangers not that long ago."

"A train depot?" She sniffled and sounded unsure.

"It's a long story and I'll tell you about it when I get home."

"You didn't phone all week."

"I know and I'm sorry, sweetheart, really sorry. It was childish and silly of me to let our argument stand in the way of talking to you and the kids."

"You haven't called me sweetheart in a long time."

"Too long," Matt said. "I've done a lot of thinking these past few days, and once I'm home I want to talk to you about making some changes."

"I've been a terrible wife," she sobbed into the phone.

"Pam, you haven't. Now stop. I love you and you love me, and we're going to make it, understand?"

"Yes," she mumbled, her reply quavery with emotion.

"Listen, I want you to think about two things."

"Okay."

"First, I want to quit my job." Not until he said the words did Matt recognize how right it was to leave MicroChip. He should have known it when he was passed over for a promotion he'd earned. Being undervalued and underappreciated had cut into his self-confidence, and inevitably, his dissatisfaction with his job had affected his family life. He couldn't, wouldn't, allow that to continue.

"Quit your job?" Pam gasped.

"It isn't as bad as it sounds. I'm going to send out a couple of feelers right after New Year's. I've got a good reputation in the industry. I can get something else. The main thing is that I spend more time at home with you and the kids. It's unfair to have you chained down with all the responsibility for them and the house while I travel. I'm going to be looking for a sales position that won't take me away for more than a day at a time."

"That sounds wonderful."

"The other thing we need is a vacation, just the two of us. I've got vacation time coming, and it's been far too long since you and I got away without the kids."

"I'd love that, Matt, more than anything."

"How about a Caribbean cruise?" he suggested.

"Yes... Oh, Matt, I love you so much and I've felt so awful about the way our marriage has been going."

"Me, too. We'll talk about that some more. Maybe it wouldn't be such a bad idea to see a counselor, either."

"Yes," she whispered.

Over the phone Matt heard a chorus of background shouts.

"Your parents just arrived," Pam told him.

"Let them wait. I want to say Merry Christmas to my wife."

CHAPTER EIGHT

"Silent Night"

Cathy made up a small bed for herself using the blankets and pillows the VFW Women's Auxiliary had distributed. By all rights, she should be exhausted. She'd been up since dawn and the day had been filled with uncertainty and tension.

Instead, she lay with her eyes wide open, mulling over the events of the past twenty-four hours. Apparently she wasn't the only one having difficulty sleeping. Matt, the sales rep, had carefully made his way across the darkened room and used the phone. It could be her imagination, but his steps seemed lighter on the return trip, as though his mood had improved. Cathy felt pleased for him. She'd lost patience with him earlier, and later...well, later, he'd proved to be an ally and a friend.

She'd witnessed more than one transformation today. The young sailor had been nervous and excited about this trip home; he'd chattered like a five-year-old when they'd first started out.

Then troubles developed, and he'd withdrawn into himself. But over the next few hours, Cathy had watched as

Len recovered from his disappointment and frustration. Before the night was over he'd been an encouragement to others.

Nick and Kelly, the young couple with the newborn, were struggling to be good parents and still hold on to the closeness they'd once had in their marriage. Those two reminded Cathy of Ron and her about thirty years ago, after the birth of their first daughter. Eventually, like most couples, Nick and Kelly would learn to work together and ease gracefully into parenthood.

Sam and Louise had kept to themselves all day, offering no advice and little comment until Cathy shared her shortbread cookies. It was then that they'd kindly come forward and contributed their oranges. Later Sam had read the Christmas story from the Bible in a way that had stirred her beyond any Christmas Eve church service she'd ever attended.

She thought again of Matt McHugh. In the beginning he'd been quite disagreeable. Easily irritated, his few remarks cynical. One would assume that as a seasoned traveler he'd be better able to deal with frustrations of this sort. Unfortunately that wasn't the case until... Cathy couldn't put her finger on the precise moment she'd noticed the change in him. About the time they'd decorated the tree, she decided, when he'd opened his briefcase and started folding and clipping memos into paper snowflakes. She'd sensed a genuine enthusiasm in him from that point on.

Cathy had been just as affected by the unusual events of this Christmas Eve as her fellow passengers. That morning, when she'd phoned for a taxi in the middle of the snow-

storm, she hadn't been looking forward to the trip. She'd
dreaded it less, however, than spending the holiday alone
in the house where she'd lived all those years with Ron.

She'd known Christmas would be difficult. After living
first with the approach of death and then the aftermath of
it, she'd anticipated nothing but pain and loneliness during
the Christmas season. And she'd been right. But today, for
the first time since standing over her husband's grave, she'd
experienced what it meant to be alive. Sharing, encouraging, laughing. Damn, but it felt good.

"Are you awake?" Matt whispered from the bench directly across from her.

"Yes. You, too." She smiled at the obviousness of the
comment.

"I just spoke to my wife." He sounded excited. "It was
the first time we've connected all day."

"I imagine she was relieved to hear from you."

She saw his nod, and then he said the oddest thing.

"You loved your husband very much, didn't you?" he
asked, sitting up and leaning toward her, bracing his elbows on his knees.

"Yes." Her voice wavered slightly, surprised as she was
by his question and the instant flash of pain it produced.

"I want my wife and me to have the same kind of relationship you did with your husband."

The comment touched her heart. "Thank you," she whispered, warmed by the praise of this stranger who'd become
her friend. "How'd you know… I didn't mention Ron, I
don't think."

"Ah, but you did," he said quietly, nestling against his

pillow. "You told Kate about the dollhouse your husband built for his granddaughters. It was easy to read between the lines and…well, I could see this Christmas was difficult for you."

"It's better now," she whispered.

He sighed and curled up against the pillow before closing his eyes. "It's better for me, too."

"Merry Christmas, Matt."

"Merry Christmas, Cathy."

Len purposely waited until the depot was silent. The even rhythm of breathing told him that almost everyone was asleep. His watch said eleven-thirty, which made it ten-thirty in Rawhide. Amy had mentioned playing the piano at the rest home, and he'd waited until he was fairly confident she'd be home.

The phone card he'd paid for on base had long since expired, so he had to use his credit card. The transaction seemed loud enough to wake the entire room, but as far as Len could see, no one stirred.

When the line connected, the phone rang three times, three of the longest rings Len could ever remember hearing. He was about to give up hope when Amy answered.

"Hello." Her voice sounded breathless and excited at once.

"Merry Christmas, Amy," he said, speaking in a whisper for fear of disturbing the others.

"Len, Len, is that you?"

"It's me."

"Where are you?"

"The train depot," he said, wishing he had other news to give her.

"Still? Oh, Len, are you ever going to make it home?"

"And miss seeing my girl? Are you nuts? I'll walk from here to Rawhide if I have to."

"Oh, Len! I can't believe this is happening."

He'd felt much the same way himself most of the day, but somehow everything had changed after Mr. Kemper brought in the Christmas tree. And after the choir had come and the ladies had brought them a meal. And Sam had read the Christmas story...

In the beginning tempers had flared and folks were impatient and short with each other. Then the kindhearted stationmaster had brought that bare, sad-looking tree and placed it in the center of the room.

Someone had commented that the stupid tree wasn't worth the buck Kemper had paid for it.

Len had agreed. It'd taken a five-year-old child to teach them. The minute Kate had placed her hair bow on one sagging limb, the Christmas tree had been magically transformed into something beautiful. Not because of what they'd used to decorate its branches, but because of the effect it'd had on all of them, the way it had brought them together.

Everything had changed from then on. Suddenly they weren't strangers anymore. Suddenly it was a Christmas like those he'd enjoyed when he was a boy. He'd spent Christmas Eve with strangers who'd become so much more. Strangers who'd become family. Granted, it wasn't the same as if he'd spent Christmas Eve with Amy, but then he expected to be with her for the rest of his life.

"I'll be home before you know it," he promised.

"I'll be here," she whispered.

The line was quiet a moment while Len gathered his courage. He'd rather propose when he could look into her eyes and see her reaction as he said the words, but that wasn't possible. He didn't think he could wait any longer.

"Did you mean what you said earlier?" he asked. "Do you really love me, Amy Sue?"

"Yes," she admitted as though confessing to a fault. "I... I probably shouldn't have said it."

"Why not?" he asked, raising his voice before he could stop himself.

"Because...well, because we've never talked about our feelings and—"

"I love you, too, Amy."

She didn't say anything for so long Len feared they'd been disconnected.

"Amy?"

"I'm here."

He could tell from the tremble in her voice that she was close to tears. "Amy, listen, I never intended it to happen like this, but then life doesn't always go the way we plan it. I decided to come home for another reason besides spending Christmas with my family."

"What?"

"I was hoping..." Despite rehearsing his proposal, he was tongue-tied and nervous.

"You were hoping..." she encouraged.

"To talk to you about something important."

"Yes?"

"About the two of us." He continued to improvise, forgetting the carefully worded proposal he'd practiced a hundred times. "I was thinking you and I...that is, if you were interested...that maybe we should get married."

There was a silence that seemed to go on and on.

"Married," she finally repeated, sounding stunned.

Len's hand tightened around the telephone receiver. His nerves were stretched to the limit. "Say something," he pleaded, all the while wondering if it was possible to get a refund on the diamond if she refused him. His heart sank to his knees; he hadn't considered Amy's refusal. In his arrogance he'd assumed she'd scream with delight, maybe even cry a little. The last thing he'd anticipated was no response.

"Amy?" he asked, humble now, wondering how he could have made such a mistake in judgment. He'd noted the reserve in her recently, the fact that he hadn't gotten a letter in almost two weeks. Other things didn't add up, either, but he'd pushed his concerns aside each time he spoke with her—although of course their phone calls had been less frequent lately. But whenever he managed to call she'd always sounded so glad to hear from him.

"Is there someone else?" he demanded, his pride rescuing him. "Is that it?"

"Oh, Len, how can you think such a thing?"

"Then what's your answer?" A proposal was a straightforward enough question. "Yes or no?"

"Who told you?"

"Told me?" he echoed. "Told me what?"

"About the baby."

CHAPTER NINE

"Home For the Holidays"

"Baby?" Len's knees went weak and to remain upright he braced his shoulder against the wall.

"Who told you?" Amy repeated.

"No one..." Len's thoughts twisted around in his mind until he was convinced he'd misunderstood her. "To make sure I understand what's happening here, I need to ask you something. Are you telling me you're pregnant?"

"Yes."

"Don't you think you should've mentioned this before now?" he demanded, not caring who heard him. "You must be at least three months along."

"Three and a half... I love you, Len, but you've never said how you felt about me. I didn't want you to feel obligated to marry me. My dad married my mother because she was pregnant and the marriage was a disaster. I refuse to repeat my mother's mistakes, although I certainly seem to have started out on the same path."

"Amy, listen, I swear I didn't know about the baby. No one told me a damn thing." He took a deep breath. "As for you being like your mom...this is different. I love you.

I want us to get married. I wanted it even before I knew about the baby." It hurt to think Amy had held back, not telling him she was pregnant. "Who else knows?"

"Jenny."

"You'd tell your best friend before you'd tell me?" he said, hardly able to believe his ears.

"Why'd you ask me to marry you?" she returned, equally insistent. "Is it just because of the baby?"

"No... I already told you that. Isn't loving you and wanting to spend the rest of my life with you reason enough?"

"Yes," she whispered, whimpering now. "It's more than enough."

"Listen, Amy. I want to be with you. And I want my baby. We're getting married, understand? Soon, too, next week if it can be arranged, and when I go back to Maine, I'm going to ask for married housing. Next month I'll come down and get you."

"Len..."

That was the reason she'd asked if she was just "his girl in Rawhide." He hated the thought of her worrying and fretting all these weeks, wondering how he'd react once he learned the truth.

"You said you love me. Are you taking that back now?" he asked.

"No..."

"I love you. I knew it after my last visit home. I should have said something then. I regret now that I didn't." Then, remembering how he didn't enjoy having his life dictated to him, he asked again, "Will you marry me, Amy?"

Her hesitation was only momentary this time. "Yes, Len, oh, yes."

He could hear her sob softly in the background.

"I knew tonight would be special," she murmured.

"How's that?" Len's mind continued to spin with Amy's news, but it wasn't unwelcome. He was ready to be a husband and had always loved children. His own parents had been wonderful and he was determined to be a good husband and father himself.

"Mr. Danbar came out of his room tonight when I sat down at the piano," Amy told him.

Len could only vaguely recall the man's name. "Mr. Danbar?"

"He's the one who hasn't spoken a word since his wife died three years ago. The man I eat my lunch with every day. I'm the one who does all the talking, but that's all right."

"He came out of his room?" This was big news, Len realized. He remembered now that Amy had written to him about the older gentleman.

"His wife used to play the piano and when he heard the music, he climbed out of bed and came into the recreation room. He sat down on the bench beside me and smiled. Oh, Len, it was the most amazing thing."

His wife-to-be was pretty darn amazing herself, he thought proudly. She could coax a lonely old man from his room and brighten his life with her music and kindness. Len meant what he'd said, about their marrying as soon as possible. Their marriage would be a strong one, based on love and mutual respect.

He felt like the luckiest man alive.

"Are you awake?" Nick whispered to Kelly in the dead of night. He thought he'd heard her stir and realized they were both accustomed to Brittany waking and needing to be fed around this time.

Nick had been wide-awake for the better part of an hour. Sleeping upright with his head propped against the wall had been awkward, but he'd managed to get some rest. It helped to have his arm around Kelly and hold her close to his side. They hadn't held each other nearly enough lately, but that was something he hoped to remedy.

In response to his question, Kelly yawned. "What time is it?"

"About two."

"Already?" His wife smothered a second yawn.

"How's Brittany?"

"Better than either of us."

Nick grinned into the darkness and gently squeezed her shoulder.

"I never thought we'd spend our first Christmas as parents stuck in some train depot," Kelly said, her words barely audible.

"Me, neither."

"It hasn't been so bad."

Nick pressed his face into her hair and inhaled, delighting in her warm female scent. He loved Kelly and Brittany more than he'd thought it was possible to love anyone. More than it seemed reasonable for any human heart to love. Little in his life had come easy, and this parenting business might well be his greatest challenge yet. But his struggles had taught him to appreciate what he did have. Tonight, Christmas Eve, had taught him to *recognize* what he had.

He'd considered the trip home to Georgia unnecessary, but Kelly had wanted to introduce Brittany to her grandparents. Besides, traveling in winter was a mistake, he'd told her over and over. In the end he'd agreed only because Kelly had wanted it so badly. He hadn't been gracious about it, and when troubles arose, it was all he could do not to leap up and tell her how right he'd been.

Nick felt differently now. Being with these people on Christmas Eve hadn't been a mistake at all. Nor was taking Brittany to meet her extended family. They needed each other. He'd stood alone most of his life, but he wasn't alone anymore. He had a wife and daughter. Family. And friends.

More friends than he'd realized.

At six o'clock Christmas morning, Clayton Kemper received word that the tracks had been repaired. He hurriedly dressed and rushed down to the train depot, not sure what he'd find. It came as a pleasant surprise to discover everyone waking up in a good mood, grateful to hear his news. While the travelers stretched and yawned, Clayton put on a pot of coffee, then dragged out the phone book and called the hotels in town to alert the passengers there that the tracks had been repaired.

"I don't imagine this will be a Christmas you'll soon forget," Clayton said as he led the small band from the depot to the train. The engine hummed, ready to race down the tracks toward Boston.

Mrs. Norris was the first to board. She smiled as she placed her hand in his. "Thank you again for all your kindness, Mr. Kemper. And Merry Christmas."

"I was glad I could help," he said as she climbed onto the train.

The couple with the baby followed, along with the young

navy man who lugged his own bag as well as the infant seat. It never ceased to amaze Clayton that one baby could need this much equipment. Time was, a bottle or two and a few diapers would suffice. These days it took the mother and two full-grown men to cart everything in. Clayton was pleased to see that the couple had struck up a friendship with the sailor. They certainly seemed to have a great deal to talk about.

The sales rep boarded next, after helping an elderly black couple with their luggage. This was the man who'd spent a large portion of the day before scowling and muttering under his breath. Kemper didn't know what had happened to him, but this morning the man grinned from ear to ear and was about as helpful as they come.

"We appreciate everything you did for us, Kemper," he said as he made his way into the train.

Five-year-old Kate bounced onto the first step and told Clayton, "Santa came last night and dropped off a present for me and Charles."

"Did he now?" Clayton asked, catching Elise Jones's eyes.

"Indeed, he did," Elise said with a wide smile.

Apparently the adults had arranged something for the children. Clayton was glad to hear it. He wished he'd been able to do more himself, but he had his own family and plenty of obligations. It was a sad case when the railroad had to put people up in a depot for the night, especially when that night happened to be Christmas Eve.

He waited until everyone was on board before he stepped away from the train. Glancing inside the compartment, he watched fascinated as the group of once-cantankerous travelers cheerfully teased one another. Anyone looking at them would assume they were lifelong friends, even family.

Was it possible, Clayton wondered, that this small band of strangers had discovered the true meaning of Christmas? Learned it in a train depot late on Christmas Eve in the middle of a snowstorm?

The question seemed to answer itself.

★ ★ ★ ★ ★

Keep reading for a special preview.

THREE CHRISTMAS WISHES is another story about searching for perfection over the holidays.

Three friends, each wishing for a perfect man, get some intriguing predictions from Santa Claus!

THREE CHRISTMAS WISHES

A brand-new novel by Sheila Roberts.

Available now from MIRA Books

CHAPTER ONE

Riley Erickson's life was perfect. Happily, there was no other way to describe it. She was engaged to a perfect man—good-looking, easygoing, kind to little old ladies, liked her friends—and they were getting married during her favorite time of year. (Christmas weddings were the most beautiful.) She had an equally great family—generous, fun-loving and supportive (now that she and her bro and sis had outgrown the sibling-rivalry stuff)—and a job she loved, teaching fourth grade at Whispering Pines Elementary School. Kids still liked their teachers at that age, so it was fun to go to work. And you couldn't beat the vacation time since teachers got summers off as well as spring and winter breaks…which made getting married in December, well, perfect.

Riley smiled as she took the small ceramic turkey off her desk and substituted a snowman. The wedding was only three weeks away. By Christmas, she and Sean Little would be hanging their Christmas stockings side by side. Humming Christmas carols as she worked, she took down the rest of the Thanksgiving decorations in her classroom and put up her Christmas-themed ones. The children would return from their Thanksgiving weekend to find the classroom all ready for the holidays.

Once her decorating was finished, she took a moment to admire her reindeer and Santas and candy canes. Yes, it looked very festive here in Ms. Erickson's fourth-grade classroom. It was oh, so satisfying to be organized.

Speaking of being organized, she wondered how her friend Emily was doing. Riley knew Emily was getting ready to visit her family in Portland for the weekend. Maybe she could use some help putting her classroom in order. Riley wandered down the hall to Emily's room.

Emily Dieb was new to the school, new to the town of Whispering Pines, Washington, in fact. But settling in well. The other teachers liked her and so did her students. Actually, all the boys in her fifth-grade class had a crush on her. This was hardly surprising, since Emily looked like a Victoria's Secret model.

Having a pretty friend was no threat to Riley. Granted, she'd never be mistaken for a model. She certainly wasn't as glam as her sister, Jo, the fashionista, whose hair was always styled and highlighted, but with her round face, and freckles and long, light brown hair, she was cute enough. Cute enough for Sean Little to fall in love with, anyway, and that was all that mattered. Sean thought she was cute, adorable even, and had told her so on plenty of occasions.

Besides, it was hard to be jealous of Emily when she was so nice. Like Riley, she loved to read and watch old movies. Unlike Riley, she enjoyed working out and had the size-four body to prove it. She was going home to Oregon for the holiday, where she'd spend the weekend playing indoor volleyball and hitting the gym. Yuck, but to each her own.

"I don't want to get too fat for my bridesmaid's dress," she'd said when Riley teased her once about being obsessed with the gym.

After Jo had gotten pregnant, she'd resigned from her position as matron of honor, so Riley had upgraded her best buddy, Noel Bijou, to maid of honor status and brought Emily on board to step into Noel's bridesmaid shoes. "I'd love to be a bridesmaid," Emily had gushed.

Emily didn't seem as gushy about being in Riley's wedding lately, but hey, Thanksgiving was coming, and Riley was sure that Emily was preoccupied with her looming family drama. Her parents were divorced and she was going to have to deal with parent rivalry and eat two Thanksgiving dinners—no easy feat for a size four.

She entered Emily's room to find her friend perched on her desk, looking gorgeous in a red knit dress and high boots, talking on her cell phone. Her cardboard Pilgrims and turkey were still hanging on the wall, and there was no sign that Christmas was right around the corner. Good thing Riley had stopped in.

Emily gave a start at the sight of her and said to her phone, "I've got to go."

"Sorry. Did I interrupt something?" Riley asked.

"Oh. No. I'm just, um, getting ready for the weekend."

"I thought you might be in a hurry to get on the road so I came by to see if you needed any help setting your room up for Christmas," Riley said.

"Oh. Well. Thanks." Emily seemed distracted.

"Is everything all right?"

"Yes. Um, everything's fine."

Poor Emily. She was obviously trying to make the best of her upcoming family visit. "Must be hard having to go home and try to keep everyone happy," Riley said.

Emily nodded.

"I wish you were going to be around. I'd sucker you into going out and getting something to eat tonight. Sean has to work at the gym." Sean owned a Fit and Fine franchise, and when you owned a business, it actually owned you. Of course, once they were married it would own both of them. Sean was giving Riley a membership as a wedding present. She could think of better ways to work up a sweat together but oh, well. She'd learn to love treadmills. Maybe someday she, too, would be a size four.

"Yeah, I'm afraid I'll be busy tonight," Emily said.

"I hope your mom doesn't try to match you up with someone again."

According to Emily, last Thanksgiving her mom had tried to set her up with her yoga instructor. Emily had just broken up with her boyfriend and had been in no frame of mind for a new man. The fact that the man had been fifteen years older could've had something to do with it. Emily's mom wasn't a very good matchmaker.

Neither was Riley. She kept trying, though. "Sean's friend Guy is going to be in town this weekend," she said casually. Maybe Emily would like to come back early. They could all go out on Saturday night.

Emily was already shaking her head. "I appreciate the thought, but..."

Riley sighed. "I know. You're not interested. But Em,

you don't want to wind up alone, do you?" Honestly, Emily wasn't even trying to fix her love life.

Emily blushed and bit her lip.

Now Riley had made her uncomfortable. "Sorry," she said. "I guess I just want to see everyone as happy as I am." Maybe Noel and Guy would hit it off. Noel needed someone new in her life.

"You're such a good friend," Emily said, her pretty blue eyes filling with tears. "I don't deserve you."

That seemed a little over-the-top but it was Thanksgiving. Everyone got sentimental at Thanksgiving. "You're right," Riley joked. "Come on. I'll help you get your Christmas stuff up. Then you can enjoy yourself this weekend without that hanging over you."

Emily stood up. "Thanks, but I need to get going."

"Okay. If you're sure."

Emily nodded. "I'm sure."

They walked to the parking lot where a few of the teachers' cars were still parked, and Emily got into her snazzy Honda Fit (even her car was fit!) and zoomed away. Riley got into her Toyota and went home by way of her sister's house.

She found Jo busy putting together a cranberry salad for the family gathering.

"That's enough to feed a multitude," Riley said after they'd hugged (not easy to do around Jo's current baby belly).

"We *are* a multitude," Jo said.

Yes, it would be a big gathering. In addition to a couple of aunts and uncles, some cousins and a grandma, Riley's brother, Harold, would be there with his wife and daughter. And, of course, so would Jo, a Wilton by marriage but forever an Erickson at heart. However, she'd be minus her husband. Mike was in the navy, stationed on a sub, which was out at sea.

Jo rubbed her back. "This kid needs to come soon."

It was her constant lament lately. Understandable, though. The baby was due any day.

"First babies take their time," Mom liked to say.

"Well, this one's taking enough time for two babies," Jo would respond. "At the rate I'm going, it'll be Valentine's Day before I have this kid."

Then Mom would say, "Maybe she's waiting until her daddy comes home."

Jo never found that remark cute. "Mike won't be here until the middle of December. Don't say stuff like that, Mom! If I don't have this baby pretty soon, I'm going to explode." Jo was a little dramatic these days.

But Riley wasn't going to point fingers. She'd spent some time on the drama queen throne a few months ago when Jo backed out of being her matron of honor. "Thanks a lot," she'd grumbled like a true loving sister. "You couldn't have waited a few months to get pregnant?" She'd been all excited about the baby—until Annabelle Rose upset her wedding plans. Not one of her finer moments, she had to admit. It became easy to kill her inner Bridezilla, though, after Jo asked how she'd like it if her matron of honor went into labor in the middle of the wedding ceremony.

Everything had worked out just fine, anyway, and she had her two BFFs to stand up with her.

"Have you made your pies yet?" Jo asked her.

Riley shook her head. "I'm doing them tomorrow so they'll be fresh."

"Ms. Organized," Jo teased.

"I want them to be good."

"They will be. You're the queen of the kitchen, for crying out loud."

"We all have to be the queen of something," Riley said. As a personal stylist, her sister had the clothes market cornered. She claimed that since this was her business she had to look good. But really, she'd look ready for an ad in *Vogue* no matter what she did. Jo had flair.

"So, are you and Sean doing anything tonight?" Jo asked.

"No." Riley shrugged. "He has to work at the gym."

Jo frowned. "He sure seems to work a lot of overtime lately."

"He has his own business," Riley reminded her. "You know what that's like."

"I do, but I still make time for the important people in my life."

"Sean makes plenty of time for me," Riley insisted.

Jo shrugged and changed the subject. "Want to stay for dinner?"

"What are you making?"

"I was going to ask you the same thing," Jo said with a grin.

"I should've known there was a catch," Riley said, but she was grinning, too.

She dug a couple of frozen chicken breasts out of Jo's freezer and baked them with an orange sauce then put together a tossed salad to go with them. It was what she'd planned to make for Sean. Before he informed her he had to stay at the gym. Sigh.

After dinner the sisters watched a movie. Actually, Riley watched it and Jo napped through most of it.

In spite of her evening nap, Jo was looking pooped so Riley cleaned up the kitchen then said her goodbyes and went home to her apartment. It wasn't all that late. Maybe Sean would like to come over for a while now. Surely he could leave the gym by nine.

She tried his cell but it went to voice mail. Double sigh.

"Hi. It's me. Just thought you might like to come over when you're done working. Call me," she added.

He didn't.

She tried again an hour later and got his voice mail. "Oh, well. I'll see you tomorrow. Mom wants us there at three so we'll need to leave by ten to. Love you."

She ended the call with a frown and plugged her phone in to recharge. Leaving voice mail was so unsatisfying when you were in love. She turned on her electric fireplace and plunked down on the couch. A fire in the fireplace was romantic, even if the fireplace was electric and mainly for show. Too bad Sean wasn't here to cuddle with her and enjoy it. Well, tomorrow night he would be. The gym would be closed on Thanksgiving, and she'd have him all to herself. Tomorrow was going to be wonderful.

The day certainly started out that way. Her pumpkin pies—the first she'd ever made, thank you very much—came out beautifully. She decided to celebrate with a home-made eggnog latte. (If she kept doing that, she'd be a size ten forever, but so what? Sean loved her just as she was.)

She was taking a sip when her cell phone rang. "Let's Hear it for the Boy," Sean's ringtone.

"Hello there, Mr. Little," she answered.

And now he'd say, "Hello there, future Mrs. Little."

Except he didn't. He said, "Riley, I need to talk to you." He sounded serious.

Oh, boy. She knew what that meant. He was going to weasel out of going to her parents' for Thanksgiving. For some reason, lately he didn't like hanging out with her family. He'd actually canceled on attending her brother's birthday party the month before. When she'd asked him what that was about, he'd used work as an excuse. "Anyway, I don't think your brother likes me," he'd added.

Which was ridiculous. Harold liked him just fine. Okay, Harold thought he was a tool. But what did Harold know?

"You don't want to go to Mom and Dad's?" she guessed.

"It's not that."

"Then what?"

"I should come over."

"You're coming over in a few hours," she pointed out. Not that she'd mind seeing him now, but it was only ten in the morning and she'd been busy baking and hadn't gotten around to showering yet and she hated it when Sean didn't see her at her best.

"I know, I know," he said, but not to her.

Now she heard a voice in the background. Who was he talking to? "Sean, what's going on?"

"I'm not sure how to say this."

Riley felt the blood start rushing from her head. Something bad was about to happen. She could feel the impending doom buzzing in the air around her. She fell onto the nearest bar stool, bracing herself.

There was that voice again, decidedly female. Riley suddenly felt as if she'd swallowed a block of ice.

"I am," Sean said, again not to Riley. "Riley…"

"Yes?" Her voice came out in a whisper.

"There's no easy way to say this. We need to break up."

"Break up?"

"I'm sorry."

"But…we're getting married in three weeks. And two days," she amended. Three weeks and two days to go and Sean wanted to break up. Now the ice was melting and pouring out of her eyes.

"I'm really sorry. But if we get married it'll be a big mistake."

It would? This was news to her. "What do you mean? I don't understand." She had to be asleep. That was it. She was asleep and this was a nightmare. She pinched her arm. *Yowch!*

"I've met someone else."

"Three weeks before the wedding?" Three weeks and two days, but who was counting?

"No, I met her before that. Things have been, uh, growing between us. Our feelings."

Three weeks before the wedding? Only a year ago he'd gotten down on one knee in front of all the other diners at Bella Bella's Italian restaurant, produced a diamond ring and declared he'd love her forever. What had happened to forever?

"How could you do this? We were in love." At least one

of them was. "You thought I was adorable." Didn't adorable count for anything these days?

"You are. Shit, Riley. I hate to hurt you like this. I feel awful."

He felt awful? "Who is it?" Who had stolen her groom three weeks before the wedding?

"This is awkward."

Awkward? This was a catastrophe. "Who is it?" she demanded.

"It's, uh, Emily."

"Emily? My bridesmaid? This is a joke, right?"

But Sean wasn't laughing. He wasn't even there anymore. Now someone else was on the other end of the call. Emily herself. Emily, Riley's fellow teacher, lover of small children, friend. Bitch.

"Riley, I'm so sorry. We've been trying to figure out a way to tell you."

"How long have you been trying?"

"All month."

All month. This whole month Emily had listened to her prattle about how lovely the church was going to look decorated with red-and-white roses and candles, how her grandma was making her garter, how Sean had someplace special picked out for their honeymoon. It was going to be a surprise.

Well, he'd certainly succeeded in surprising *her*.

"You were supposed to be my bridesmaid," she protested. *You were supposed to be my friend.*

"I know. I really am sorry. It just…happened."

"Where did it just happen?" Oh, wait. She knew. Sure enough. "At the gym."

That explained those extra-long hours Sean had been putting in. When you owned a business...blah, blah. The only business going on had been Emily in the business of stealing Sean. "You thief! You rotten, man-stealing thief. I thought you were my friend."

"I was. I am."

Not anymore. "Have you been sleeping with him?" It was Silent Night on the other phone.

"You've been sleeping with my fiancé. Seriously?"

No wonder Emily didn't want Riley to match her up with someone. She'd already matched herself. Was that who she'd been talking to when Riley walked into her class-room the day before? *I need to get going.* Yeah, she'd gotten going—right over to see Sean.

"Riley... Oh, here's Sean."

"I hate you," Riley said as soon as he came back on the line.

"Come on, Riley. Don't be like this."

"And why isn't she in Portland?" Or Timbuktu. Or Antarctica. The North Pole. No, scratch the North Pole. Santa would ban her.

"She was going but her plans changed."

Just like Riley's. No more wedding, no more wedding reception, no honeymoon with the perfect man who'd turned out to be anything but. No more life. And breaking up with her on Thanksgiving? Who did that?

Sean Little, that was who, the man she'd loved with all her stupid heart, the man who'd just broken that stupid heart. All that was left of her perfect life was her pumpkin pies. If Sean and Riley were here, she'd hit each of them in the face with one.

"Riley, I wish this hadn't happened," he said.

That made two of them. "I can't talk anymore," she said. "I have to get ready to go to my parents' and be thankful."

CHAPTER TWO

Riley ended the call but made no move to go anywhere. Instead she stayed on the bar stool and hyperventilated. *Get a bag. Breathe into a bag.* All she had was plastic bags. Probably not the best plan.

So she switched to crying at the top of her lungs. Good thing most of her neighbors at the Pine Ridge Apartments were out of town for the long weekend, having fun with their families.

Or their boyfriends.

Her crying increased in volume. How could this have happened to her? It was like getting hit by a tidal wave. She grabbed a box of tissues from the bathroom and, hugging it like a long-lost friend, planted herself on her couch and cried some more.

The fold-out turkey centerpiece she'd found at Daily's Drugstore sat on her dining room table, mocking her. She'd envisioned Sean and her starting their happy life together, sitting at that table every morning, having breakfast before they went off to work, then enjoying a cozy dinner for two when they returned home.

Sean would still be enjoying a cozy dinner for two. Just not with her. She grabbed another tissue.

It only took her half an hour to go through every tissue in the box. She needed something sturdier. Paper towels.

There on the kitchen counter, next to the paper towel dispenser, sat the pumpkin pies. She wished she hadn't offered to bring them. It had seemed like a good idea at the time. She loved to bake, and Mom had her hands full with the rest of dinner. She'd been excited to show off her culinary artwork to the rest of the family, imagined the oohs and aahs as everyone savored each pumpkiny bite.

No way did she want to go to the family dinner now, not when life as she knew it had come to an end. She put the pies in the fridge and called her sister.

"Hey, there," Jo answered. "Gobble, gobble."

Gobble, gobble. Happy Thanksgiving. "I can't go to Mom and Dad's," Riley wailed.

"What? What's wrong?"

"You have to come get the pies."

"What do you mean? Are you sick?"

"It's Sean. He...he..."

"He's sick."

"No."

"He's dead!"

"Nooo."

"Then what? Oh, no. He broke up with you," Jo guessed, quickly arriving at the correct conclusion. There was only one thing as bad as Sean dying, and he had done it.

"Y-yes," Riley sobbed.

"What's his problem?"

"Emily."

"Emily?"

"They're…they're…" Riley couldn't finish the sentence.

"That be-atch," Jo growled. "That sneaky, little fake friend. I'll be right over."

The pie problem solved, Riley took the roll of paper towels and returned to the couch. Maybe she'd see if Jo could bring home some leftovers for her…in case she ever wanted to eat again. She hated to miss Thanksgiving dinner but the thought of facing everyone was more than she could bear. She'd be a real dinner buzzkill, sitting there like the world's biggest loser, crying into her candied yams.

Ten minutes later Jo was at the door. And not only Jo but Mom and Grammy, too, neither of whom would leave the kitchen on Thanksgiving Day unless the world was coming to an end. Oh, no. This was so humiliating.

Until they rushed her and gave her a group hug, everyone standing in the entryway like a giant amoeba.

The amoeba slowly moved to the living room, Grammy and Mom flanking Riley on the couch, and Jo and her giant tummy settling in a nearby chair.

"That boy," Grammy said in disgust. "I never liked him. He was selfish." This was because at Thanksgiving the year before, Sean had eaten the last piece of huckleberry pie, which Grammy had planned on taking home and having for breakfast the next morning. It hadn't mattered that he'd been unaware of her plans for that piece of pie. As far as she was concerned, he still shouldn't have eaten it.

More evidence of how unworthy Sean was began to come out. "Remember how cheap he was on Valentine's Day?" Jo reminded Riley. "A bag of M&Ms instead of a box of chocolates."

"But I like M&Ms," Riley said.

"It was still cheap. And he didn't even take you to a nice restaurant. Bubba's Bar-B-Q? Really?"

"You're well rid of him," Mom agreed. "Heaven knows who else he's cheated with this past year."

"Now, there's something to be thankful for," said Grammy.

"That he cheated on me?"

"That you discovered what a weaselly cheater he is before you got married."

"He had to wait till three weeks before the wedding to do it?" The humiliation, the disappointment. Oh, the wrongness of it all.

"That is a little inconvenient," Mom conceded. "But nothing we can't handle. We'll start calling the guests tonight."

"I'll text all the cousins," Jo offered.

"See? It's going to be fine," Mom assured Riley.

"And look on the bright side," Jo added. "Now you don't have to work out at the gym."

No. Emily would be doing that, right alongside Sean. Riley sniffed.

"One less Christmas present to buy," Grammy said with a nod that made her glasses bob on her nose.

Christmas. Riley had been envisioning their first Christmas as a married couple—getting up in the morning and drinking hot chocolate, opening their presents. She'd already bought Sean's, a tool set she'd found online with everything from wrenches to Phillips screwdrivers. Well, she needed a tool set. And she could still drink hot chocolate.

All by herself. She burst into fresh tears.

"We're not going to let this ruin our Thanksgiving," Mom said firmly.

Was she kidding? "I'm not coming," Riley said.

"Not coming!" Mom and Grammy chorused.

"I can't." How could they expect her to face everyone after what had just happened?

"Now, baby," Grammy said, putting an arm around Riley's shoulders. "When you take a fall you have to climb back on the horse."

"I didn't fall," Riley protested. "I was dumped."

"Doesn't matter," Mom said. "Your grandmother's right. You don't want to be alone at a time like this. You need your family. And besides, if you sit here and mope, think of the power you're giving him."

"I'm not giving him any power. I'm just... Guys, can't you let me mourn?"

"Absolutely not," Mom insisted. "Now, go shower and dress. We'll wait."

Once Mom and Grammy made up their minds, arguing did about as much good as trying to stick to a diet in a bakery. Riley trudged off to the shower.

As she went, Grammy started singing some old song about washing that man right out of her hair. Funny.

After Riley was cleaned up, Mom and Grammy loaded her and the pies in Mom's car and hauled her back to the house while Jo went home to put the finishing touches on her cranberry salad.

"How's my girl?" her father asked, folding her into his big arms.

"Miserable."

"Don't be. Forget about that clown. Anyone stupid

enough not to want to be with you doesn't deserve you. I never thought he was good enough for you, anyway."

And that was the general consensus as the family gathered for their annual Thanksgiving feast.

"Men are beasts," said Aunt Gertrude, making Uncle Earl frown.

"Good riddance," said Riley's brother, Harold. "He's a tool."

"That's bad," explained his seven-year-old daughter, Caitlyn.

Harold worked out at Sean's gym a lot. "Did you know he and…" Riley couldn't bear to mention her false friend's name. "Did you know what he was doing?"

"Would you pass the stuffing, Aunt Gert?" Harold said, trying to dodge the question.

"Harold, did you?" She knew the answer before he even spoke. Guilt was painting a red flush on his face.

But he shook his head. "Not for sure. There was a lot of flirting going on and I thought that was tacky. You're well rid of him, sis."

Maybe she was, but the loss hurt all the same and it was hard to be thankful.

Still, by the end of the day she felt somewhat better. Everyone had complimented her on her pumpkin pies. Her aunt Ellen told her how nice she looked and asked her if she'd lost weight. She'd played Go Fish with Jo, her sister-in-law and her niece and had actually managed to forget her miseries for an hour or two.

Until she got back home to her empty apartment and realized it was going to stay empty for a long time to come. Maybe forever. Oh, there was a comforting thought.

Mom had sent home the last piece of pie with her, along with some stuffing and gravy and turkey. She'd planned to have them for lunch the next day. But, like the saying went, life was uncertain. She decided to eat dessert first. Maybe tomorrow she'd bake pumpkin squares. To heck with never eating again. She was going to eat away her sorrows, turn herself into a blimp. Who cared?

She took one bite of the pie and then tossed it in the garbage. Pumpkin pie was a poor substitute for a fiancé.

She was working up to another good cry when her sister called. "I know you're feeling sorry for yourself again."

Sometimes older sisters could be real stinkers. "I'd say I have a right to."

"Yeah, you do, but I have a better idea than sitting around feeling miserable for the next six months."

She wasn't planning on feeling miserable for the next six months. More like the next six years. "What?" Riley asked suspiciously.

"Girlfriend party. Pack a bag. Noel's on her way to pick you up."

"You told Noel?"

"Yeah, since she's your oldest friend and your maid of honor. Thought she'd need to know."

Yes, of course, Noel had to be told. Still, this felt as if her sad news was spreading faster than gossip on Twitter. In fact, it would probably be on Twitter before the day was over. Maybe it already was. Maybe Sean had tweeted. *Happy Thanksgiving. Dumped my girlfriend. Gobble, gobble.*

"You wanted to give her the happy news yourself?" Jo retorted.

Good point. She supposed she should be thankful her sister was telling people so she wouldn't have to.

"Come on, we'll drink eggnog and play Farkle. Then tomorrow we can hit the Black Friday sales and get you some new clothes, give you a break-over."

A breakup makeover; that did sound tempting.

"You don't really want to be by yourself, do you?" Jo continued.

"No," Riley admitted. She had enough of that being-by-herself stuff looming in the future.

"Older sister knows best," Jo teased.

"Sometimes." In this case she probably did. Who better to help Riley recover than her sister and her best friend?

Noel, who had gone through a breakup a few months earlier, understood exactly how she felt. "It sucks," she said as Riley dropped her overnight bag in the trunk of Noel's old clunker. "I swear there aren't any decent men left out there," she said once they were in her car and on their way. "Jo got the last one. No, I take that back. My sister did. Which is great, of course. I'm happy for Aimi." Noel sighed heavily.

Great. She was almost as depressed as Riley. Before the night was over they'd probably both wind up stretched out on Pine Street in the middle of downtown, praying to get run over by a reindeer. Except it was too early for Santa and his reindeer to be out cruising.

"I think the male population in Whispering Pines is shrinking." Noel heaved another sigh. Then she cast a guilty look in Riley's direction. "But you know what? We're not going to think about that tonight," she said with a determined nod.

★ ★ ★

"Thirty-one, and there's still no one, not even a glimpse of someone on the horizon," Noel said a millisecond later.

Jilted brides and empty horizons—oh, yes, this was going to be a fun evening.

Another guilty glance shot Riley's way. "I'm sorry. Listen to me, going on like Princess Pitiful when you're the one who's suffering. I'm sorry, Riley. I'm sorry Sean was such a jerk and Emily was such a rotten friend. But like I said, we're not going to think about that. Tonight we're going to have fun."

Fun.

Noel pointed a finger at nothing in particular. "You know, I never really liked her. Remember when we were at her place and she had that box of chocolates on the counter? She never offered to share. And they were Godiva! What kind of friend doesn't share her chocolates?"

That had been last month. Had those chocolates come from Sean?

They drove through downtown (which took all of five minutes). Santa's elves had already been busy because twinkle lights now dangled over Pine Street, and the lightposts were decorated with giant candy canes and red ribbons. Everything looked festive and happy. Happy holidays. *Bah, humbug.*

"But you know what?" Noel continued as they turned the corner onto Jo's block. "Tonight is all about forgetting your troubles, and we're not—"

"Going to think about it," Riley finished with her. She was glad when they reached Jo's house. Maybe now they really *could* stop thinking. And talking.

Jo was still looking picture-perfect in her maternity jeans and black sweater, an Italian charm bracelet dangling from her wrist. No matter how tired she got, she always managed to look perfect. The eggnog was ready, spiked for Riley, alcohol-free for herself and Noel, who wasn't much of a drinker.

"Eggnog!" Noel cried happily. "That's enough to make us forget our troubles."

"Until we step on the scale tomorrow," Jo cracked and took a sip of hers. "Except I'm drinking for two. Probably for another nine months at the rate I'm going. This baby's taking her own sweet time."

"She'll be here any day," Riley said. Her sister was having a girl and had the ultrasound to prove it. She also had a dresser full of cute outfits so her little girl could be as stylin' as she was.

"I'm ready. I'm more than ready. I have cleaned this house from top to bottom."

"It looks great," said Noel.

Jo's house always looked great. It was like an ad for Crate&Barrel. Chocolate-brown leather sofa and matching chairs, an expensive, thick throw rug over hardwood floors, her cupboards stocked with artisan stoneware. Tonight an arrangement of fall flowers in a long vase sat on her antique dining table, and she had a balsam-scented candle burning.

"I even cleaned the grout in the shower," she told them. "Mom says it's that final burst of energy before the baby comes. I sure hope she knows what she's talking about. I'd like to see my feet again."

"I thought expectant mothers were supposed to, like, glow," Noel said with a frown.

"I left glowing behind two months ago," Jo informed her.

"But you're going to have a baby!"

Jo did smile at that and rubbed her bulging belly.

Wait a minute. What was wrong with her sister's smile? The lips were in the right position but something was missing.

"Are you all right?" Riley asked her.

"Me? Of course I'm all right."

"Are you sure?"

Jo's chin went up a notch, a sign that she wasn't all right at all.

Riley's stomach started churning her eggnog. She set down her mug. "What's going on?"

Jo shrugged and downed the last of her drink. "Nothing."

"Okay, something is definitely wrong," Riley said.

"Not really wrong, just...not right. I don't know if I want to stay married to Mike."

Riley could feel her eyes bugging. "*What*? You and Mike have a great marriage. What are you talking about?"

"There's nothing great about him being gone all the time," Jo snapped. "He wants to re-up."

"Reenlist? You guys already talked about that," Riley said.

"We did. And I thought we had it settled. Obviously, we don't, not according to the email I just got." Jo frowned. "All he can see is that big bonus he'll get. He thinks we need it now that we've got the baby coming."

"Well, his motives are good," said Noel.

"No, they're not. He's just being greedy."

"Maybe he's worried about finding a job once he gets

out," Riley suggested. Mike was a nice guy. He would never cheat on his woman. Jo had no idea how lucky she was.

"He'd have no trouble getting a job. He'll be in high demand. That's why they're offering him such a big signing bonus. I told him it's either me or the navy. If he re-ups it's anchors aweigh. We're through."

Jo had dashed all over the emotional landscape during the last few months. Riley was sure this was simply one more case of whacked-out hormones. "You shouldn't make any big decision like that right now. And anyway, Mike loves you. And you're about to have a baby, for crying out loud."

Tears started leaking from Jo's eyes. "I don't want to raise this baby alone."

"You won't be," Riley assured her. "Yeah, Mike goes out to sea but he always comes back to you."

"He's gone for months at a time," Jo said, wiping her eyes.

"But we're all here."

"It's not the same. In the end it'll be me and Annabelle alone in this place. It'll be me up all night when she's sick, just me at the PTO meetings and the school plays. He'll be off...somewhere, keeping the world safe. Super Squid in a sub," Jo said bitterly.

"But think how noble—he's serving his country," Noel pointed out.

"I know, but he's been doing it for eight years. Isn't that enough? Can't he let someone else take a turn?"

This was obviously a rhetorical question, so Riley didn't respond. Instead she said, "You really need to think about this, sis. If you split with Mike you'll be even more alone."

"I'll replace him."

"You don't mean that," Riley said sternly.

Jo sighed. "I don't know what I mean. I'm just so…mad."

It was all Riley could do not to tell her to get over it. But that would be unkind and not very helpful. This was hormones talking. Had to be. So she decided to say, "Mike's a good man, and it's darn hard to find a good man." This was something she was now an expert on.

"Yeah, he's practically perfect," Noel added.

"There's no such thing as a perfect man," Jo said in disgust.

"I'll settle for *almost* perfect," Noel said.

"I'll settle for playing Farkle," Riley said. Sheesh. This was supposed to be a girlfriend party to cheer her up. At the rate they were going, they'd *all* be lying down in the middle of Pine Street waiting to get run over by a reindeer. "Come on, let's have fun. No more talk of men. Okay?"

Noel nodded. "I agree."

"Me, too," Jo said and fetched the game.

For the next two hours they played games. Then they turned on the Hallmark channel and watched a Christmas movie. "The guys in these movies are all so great," Noel said with a sigh as the ending credits rolled.

"That's because they're not real," Jo said. "If you sit around waiting for the perfect man you'll be on your buttsky for a long time."

"Thanks," Noel muttered. "You sure know how to inspire a girl."

"Just sayin'." Jo heaved a sigh. "Oh, never mind me. I'm cranky. And I'm pooped. You guys feel free to stay up as long as you want, but my daughter and I are going to bed so we'll be ready to hit the mall tomorrow." She waddled off to her bedroom, calling over her shoulder, "Leave the mess. We can clean it up in the morning."

"I'm tired, too," Riley said. It had been a long day and she suddenly felt the weight of all her misery. She stacked the empty popcorn bowls and grabbed a couple of glasses.

"Me, too," Noel said, picking up the rest of the mess. "Do you think your sister's right?" she asked as they loaded the dishwasher.

"About what?" Not about Mike, that was for sure.

"About there being no such thing as a perfect man."

"Well, none of us is perfect, but I hope there's such a thing as the perfect man for me," said Riley.

Maybe someday, somewhere, she'd find him.